After escaping fr
Epsilon 17 finally ⏤⏤⏤ ⏤⏤⏤ ⏤⏤⏤⏤ ⏤⏤⏤⏤⏤. ⏤⏤⏤⏤⏤⏤⏤⏤.
Helping to build a new city in the wake of the destruction
of the Institute should be all they're worrying about, but
Epsilon 17 has a horrific secret that's getting harder and
harder to hide. Cassandra isn't dead, she's locked up in
the deepest, darkest corner of E17's mind. Pushing E17 to
the brink of madness, Cassandra is determined to take
over E17 entirely and destroy the rebellion.

Can Epsilon 17 overcome their hidden enemy and learn to
trust the people around them? Unwilling to wait for
Cassandra to force their hand, Epsilon 17 decides to take
control: to go to a city where the Institute still holds sway,
and try to destroy them once and for all. Toby, forbidden
from joining the mission, has to find his own path
forward. Their connection is as strong as ever, but the
distance between them keeps growing.

THEY ARE THE TIDE

TIDE

The Psionics, Book Three

Tash McAdam

A NineStar Press Publication

Published by NineStar Press
P.O. Box 91792,
Albuquerque, New Mexico, 87199 USA.
www.ninestarpress.com

They Are the Tide

Printed in the USA
First Edition
June, 2019

Print ISBN: 978-1-950412-92-1

Also available in eBook, ISBN: 978-1-950412-91-4

Warning: This book contains scenes of violence, child abduction, memory wipes, depictions of PTSD, depictions of disassociation, suicidal ideation.

For Anne and Glo, who helped make Canada my home.

Chapter One

E17

Sometimes I think all I have ever done is hide.

I hid in the Institute, shielding my memories, my soul from those who wanted to take it from me. Now I hide here, from those who want to help me. They *want* to help me, but they're also afraid of me. I had a reputation before I was "saved." Their thoughts call me "the Hunter." Even though they try to cover them, I catch their fear and distrust echoing in the air all around me, and in the slant-eyed gazes they throw at me. They don't know I can still hear them. I've always been stronger than people predict. I understand why they feel this way, but it burns me still. So, I avoid them as best I can.

I'm sitting alone in the lush garden that circles the new ARC headquarters. It's beautiful here, a swathe of luscious green studded with vivid color, trees and flowers in carefully designed paths that lead around a low-slung, glittering white building. The whole area is sheltered with cunningly joined transparent sheets that filter out the worst of the dangerous sun. If you squint, you can see the shape of them, hexagon upon hexagon, tessellated together. Last week they were tinted dark for the brutal summer months, now they're clear and nigh-on invisible. This used to be the Governor's house, but he fled during the fall of the Institute and took a lot of the military police with him, leaving the city reeling. ARC stepped in, stepped up, tried to retain normalcy, but the shiny surface of city life has worn thin. The power vacuum caused by the disappearance of most of the higher-ups is exacerbated by the growing discontent of the township peoples. Without the Institute dampening them down, hunting for the worst of the malcontents, the slums are rumbling, and the people of the city are frightened and confused.

Several of the factories that produce luxury items for the Citizens have gone on strike, the poor workers no longer numbed to the imbalances in their lives. ARC has worked in secrecy for so long they don't know how to take charge like this. There's no direction, and that is frightening. Shivering, I turn my thoughts away from such darkness, and I look up into the bright-blue sky.

I can't get enough of being outside. Simply sitting in the air is still incredible to me. Several nights I've been woken by Toby or Darcy shaking me gently, urging me to go inside to escape the heavy chill of the night. I don't have nightmares when I'm outdoors. I seem to have developed a sort of claustrophobia that makes me edgy and jumpy when in a closed environment. Strange, when I lived below ground for years, to think that now I'm free, the walls press on me.

It's been two months since I tried to kill Cassandra. Looked her in the eye and stopped her heart inside her chest but failed to end her. My thought-blind brother carried me out of the wreckage of the Institute, not knowing what he couldn't see. That she didn't die, not really. I bear her with me, a nebulous tumor nestling in the secret place that was once my salvation. The bunker I built to save my memories from the Tank, from the wipes that would remove my personality and feelings. She hides in there; I know it. For two months I've fought her for possession of my mind, control of my body. The fear is with me, always, but it lessens when I'm outside. I like to sit under the apple trees most of all. The fresh, sharp smell permeates the air, and I fill my lungs until it feels like they must burst from the strain. The filtered sunlight bathes me, trickles honey warm down my spine and soothes my troubles until I can almost forget them.

But no one here wants to forget what I've done. The few people who I don't feel the need to hide from are Toby's personal group of close friends. They accept me as he did, unquestioningly. Their shields are strong enough that I don't get inundated with their private thoughts against my wishes, and their open faces tell me they trust me not to pry. That trust is an incredible thing. It feels tangible. I treasure it, as though I can cup it in my palms and feel a tiny heartbeat. The smallest act could snuff it out. I keep the tightest lock on my powers possible. Awareness of that trust helps me control myself and win the fight that always tears at the back of my mind.

Darcy is my favorite. There's something about her that soothes me. She's so calm and accepting. In a strange way I feel mothered by her. She always checks in on me, makes sure I'm managing but never makes me feel like I'm not enough, not trying hard enough or being normal enough. She doesn't mind that I'm quiet. Sometimes she'll come to sit with me and draw while I think. I love watching her draw, watching a thick black line roll over a blank screen and seeing pictures come alive.

I've tried to draw. I'm able to produce accurate technical sketches, one of the many skills the Institute has written through the core of me—regardless of any innate ability—but I don't know how to take what I see of beauty and translate it into an image. My drawings are dead. And really, it's the stillness of Darcy's consciousness when she draws that I envy. I want to find the thing that stills me, settles my heaving insides. There must be something. My brother doesn't rage inside as I do. Which is a blessing, I suppose. If he did, with his power, everyone would feel it. We'd probably die from it.

Toby is... Toby is Toby. His naiveté often dazzles me. His shields are firm for the most part, having pinned them down, knowing how dangerous it is to be open, but he still projects this aura of hope, of trust. He believes that people are good, and pure, and they all deserve to be safe and happy. He's been so untouched by loss, disregarding the past year of his life, that he's still untarnished by the harshness of existence. As well, being unable to read protects him from the more bitter realities of what lies below the surface. It's a beautiful thing, and I know I'll do anything to protect that in him. Not a day goes by when I don't regret my choice. Not Cassandra's death itself; the woman was, and is, a poison. Now one that seeps inside me, which I believe is better for the world. I regret the innocence I took from my brother, and the price I pay is for that.

My penance is clear; carry Cassandra inside me and never, ever set her free from the prison she is trapped in. Never allow her to take hold of me, or find a way out. I'm her jailer as she once was mine. It seems like a fair trade.

The soft material of my shirt scratches the short hair at the nape of my neck, tickling, and I rub it for a moment, allowing my thoughts to drift across to the training rooms where I know most people will be at this hour. Toby and his friends. I like them well enough, but I find Serena too loud and abrasive to spend long periods of time with; she grates on me, although I know she means well. She's an explosion of energy and sound, too wild to contain. I'm happy for her swift recovery, and grateful she's around, but she sets my teeth on edge. Too much, too friendly, too loud. As for Jake, who seems to think himself my honorary brother, he has more energy than I know what to do with. He's fascinated by the Institute, and asks me questions all the time, which wears me down. He's become good friends with Damon, Gamma 26, the little boy I pulled back from a coma.

In a strange twist of events, Damon turned out to be Serena's half brother. I get the story in bits and pieces, coded thoughts and sentences. Damon was taken when he was just five years old. They had him for five years, and he'll never get those memories back. Not that he'd want them. I know Serena is working with India and Oman to reconstruct his memories of the time before he was taken. I can't help but feel a little jealous that for him there *was* a before. For me, my everything has been the Institute. Sharing Toby's life may have saved my mind, but it's not the same as a real past.

Damon still seeks me out, preferring my quietness over the edgy energy of ARC, but less and less as he settles in. I like spending time with him, when he wants to be silent together. I think that alone cemented me on Serena's "team" as she describes it. There is a level of "debt" that ties me to this strange family, but the harnesses don't sit comfortably on my thin shoulders.

At least I can go where I want to. I'm sure I could even leave, if I chose. For now, here, I've taken to spending a lot of time with Kion, one of ARC's operatives, a quiet, accented man in his midtwenties or thereabouts. He was born in the deadlands and recruited to ARC after an

Institute team tried to take him in from the townships, not realizing that—as well as being a powerful telepath—he made his income by street fighting, or that he had a loyal gang of friends who weren't going to stand by as he was dragged into a hovering elec-car. He's an interesting guy, the sort who doesn't say a lot, but when he does, it's worth putting credit on. He's been teaching me self-defense and helping me put together a training regime. It's working pretty well. Regular exercise combined with endless amounts of food have made me unrecognizable as the birdlike human who once lived underground. I have curves and swells of muscle where before only nubs of bone and stringy tendons were visible. My skin has darkened, no longer looking gray and thin, and my hair has grown in, to the extent that my Institute tattoos are hidden. I like to run my fingers through it, but I can't deal with hair longer than an inch or so yet. It makes me feel panicky and off balance, but I'm working on it.

As I sit, comfortable on an ancient and worn marble bench, I swing my feet and contemplate my outfit. I've taken to wearing smooth and slinky UV proof cloth, it's a little shiny and feels luxurious against my skin. My shirt is blue with a raised collar snug around my throat and long sleeves that I can tuck my hands inside. I have a nanofiber-reinforced vest over it, white, to reject the heat from the sun. It's stab proof, and quite expensive. A present from Serena. She left it on my bed without a message, but the days I spent tracking her essence have tuned me to her. I knew who it was from as soon as I touched the ridged material, and she didn't go to great lengths to conceal it. My trousers are standard issue combat style, meaning they have dozens of pockets to keep things secreted away. I like to keep my possessions on me. Having things that belong to me is so unreal I hate leaving them anywhere. In my left hip pocket, my datapad is snug against my thigh, my Ident and credit card are tucked into the side of my waistband. A heavy-duty combat knife with a sharp blade and a ridged section for sawing through things is locked into its sheath on my right thigh. The blade is impossible to remove from the black aluminum casing without my thumbprint on the hilt, making it a secure weapon to carry without fear of it being lost or stolen. I trail my fingers down its spine.

Toby hates that I carry a knife, but he has no idea what it's like to be helpless. It's ironic that he feels that way, as he himself is a weapon more powerful than any I could carry. I'm getting stronger, faster, better at squirming away from Kion's tight grips and locks, but I'll never be powerful. And I would rather die than be captured again. Cassandra whispers that if only I would take Toby's power, stream it out of him and fill myself to the brim, then I'd never have to be afraid of anything again, not even her. I could use that power to expel her into the nothing space, she murmurs happily, tormenting me. I crush her down as best I can, distracting myself with the rebellion and training.

According to Sander, ARC's computer tech, there are descriptions and files on all of us floating around the other Cities. We're wanted terrorists. They've yet to mount a full-on assault, but we've been dealing with attempted infiltrations and several stealth attacks. My file says I should be brought in at all costs. No harm to come to me. The knife on my hip will stop that from happening, if ever it comes to it.

The sharp scuff of leaves crunching on my left breaks me out of my idle thoughts, and I turn to see who's approaching. Jake is hovering off the ground, running and flipping over in random directions; he looks like a floating gymnast. Damon tries to evade him, scurrying backward on his hands and feet with a wide grin on his face. Jake whoops and waves at me before diving toward Damon and for a moment they're just a blur of ridiculousness and laughter. A smile creeps over my face watching them. Damon seems to have recovered well from the ordeal of the Institute. Oman and India have been working themselves into the ground with all the sheep they pulled out, and most of them are doing okay. They've lost the empty, vacant look completely, and they squeal and run and act much like the kids who grew up the normal way. They'll never get their memories back, but who would want them? Now they can build new ones, start fresh. They don't need to know what a bone saw drilling into their temple feels like. No one does.

I'm an exception, I suppose. My memories haven't been blotted from me, so I can't just move on from them. If I didn't remember, though, who knows if Toby and I would have connected the way we did? We could have both died down there, with all of the others. Trapped. I give a mental shrug and lean against the cool stone of the bench, pulling my legs up underneath me and enjoying watching the children messing around. Totally worth it. I'm managing, after all.

As I watch, the distinctive, stocky figure of Kion appears from around the side of the building. He zeroes in on me and raises a hand; he has a large bag slung across his broad shoulders and I know what that means. I slide off my bench and pad across the grass to meet him.

"Hey, Thea. How's it?" My new name sits awkwardly in my ears, still. I chose it myself, after reading a book of ancient myths. I haven't told anyone the origin, but sometimes I whisper it to myself. Prometheus, eternally punished for stealing fire from the Gods. In some myths Hercules saves him. Someone could still save me. Taking a mythological name, in the style of the Institute, might feel odd to the others, but it makes sense to me.

Kion watches me with a gentle expression. His gravelly voice always makes me laugh. He's two inches taller than I am and has an open boyish face, teeth flashing white against his dark skin. He's about three times as wide as me, though, and he speaks calmly and sparsely. He reminds me of the images I've seen of bears, soft-looking but with immense amounts of power and an aura of danger. He rakes his banded dreadlocks out of his face and grins at me.

"Hey, Kion. Can't complain. Just watching the monsters." I jerk my chin at Jake and Damon who are sprawled in the grass poking each other in the face for no reason other than that they're young.

He grunts, squinting at the wriggling forms, and gestures toward the low outbuilding that has been turned into a training area, and I nod in agreement.

We try to train every other day at least, but Kion often has to go out on missions, and I work with Marty or Serena instead. Marty is still raw with grief over his partner's death, his face so stark sometimes I can't stand to look at him. He doesn't say much, but he's a good trainer, patient and skilled. Serena and I don't click so well; she likes to banter and chat while I prefer to focus and stay quiet, which makes her uncomfortable, and in turn she talks more, making me shut down even further. She knows a lot about fighting, though, even if the way she uses her power will never be something I can do.

Kion's the best. I don't know why he's training me—he has much better things to do as he's the head of the ARC operations branch—but I don't ask him 'cause he'd just grunt in response. I never realized how expressive a grunt could be until I met him. I've started counting them and giving them numbers. I might print a translation guide for people.

We amble in companionable silence over toward the training rooms, and I once again marvel at the efficiency of the ARC personnel. They train people to shield in a different way than the Institute does. For a start, there's no punishment if you lose concentration and drop your shield, so the fear factor is absent. The minds here are ordered and closed down, as a general rule. I still pick up a lot of stray thoughts and feelings, but when I lock myself down, which is nearly all the time now, I get to relax in the privacy of my own mind, without others intruding. A lot of the people here don't seem to believe that I'm not sifting them, but that's fine. I don't need a lot of friends, or any, maybe. I'm happy to just be left alone. I prefer the still quiet.

We slide the heavy door open, Kion with telekinesis, me with my bare hands, new calluses scraping on the metal, and head into the large room. There are changing areas at either end, but Kion insists we train in whatever we're wearing and change into clean clothes after. He's told me time and again it's no good learning to fight in tight-fitting operative clothes if you're not going to be wearing them.

I smile at the men and women who are already training. Jamal is pummeling a heavy bag in a corner while Zeb holds it in place, and Grace is running wind sprints down the edge; all of them spare a momentary sign of acknowledgement for me. There's a few others scattered around, working weights or training in pairs on the floor mats. A loud drop makes me wince on behalf of Daine, a skinny blond guy who's just been slammed to the ground by Ria, one of the female soldiers. She's one of those people who look pretty thin and fragile until you see her without long sleeves and realize every inch of her is rock-hard. Also, she's a fierce Projector, which helps even the scales in terms of strength.

When I train with Kion, it's always a battle not to draw on Toby's power to help me, but I'm trying not to do that. It still happens when I get scared or lose my focus from pain. Johan has been very clear in our meditation and shield-building sessions about the negative effects of drawing Toby's power out of him. He might be bursting with it, have so much he doesn't even notice me pulling a little off, but if I take too much, I could kill him. Also, if I'm reliant on that connection between us, if I ever can't access it, from distance or something, I might panic and not know how to handle myself without that crutch. I'm not sure I believe him, but the fact that Cassandra seems to think taking his power is a good idea is enough to put me off.

Kion heads to a free floor pad and begins loosening up, expecting me to follow suit without any idle conversation. One of the reasons I like spending time with him so much; there's no unnecessary chatter. I'm unused to small talk, and the social nuances escape me. I often end up fumbling for words and find myself hot and uncomfortable. Another interesting fact I had no idea about. I've never been in a position to experience social embarrassment before, but it turns out both Toby and I blush easily and far more often than either of us would prefer.

We stretch out for fifteen minutes, warming our muscles and then Kion turns to face me, bouncing on the balls of his feet. I take a deep breath and find my center of balance, bending my knees and lifting my hands. Sometimes we wrap our hands up, which means we're focusing on hitting, but on days like this, when we're just facing off, it means grappling and holds.

Two of the male operatives stop working out on weights and start shaking their muscles out, watching with interest. It's become a sort of running joke that Kion and I fight pretty brutally. The Institute unarmed combat lessons focus on pressure points, and I have been drilled in them over and over. I asked him early on not to go easy on me because I'm weak and not a Projector. The enemy won't, so I need to learn to react properly. My training is for war, not for fun or because I have to. He tries not to break my bones, but it's a rare day for me to leave without some nasty bruises.

He feints left and then comes in hard for a leg sweep. I read it on him, a split second before it would have been too late, and lift my foot, aiming a wicked stamp down toward his knee. He reacts fast, sliding a little on his braced foot so my strike bounces off the rubbery muscle of his thigh. It won't have hurt him. I don't have enough power to damage a full grown man unless I hit a delicate point. Elbows, knees, throat, eyes, groin, feet, wrist locks and arm locks. Kidneys. A strike to the nose will slow down someone untrained, but a soldier will walk right through a broken nose. I've seen Kion shake off blows that would have landed me in the hospital with cracked ribs. It's physiology, not something I can change except by building more muscle where I can. My main advantage in fights is my reading of intent, and that's what I concentrate on. Sometimes Kion makes me fight him blindfolded to work on that, perception of surroundings, blind vision, they call it. A Reader as strong as me should develop accurate 3-D awareness that Projectors just can't match. I should be able to fight in the pitch dark, if necessary.

I jump back, fast, avoiding the follow-up. Another thing I have learned is he'll strike back immediately, so don't back off—it cedes the advantage, lets the opponent dictate the pace of the fight. I wait again, my fight is reaction not aggression. I use his movements against him, his weight and power my advantage. He grins at me, eyes narrowed in mock anger. He flows forward again, moving as smooth as oil.

When Kion fights with other people, he uses his Projector strength. In training fights we don't use our power to hammer our blows harder, as we'd just injure our opponents all the time. We use it to drag their feet out, trick them into blocking a ghost blow, hit in dozens of places at once so they have to shield their whole bodies. Kion likes sparring with me because it makes him "inventive." He can't simply cycle through dozens of well-practiced sets of movements, designed to complement one another. As I read his intent, I know where he will be exposed, where I can slide an open hand in, jabbing my stiff fingers into his kidneys. I know the split-second moment his throat will be exposed. With me, Kion has to fight without thinking, which is something strange to him.

I slip away from him, my hands hovering in a guard in front of me. My technical skills are still developing, and reading Kion's subconscious analysis of my stances and guard provides me with better information than just being told. I feel him clocking the three-inch gap behind my left elbow, where a swift roundhouse kick will knock the wind out of me, and tighten my guard. He grins wryly, acknowledging it. His hand snakes forward in a lightning-fast jab toward my nose, but I'm ready, and I block it with a butterfly grip, pulling him off balance and slamming my knee into his ribs and following with a double fist to the meat of his arm, knocking him off balance and giving me space. Then I back off fast. He's too dangerous to try to chase down unless I strike a crippling blow that will put him on the floor.

He tensed his muscles in time to take some of the power out of the hit, but I have bony knees and a double blow from my hands is pretty hard. He's thinking, ruefully, that he'll have some bruises. His thoughts skitter through moves, trying to hide his intent as he comes at me again, and I miscalculate, falling for a feint and taking a powerful fist to my solar plexus for my trouble. I go down, gasping for air that doesn't exist. The fight is won, but Kion is not smug as he crouches down to check on me. He always worries he'll hit me too hard. But I want to learn to fight through it. There are worse things than pain. I'm sure that's the only way I can ever be a successful fighter.

My lungs spasm uselessly before he thwaps me on the back, shocking my body back into breathing. The air burns my throat, and I hack a few times before collapsing onto the mats and smiling up at him.

"Ugh. I hate you." The more time I spend with Toby and Serena, the more I start to speak like them. He grins and flicks his hair back. He's not even sweating properly; our fight lasted less than a minute. My aim is to stay viable for three, but I'm nowhere near being able to hold him off for that long.

"You're still falling for feints." His voice is mellow and non-accusatory as he helps me up.

"Yeah, well. Usually people aren't trying to lie to me and hit me at the same time." I find my feet and shrug. I've got a lot to learn, but training every day is helping in a myriad of ways. Cassandra even remains quiet while I'm fighting. I don't know if she feels the pains of my body, but she doesn't seem to want to distract me into getting punched more than necessary.

I rub my upper stomach and wince as I feel the swollen heat beneath my skin. The corner of Kion's mouth dimples, the closest he'll ever get to gloating, and he chucks me on the shoulder affectionately.

"Stretch, then light weights." He means "Go and do a proper cool down. I'll see you later," and I grin at him, heading for the weights area, before starting to stretch my body out so my muscles don't cramp.

Kion hooks his hands behind his neck, biceps bulging even through his shirt, and spreads his legs. While he waits for another sparring partner, he forces his head down so his nose touches his knees. I pull a face involuntarily. I can, after four months, just about touch my toes with the tips of my fingers.

Ria was doing crunches in the corner, Daine having retreated after his ignominious defeat, and she gets to her feet and saunters over to Kion, lifting a foot to poke him in the rear. He says something to her from between his own legs and then straightens and the two square off. I reposition myself so I can see them more comfortably, and start doing some light bicep curls. I love watching Ria and Kion spar. She's brutally fast, even though he's stronger and more thoroughly trained.

Their match is, as I predicted, a good one to watch. They're both bleeding after the first flurry of blows—Kion from a split lip and Ria from a cut above her eyebrow. He probably caught her twice in quick succession, the first blow to swell the skin and the second to split it. He bares red teeth and closes in again, trying to use his superior strength to force her into a wrestling match. Neither of them have used their powers yet, which isn't unusual for them. They're evenly matched in projection terms, so they'd just run out of energy faster with a similar result. If one of them gets in a tight spot, that's when telekinesis will change the game. They test each other with punches without closing up too much, and then Kion barrels forward again.

As I watch, Ria ducks under Kion's leading punch and digs a blow into the line between his hip and stomach, her fingers and thumb stiff and pushed together like the beak of a bird. Kion crumples to the floor like she cut his leg off, but manages to sweep her with his other ankle, sending her in a tumble on top of his legs. For a moment it's all flurrying limbs; then Ria manages to get Kion's arm up behind his head, and with his numbed leg as well, he's out of the fight. He taps the floor in submission, and she holds him there for a moment longer before releasing his arm and collapsing next to him, laughing. Her nose is bleeding a little now, and Kion is moaning in exaggerated agony as he tries to massage the feeling back into his thigh.

"Dirty!" He growls at her, grimacing in pain as pins and needles torment him.

She snickers and shuffles around to help him, massaging the thick muscle above his knee in apology. "Well, you did say 'no holds barred.'"

Kion grunts in response, and struggles to his feet, miming a kick at her face but with a grin to show he doesn't mean it before limping off in the direction of the hot water pool and flicking her the finger over his shoulder. Kion's not a sore loser, but he and Ria are the top two ranked operatives, and as such, they have a lot of competition between them. Kion beat her out in an in house training tournament recently, and since then, Ria has been merciless in their sparring, but it's all good-natured.

I finish up my weight work and crack my neck from side to side, scooping a bottle of water from the floor on my way to the dry showers. Ria falls into step with me, blood gleaming on her forehead, until she swipes at it with a hand, leaving a dull smear in its place.

"You were looking pretty good out there today, Thea." I lift a shoulder in response, realizing I've taken to echoing Toby's common gesture.

"Thanks. I'm still too slow, though, and weak." I gesture at her face, changing the subject from me. "Doesn't that hurt?"

She grins, extra wolfish with blood staining her teeth from her nosebleed, swinging her arms as she walks. "Nah, not really. I bet Kion's leg does though. I wouldn't have got him with that if you hadn't bruised his arm earlier. He was a touch slow on his blocks. Thanks!"

I smile tentatively, pleased by her comments and cheerfulness as we slip into the dry shower room. We strip off our clothes unselfconsciously, and I pout as I see the shape of Kion's fist, reddish bruising clear just under my sternum.

"Yowch!" Ria raises her eyebrows and slides into the shower, clicking it on and shouting to be heard over the roar of the air blast. "You caught a live one. Don't show Kion, he'll feel terrible!"

"Don't show me what?!" The voice echoes over the dividing wall between the changing rooms, and Ria wrinkles her nose and mouths "oops" at me. We share a quiet giggle, and Kion snorts from the next room.

I shower rapidly, blasting the salty sweat out of my short hair and from my skin. We dress in companionable silence and head back to the main building. Jake and Damon are still rolling in the grass and I control the urge to siphon off some of Toby's powers and lift them both into the air by their feet, just for fun. When we get back to the main building we part ways, Ria clapping me on the shoulder in a friendly fashion. I head back to my room and drop my sweaty training gear in the laundry chute on the way. It's lunchtime, so I just drop my kit bag and head down to the canteen.

Toby and Serena still aren't back from their mission, so I sit with Darcy and Aly. Aly is an interesting character. She grew up in the slums, but is whip smart even without any formal education. Smarter than me by a good deal, I think. She reads voraciously, never to be seen without a device in her hands or pockets, and has a wealth of knowledge about the most random things. She's been teaching me about world history and geography in our free time, and her face lights up as I slide my tray onto the table opposite her.

Darcy looks at my tray and raises an eyebrow, and I sigh, spinning on my heel and returning to the queue. When I get back to my seat, I have twice as many of the slimy things that seem to be passing for vegetables these days, and one fewer dessert. She laughs and pats my hand as Alyssa twists her data screen so I can see it and we tuck into our food while watching an animation of the way global warming and natural disasters reshaped our world over the last five hundred years. I know I'll be tested on it later, so I pay close attention, a warm glow of companionship deep in my belly that can't even be cooled by Cassandra hissing in my head.

Chapter Two

TOBY

My calf muscle knots with an intensity that makes me screw my face up in pain, but I swallow the sound I want to make and clench my jaw, wrapping my hands around the spasming muscle and digging my fingers in. It's excruciating, and worse is that I'm gonna have to stay here, crouched down and silent for at least another few minutes. I knead until the knot releases, but it will return in a matter of moments if I don't change my position. Stealthily, I extend my leg, using my telekinesis to balance, then shift my weight as quietly as I can and move from crouching on my feet to sitting on my bum. It'll take longer to get up, longer to move, but the alternative is a return of the intense pain, and I won't be able to move fast with a dodgy leg anyway. I let myself sink back against the wall behind me and keep my ears perked for the sound of Serena's return.

She's another fifteen minutes, making me thank my lucky stars that I moved when I did. I would probably have fallen sideways, which would have made my position clear to the men milling around below me. Serena's so stealthy I don't notice her until she's right next to me, and her cold fingers pressed against the back of my warm and clammy neck make me jump. We push thoughts back and forth lightning fast, her filling me in on her sneaky look around, me showing her the men below, adding my own commentary on who's worth bothering with. Although I try to keep it from her, she catches the pain from my thought shapes and glowers at me in the darkness before wrapping her power round my leg and kneading it with telekinesis. The violent massage causes a return of the cramp, but it's alleviated immediately, and this time I don't feel like I've just been waiting for it to return. I think my gratitude at her, and she grins, teeth flashing in the firelight from below.

The "room" we're spying on is more of a ramshackle warehouse than anything. About a dozen men are shuffling around, exchanging greetings and muffled conversation. The fellow we're after, a dealer named Jean Pierre, is leaning in the self-assured way that only very, very confident people can project. His right shoulder is against a metal pole, his feet crossed at the ankle, but still he looks like he's about to pounce on something.

In the days since the fall of the Institute, the City has fallen apart. After seeing what they were doing, torturing children and invading people's most private thoughts, I'm definitely not saying I think they were in the right, but...without their controlling presence, things have gone a bit mad.

The townships were rough before, but these days they're a cesspool of murder, drugs, and corruption. I don't know what the body count is, but I know that the mass graves being dug on the edge of town have a purpose. Jean Pierre is one of the people who have managed to come up into the new world swinging. How he slipped below the radar before is no mystery, Serena tells me he's a natural Blank, as I was once thought to be. His drug deals go down with a front man; he's just here to observe the trades and make sure it's all legit. Now there's no police presence in the slums at all; he's not even really bothering to keep a low profile.

I send Serena my weapon count for the floor. I see four illegal Zap weapons clipped to hips or bulging below people's armpits. There's probably at least four more in better concealed places. She pats my shoulder and for a second as our eyes meet I feel the old jolt deep in my stomach, but the moment is fleeting. Our friendship is more important than any attraction I may have left. Serena smirks, giving the impression of something like "Yeah, yeah, I'm a babe, but that's not the issue at hand."

Our plan is pretty simple. We see where the drugs go, relay those descriptions to the two teams on the ground, and we follow Jean Pierre, hopefully back to wherever he's producing the twitch he's been flooding the streets with. We take him down, destroy his lab, and disappear him. I dunno what'll happen to him after that, but the two bodies I saw in an alley on the trip out here weren't older than ten, and both young girls had the distinctive muscle rictus of twitch users. I doubt it was their idea, either. I don't care if they decide to put him down, or jail him, or whatever. I just want to do what I can to try to undo some of the damage that the sudden removal of authority has caused.

Something I was told a lot at school is that I have a worrying tendency to follow along with other people's bad ideas. I was never an instigator, but I'm easily swept up in people's enthusiasm. However, in this case, I may not know too much about the big picture, but I do know these drugs are bad, and I trust David Jacobs to have figured out the most effective way to take down this dealer-supplier.

Down below us, two bulky guys are doling out wraps to the crowd, taking nothing in return. Serena puts her hand over mine so we can communicate. *It's on tick. Jean Pierre knows his loyal customers aren't gonna nuke him over.*

I nod in understanding, and Serena furrows her brow in concentration and moves her hand. I know she's sending descriptions and directions to the teams waiting outside. The first recipients start to filter out, some of them jostling one another in an aggressive fashion before they're even out the door. Serena's eyes flick from side to side, working out which teams should go in which directions. Our job is to wait, and follow the big fish. I get picked for quite a lot of sneaky following missions nowadays. I was also subjected to an embarrassing talk about using my perception warping power for nefarious purposes. I *think* David Jacobs was suggesting that I restrain myself from getting any visuals I shouldn't have access to, and it was pretty uncomfortable for both of us. Thea can always tell where I am, and I doubt she'd keep quiet if she thought I was slipping into the girls' changing room. Not that I *would*. Besides the fact that would be pretty messed up, they'd kick my ass if they caught me.

The room empties rapidly, no one wanting to linger in a precarious situation, and soon Jean Pierre is left with his two companions, a guy with arms as thick as my torso, and a scraggly, short-haired woman. They confer briefly, and Jean Pierre waves a dismissive hand at them, unfurling his body from the pole and stalking toward the exit. He moves like a predator. A few moments after they have disappeared into the darkness, Serena slides to the edge of our ledge, and drops into the alley outside. I follow, somehow managing to scrape my stomach against the jagged metal on the way down. Serena rolls her eyes at me as I lift my shirt to examine the graze and flicks me in the ear. I pout at her, wounded, and she gestures at her body. The meaning is clear. My eyebrows draw together and I chew the side of my lip as I cloak us in my power. Feeling it settle into place, I nod at her. She pokes me in a painful spot on the side of my belly and I thwap her hand indignantly. Smirking, she slips into the shadows and sets off at a fast soundless walk after our targets. Grumbling silently I slip after her. She can be such a brat sometimes.

We catch up with Jean Pierre and his bodyguards just moments later, keeping them in sight but staying well back in case I make a noise. Serena is a *lot* stealthier than me. I've never considered myself clumsy, but next to the people who grew up with ARC, I may as well not even be trying. I've barely mastered walking on the outsides of my feet to muffle my footsteps. I've experimented with creating a sort of cushion of my power under my feet, but it doesn't quite work. Something to do with the science of telekinesis. I keep meaning to sign up for that class.

We follow behind them for about twenty minutes, keeping our footsteps light on the broken, gravel concrete. The slums are busy, people scuttling along, others gathering on corners. The moon lends a silvery light to proceedings, and I nervously wonder if our shadows are covered by my perception altering when Serena grabs me and gestures up ahead. Jean Pierre has stopped and is deep in conversation with a man clad in shadowy grays. It takes me a minute to figure out what Serena is motioning at, and then I see that the guy has close-cropped hair. In the moonlight flooding down from above, it is relatively easy to make out the distinctive black lines of an Institute tattoo. I flatten myself against the wall, heart rate soaring.

The Institute agent turns in our direction, and I redouble my efforts to project nothingness while trying to make sure my shields are in place. His eyes are sharp and dark, weathered lines at the corners. I've never seen him before, but he carries himself like a warrior.

Serena grabs my hand as the agent looks right at us. I gather my power, preparing to thrust it out at him, readying myself for the inevitable fight. Jean Pierre will probably escape during the chaos we're about to unleash. At my side, Serena is trembling with anticipation, I know it's not fear, I've rarely felt her afraid. The man meets my eyes, it seems, for a few, bladder-tightening moments and then frowns for a split second before returning his attention to a concerned-looking Jean Pierre. He says something to his bodyguards, indicating they should head up this way and check out what's going on. The Agent raises his voice a little. I still can't make out what he's saying, but he looks agitated. Serena tugs at my hand and we tiptoe backwards trying to go speedily but silently. We press against a wall as far away as we can while still keeping our target in sight. The bodyguards check out a couple of the nearby alleys, but don't get that close to us. To my dismay, we see Jean Pierre disappearing round a corner with the Institute Agent. I figure there's no way the bodyguards will be stupid enough to lead us to the lab if they suspect someone's here. Serena's face twists in dismay, and she squeezes my hand to get my attention.

We should head down here, and split up if we can't see him. If you find him on the other side of these guys, send a beep. Comms mind—not psi—the creep'll hear us if we psi each other noncontact.

I nod my agreement and turn, ready to trot down an alley. Serena holds on for a second, continuing her message.

Be careful; beep as soon as you see anything. Drop the cloak as soon as that guy turns.

I see the guy she means; he's walking toward us, but clearly about to slip down a side street. We don't want anyone to see us appearing from nothing, obviously.

He turns, and I uncover us. Serena drops my hand and bolts down an alley, running like a street kid, not a soldier, all knees and flailing arms. I break into a lope and scruff my hair up, hoping my clothes blend enough to look like a local. It's a few minutes before my comm vibrates against my wrist. I duck into the most shadowy alley I can see and wait for a pair of teenagers to pass me by before peeking at the screen and select the option to show Serena's position relative to mine. If anyone sees my tech, I'll be on the ground before I get a chance to do anything about it, so I commit the image to memory and pull my sleeve back down before I start jogging toward her location.

When I get to where I think she should be, I look around. I'm about to check the screen to see if she's moved on when something hits me right in the back of the neck. I jump about a foot in the air; fearing an attack I whirl, my hands up, but there's no one there. I shuffle awkwardly, hoping none of the locals saw me, or if they do that they assume I'm twitching and keep clear. That in mind, I hunch my shoulders and try to look high. Something moving hits me in the nose before I can react, and I swing my head around, trying to figure out what's going on. Then something nudges my hand and I look down. A piece of stone is hovering by my little finger. Swiftly, I wrap my hand around it, and follow its pull. It yanks me toward a broken-down, crumbling shack made of old food cartons piled up like bricks, with a piece of cracked plastic sheeting forming a roof. Serena is crouched inside, there's no one else there. A pile of old rags makes up a bed, stacked on top of a pallet formed from cottonboard. It's pitiful, and something twists in my stomach.

Serena sees my expression and nods, eyes glittering hard in the low lighting. I squat next to her, and she sketches something out on the screen of her wrist comm before showing me. I still can't get over some of the tech Sam invented. The comms are a black, liquid-looking plastic that's so soft and malleable it conforms to our wrist contours. The screen is a bright display, although Serena has hers turned down so low I struggle to make out the picture she's scrawled. That was smart; I'll remember that for next time we come into the townships. In her drawing, which looks like a three-year-old did it, there are two stick men she has labeled as "me and you" in a box and then another box opposite, with some lines that have been marked as "stairs" with an arrow. So our targets are in the shack opposite, either up or downstairs. I draw two arrows next to her arrow, one up, one down, and a question mark. She scowls and takes my hand. Nuke knows why we didn't just do it that way to start with; sometimes being stealthy plays tricks on your brain. Or maybe she just wanted to show off her art skills.

He's downstairs with the Institute guy; that woman turned up and is sitting at the top; she looks pretty comfy. I dunno where the big guy is. Did you see him?

I shift position and reply. *Nope, no sign. D'ya think this is the lab?*

Serena flares her nostrils. *It's gotta be, I reckon. I mean, he probably has a bunch more, but that's for someone else to find out. I fired a mail off to base while I was waiting for your lazy ass.*

I punch her in the shoulder, but gently, and she grins winningly at me.

So, what's the plan? I'm impatient to get on with things.

She sniffs, hooking her hair behind her ear. *I wish we knew who that Agent was. We should take him in, if we can. He's obviously working with the lowlifes here. Trying to give us more to deal with, I guess.* Her mouth twists in thought and then sets in an expression I recognize as "We're doing this, whether or not it's a smart plan."

Shouldn't we wait for backup? I venture, and she shifts a little, flashing a smile at me.

For all we know, he's already called in HIS backup. We can take down two no-Tals...she catches my question and rolls her eyes...*no-Tals—no Talents—anyway, two of them and one kweedy Agent. I'll take the prick; you knock Jean Pierre out. It'll take us two ticks, and we'll pull them out and drop into the low roads. No one knows 'em better than me, remember?*

I chew my lip and then lift a shoulder. She's right: a team could be about to descend. We should go in fast, we can be out of there in five minutes.

What about the bodyguard at the top?

Serena has a dangerous edge to her grin. She waggles her eyebrows, straightening up and moving quietly to the entrance. I huff air out of my nose and follow her. I'm not convinced it's the greatest plan, but I don't have anything better, and the presence of the Institute Agent is making me antsy. She's right; if we wait for backup we could have an army on us.

We're outside the shack, and to my surprise, Serena walks straight in. The guard leaps to her feet, the chair skittering backward, and opens her mouth to shout, but nothing comes out. She reaches up, clawing at her own throat and making a choking noise. In the nick of time, I manage to catch the chair with my power, stopping it from making a noise, and Serena holds onto the guard with her power for a solid two minutes before the woman slumps in her Psionic grip, her face swollen and taking on a purple tint. Serena pads forward and checks her pulse, looking concerned for a moment and then relaxing. The woman's color starts to drain and she moans very quietly. Serena matter-of-factly gags her and ties her up, zipping her wrists together with plasticuffs before tiptoeing to the maw of the stairs and squatting, listening.

I set the chair down, with my hands now, not my power which still gets away from me sometimes. The whole process was close to silent, but my heart is pounding and adrenaline has flooded my system. I wait for Serena's signal, and we position ourselves on either side of the staircase. Satisfied that those below haven't heard anything untoward, Serena holds up three fingers and counts down. On one, we both slip over the edge and barrel down the stairs, stealth abandoned in favor of surprise. The men at the bottom whirl toward us, both raising Zaps, the Institute guy also reaching for his comm. I force Jean Pierre's Zap up before he gets a shot off, and the blast thunders into the ceiling, shattering a hole the size of my fist in the concrete and sending a rain of chips and dust down on us. I waste no time picking Jean Pierre off the floor telekinetically and slamming him into the wall. His head thuds back, and I let him drop, seeing his eyes roll up in his head. I twist to analyze the situation next to me. Serena is on top of the Institute Agent, who looks unconscious as well, blood pouring from his nose.

She's busy plugging his comm into her wrist unit, I guess trying to see if he got a message out. She looks up at me, eyes wild with the rush from the fight, and grins. I see she didn't get off unscathed; her hand is bloodied like she hit the wall or the floor, but she seems fine.

We slap cuffs on them both and yank them upright, with a combination of powers and brute force. Hastily, Serena checks the room, and the room next door while I dose the men with a knockout needle and watch the stairs. She comes back with a datapad and some memory cards in a case, stuffing them into her flatpack where it lies concealed under her shirt, resting in the small of her back.

"It's the lab all right. I've left some plastic; we gotta bounce before the place comes down!" She's lit up, practically vibrating, and I nod.

She takes the lead, pounding up the stairs. I spare a moment to hope there's no one up there waiting for us before yanking the two men with my power and thrusting them in front of me. Serena grabs the door guard and dumps her on the street, so she won't die in the explosion, then takes point, flitting from shadow to shadow. We trot in tensed silence, me focusing on making the men in front of me unnoticeable and her keeping an eye out for trouble.

We make it to a manhole cover and wrangle our captives down before sliding the cover back into place. Relaxing a little, I slump against the wall and wipe my sweaty forehead.

"How far do we have to stay under?" My voice sounds thready, a little high-pitched, and I swallow roughly.

"We'll never get them through the rabbit hole without breaking their necks." The rabbit hole is the secret passage under the Wall, allowing illegal entrance to the City, I remember. "We'll have to get to Tudor's new place and then surface, go through the gates on the East. I'll beep ahead so they're expecting us, get them to bring some phenolum. I wish we had some now. If this guy wakes up, even for a minute, he's gonna get a message out."

I twist my mouth in agreement. "Let's hood him; he didn't get a good look at us, and if he doesn't know where he is then he can't bring them straight on us, especially if he's a bit scrambled. You left his comm, right?" Without waiting for her answer, I yank a black fabric strip out of my own flatpack and wind it around the Agent's eyes.

She fires a withering look at me. "This isn't my first dance, rookie." I poke my tongue out at her and she mock grabs for it before slapping me on the shoulder and hoisting Jean Pierre up. She looks ridiculous with him over her shoulder; he's so tall his fingers are dragging on the ground. She grins and then stiffens, her face hardening and cocking her head in the way that means she's casting out psionically.

"They're here. There's a team scanning for him. Let's move out."

I smother a brief smile at her military terminology but haul the Agent over my shoulder, bolstering him with my power. It requires a bit of concentration, but it's easier than wrangling him in front of me in these narrow tunnels.

We pass the walk in tense silence, stopping periodically for Serena to do her thing. I'm patient, not asking her to fill me in. Sound carries pretty strangely in the low road, and if anyone's down here, we don't want to alert them to our presence. Our scuffing footsteps echo eerily, and we are filthy, gross mud splashing up to our knees. My mind flashes back to our run through the sewers the first night we met, when she saved my life, and I grin a bit as I trudge through the inch or two of muck. I have no idea how it's always so wet down here, since we're in the middle of a seven-year drought. The coasts get hammered by torrential rain year round, hurricanes brewing up in the ocean and smashing themselves to pieces on the shores, but in the inlands it's bone dry. Pondering the mystery of my damp feet and frequently adjusting the awkward weight of the man draped over my shoulder, we wind down the low road.

I'm aching, calves and neck tense and painful by the time I walk right into Serena, who's stopped under one of the terrifying, rusty ladders that comprise the way in and out. She pads up it while I take a rest from carrying, letting both the men soak in the stinky water and not feeling bad about it at all until I realize I'm going to have to put him back over my shoulder soon. Cursing my bad decision, I wait for Serena to wave me up. I channel my Talent to wrap around the dripping captives and hoist them up, one at a time, paying close attention for any signs of life. I'm not above concussing them if the knockout needles don't seem to be cutting it. We manhandle them through the narrow entrance, and I grin when I see Tudor at the top, hauling them out with his massive hands.

"Awright, kid?" He greets me in his gruff tones. He looks the same as he did when I met him, on the run from the exploded ARC facility. Thinning brown hair, bulging muscles, and the sort of face that is just kind of irritating.

"Yeah, not too bad. Just been out for a nice morning jog in the sewers."

He snickers and hooks a paw under my armpit to lift me out of the manhole and then kicks the cover back into place. He slings Jean-Pierre over his shoulder, and I hoist the Institute Agent back up, sighing as his stinking weight settles on to me. I need a hot shower and a massage. While we've been under, dawn's gotten busy, streaking the horizon with pretty colors, and I look at it for a moment.

Serena smirks and taps something into her wrist unit after checking for anyone showing any interest in our activity. Then she cracks her neck, gives a huge yawn, and starts sauntering off down the street. Tudor and I follow just a pace behind.

There are more people on the streets as we get closer to the Wall, and Serena waves a hand at us to stay back. We wait in the shadow of a collapsing building while she jogs off into the gathering crowd.

I'm just starting to worry, when she reappears, sweat streaking her dusty face. She's chewing her lip and lets it go with a pop when she catches my eyes.

"It's the makings of a full-on riot up there. The Gate's been shut. Dad says we should just wait it out, but it looks to me like it might get pretty nasty round here. The dwells want in; there's fights kicking off. I heard someone say something about a factory bombing, but I couldn't pick up if that's past, present, or future."

Her lip is raw where she's been worrying at it, and a bead of blood wells up.

Tudor grunts, and kicks the unconscious drug dealer on the floor, just for fun, it seems. "Awright then, kids. Have fun." He turns on his heel and starts to walk away.

"Hey!" He looks back over his shoulder and grins at me, waving, before turning the corner. I frown, letting my shoulders hit the wall. "What do we do?" He's such an asshole.

Serena sniffs, and undoes her horse tail, redoing her hair as she answers me. "To be honest, I'm not sure. We can't let these guys go, and I don't think we'd be able to get them through this lot." She jerks her chin at the crowd by the Wall. Several small fights have broken out, and there's an ominous. heavy feeling in the air. The atmosphere is oppressive; people are desperate, starving. Inside, there's food, and not many people left to stop them taking it. Just the Wall. ARC is trying to organize a system so everyone gets fed and watered, but it's difficult, and the dwells aren't inclined to be patient, understandably. If everyone just came in, then the city would be destroyed, pipes and water purifying factory alike, possibly. And I'm sure more food would be wasted than anyone can afford. It'd be a blood bath. The transition needs to be slow and steady, but for the people outside that isn't appealing.

I nod and wish I hadn't finished my water. "So what, we lay low somewhere away from—" A shattering noise cuts me off, making me jump. Serena and I both twist toward the sound, hands up in preparation. It looks like someone has thrown something against the Wall; a brown stain is marring the surface a few feet above the heads of the crowd, which has started roiling, movements washing through the people like waves. I see a thin woman fall, but she's trampled before she can get to her feet again. I wince, instincts shouting at me to help. Not for the first time, I wish people knew about our powers, so I could use them to pull her out. There's so many people I'd never make it to her in person. I can't even see her anymore.

Serena looks at me sadly, and cocks her head in the direction of a ruined wall corner. I clench my jaw and haul one of the men off the floor. Serena waits with the other, and I pad over to the possible entrance. It's dark and musty inside, but it's out of the sun and out of sight. I poke my head out and nod. Serena joins me in a moment, and we arrange the men against some rubble. Serena pokes one with her toe and huffs.

"We might have to dose 'em again. It's good for four hours only, and I do *not* want this dude waking up." She pokes the Agent again for emphasis.

I sigh, leaning back and making myself as comfortable as possible. Serena scoots over so our shoulders are touching and unclips her wrist unit.

"Wanna watch a movie?"

I snort, surprised, and nod. She drapes the screen over my left knee and her right, and we watch a movie with subtitles on so as not to draw attention to ourselves. Aside from my butt going numb within ten minutes, and the bits of gravel digging into my thighs, it's a pretty nice way to pass the morning.

By the time we've finished the movie, watched another one, and periodically stretched and checked on the increasing crowd, I'm not as enamored with the situation. Serena has re-dosed the prisoners, and is now lying sprawled on the ground, catching up on the sleep we missed last night. I'm struggling to keep my eyes open myself, and I'm getting ravenous. I've checked my pockets and eaten the unappetizing-looking cereal bar, which was all I had left, and I'm mournfully finger dipping the crumbs out of the corners of the package when a large shadow appears in the "doorway."

I scramble to my feet, interposing myself between the shadow and Serena, when I recognize the person standing there.

Tudor grins at me and waggles his hands in a pantomime of a Psionic attack and I roll my eyes.

"Awright? Davey said ya were still stuck, so I brought ya some snacks and things. You can thank me by stayin' outta trouble." He holds out a wrapped package, and the smells emanating from it make my mouth water. I grab it eagerly, and by the time I've loosened the binding, Tudor's gone again. Serena, amazingly, has managed to sleep through the whole visit. As the delicious scent rolls over me, I take back every nasty thing I've ever said about the big Blank.

I kick her on the ankle, and she rolls to her feet immediately, looking around. That never gets old. It takes her a second to remember where we are, and she pokes her tongue out at me, looking disheveled. I suppress a snicker at her expense and wave the packet.

"Breakfast. Or...lunch, I guess?" Looking at the time, I see it's more of a lunch hour. I plop down on the floor and rip open the fiber paper. A bottle and two brown pies nestle in the packaging and my mouth starts watering immediately. "I'm dreaming!" Putting the pack to one side, I waste no time stuffing my face.

Serena daintily picks up the remaining pie and takes a neat bite, somehow managing to avoid getting piping hot gravy all around her mouth. I'm finished before she's halfway done, and I wipe my mouth with the back of my hand, then burp happily. Serena flips the packaging at my head psionically, but I bat it out of the way with my own power without missing a beat. The water in the bottle is brackish and warmed from the pies, but tastes delicious. I limit myself to a few mouthfuls, and then bounce to my feet, rejuvenated. "I'm gonna check out the sitch; be right back."

Serena nods, concentrating on her pie, and I check both sides of the street before slipping out the hole in the wall. The crowd seems to be dissipating; there're far fewer people than there was earlier. I duck back inside. "People are leaving. I reckon we can make it through, assuming they'll open the doors for us? Have you heard from the boss?"

Serena burps, louder than I did, and looks smugly at me before replying. Everything's a competition. "Nah. How many people are still out there?"

I think for a second, running my mind back over what I saw, and hazard a guess. "There's maybe twenty or so left, and they seem to be milling around in groups rather than hammering at the Wall now. Want to take a look?"

She stretches forward, cracking her spine before getting to her feet and heading out. She's back inside a minute and says decisively. "Yeah, I'm nuking bored of this shithole. Let's go." Just before we're ready to step out into the brutal sunlight, a huge noise thunders, and the ground shakes under my feet, dropping me on my butt. To my horror, the walls above us start to crumble. The rocks are tumbling down toward us. Crawling toward Serena, I reach out for her, thrusting my power above us and trying to create a pocket of protection—a globe-like shield to stop us being crushed. My Talent, flighty and overpowerful as always, bursts a great deal of the rubble up in the air before gravity takes hold and starts dragging it back toward us. Frantically, we manage to link hands and weave our power together. Serena's control and my strength combine to hold up the mess of concrete and plastic, not to mention metal poles trying to crush us. It takes a moment to get it stable—it's heavy and awkward—but we manage to squirm through the dust and debris. We're outside before I remember our prisoners. We look at each other for a moment, and Serena pulls a face, blood bright on her cheekbone and matted in her eyelashes.

"Oops?" Her tone is wry, belying the silliness of her response.

It takes us two hours to dig the men out. They're in pretty lousy shape but still alive. Still, one's a torturer and one's a murderer, so I don't cry about it. The crowd's disappeared from the Wall, leaving a gaping hole fifteen foot across. Explosives. The square's a mess. I can see dozens of people bleeding from various wounds, and everyone is coated in a thick layer of grime. People are screaming on the ground, clutching crushed limbs or worse, lying silently, staring up at the unforgiving skies. We haul ass through the gate, soldiers letting us in immediately. We're quiet as we head back to ARC base, hauling our prisoners on stretchers with the help of two soldiers.

Serena tries to talk to me, but I can't find any words. I'm caught up in my own head, hollowed out by the sight of the injured and dead. I don't know what to think about anything anymore.

Chapter Three

E17

I'm sitting in front of a small fire, its warmth bathing my front to the point of discomfort, and my back icy cold where it's pressed against a rock. As I look around, I jerk in surprise when my gaze lands on a profile I would recognize anywhere. The cruel metal needles bursting out of the bones of the skull, framing a hairless head. Pollux. My body doesn't move as I cringe backward, and I realize the feeling is familiar. For a moment, I think I'm dreaming Toby's life again, trapped in the meat of his body as he goes about his day and I sleep somewhere else. Then the reality of the man's crumpled form opposite me, and the unfamiliarity of my surroundings sinks in. I'm not in Toby's body, but somewhere else. I shiver, and Cassandra twists inside me, like muscles in my brain are pulsing. Like my mind has a snake coiled inside, sinews pushing against the confines of my skull.

I look down, and these hands are curled on my knees, pale, fragile and delicately boned, though far larger than my own. The nails are chewed down to the quick, the flesh on each side red and ragged. I recognize the hands, but I don't know why, and Cassandra squirms again.

My son.

My mouth falls open. I imagine my body back at the ARC base gasping in its slumber. I'm dreaming of Icarus, somewhere outside of the city, huddled and cold, sleeping with Pollux at his feet like a loyal servant.

I can feel the tension in his body, even as he sleeps, his shoulders locked and tight, and even though it could be the cold, I feel a twitch of sympathy for his misery. I swallow convulsively, wishing myself away from here. Cassandra winds inside me, more determined than I have ever felt her, and I try to push her back but it's like stopping water from slipping through my mental fingers. She pulses in triumph as she forces me back, and Icarus awakes with a shuddering cry.

It sounds like the moment I am dragged from the Tank.

His-my ribs are heaving, and he runs his hands down his body, as though to check he is still present, solid. The familiarity of it judders through me, and I huddle in his head, small and afraid.

Pollux comes awake lazily, stretching spidery limbs with a sigh, moving with such awareness of the metal gear attached to his head I wonder how long it's been since he was able to sleep in comfort. He smiles at Icarus-me across the fire, unsettling in the flickering light.

"She's hereeee," he hisses, his voice sibilant. I'm afraid. I don't know if he means me, or Cassandra, or how he can sense our presence, three minds stuffed inside one body, like one of those toys wherein a doll fits inside a doll and inside a doll again.

Icarus ignores him, oblivious to the hijacking of his mind. Judging from the lack of awareness Toby has exhibited during my sojourns into his mental spaces, I hope that here, in Icarus's mind we have a similar lack of affect and control.

He groans, the feeling reverberating through my awareness, and then turns to warm his back against the fire. He drops his head into his hands, and presses his fingertips to his eyelids hard enough to flare green spots into our vision.

"Now, now. It's impolite to ignore one's relatives." Pollux frightens me, but he does not seem to frighten Icarus. It takes a moment for his words to worm their way into me, and my heart, far away though it may be, stutters. Relatives? Like I'm part of this twisted group? At its heart, the Institute appears to be a family business. I remind myself to pass this information on. It could be important, and it argues for the case that Psionic abilities are a genetic predisposition.

Cassandra feels smug inside me, and I hate her more at this moment than I ever have in the past. I look at Pollux's headgear and remember the tension in Icarus's spine as he woke, gasping for air. I wonder if Cassandra has ever been in the Tank, if she remembers it at all, subconsciously or otherwise. I wonder if she dreams of drowning.

She laughs inside me, and I grit my teeth, trying to force her back. For some deep, instinctive reason, I do not want to let her be here with her son. There is something empty about her pleasure at seeing him, something ugly.

Icarus gets to his feet, changing my perspective, my vision lurching. I see they're in a canyon or something similar. The sky is visible through the crevice a few feet above Icarus's head. The stars are twinkling, and I realize he must be far from the city to be able to see them like this, without the pervasive orange glow shielding all but the brightest from our eyes.

He rolls his shoulders, and pads into the darkness. His hands go to the ties of his trousers, and I mentally recoil. Cassandra laughs again, and I do my best not to pay attention as he answers nature's call. It is impossible to detach myself completely, though, and I feel the heat in my cheeks as if I'm standing there in my own body, watching his private moments.

He turns, and heads back to the fire. Pollux is crouching on his heels and warming his hands over the low flames. The smoke eddies in front of him, turning him into a ghost creature, freakish and dangerous. I try to will myself back, into my own flesh, the meat that remembers me, fits around me properly, but it is in vain. I resign myself to this piggyback ride, and resolve to gather as much information as possible about where they are. I wish I could read Icarus's thoughts, but when I'm out of body like this, I have never been able to access my powers.

They eat in silence, although I can feel them communicating psionically. It feels like someone is breathing on the back of my neck. I can't tell what they're thinking to each other, and I squash down the frustration. Cassandra can't hear them, either, I know, as she tries to push against the ephemeral membranes keeping the three of us from bleeding into one another.

Icarus rummages in a pile of packs, and comes up with something heavy and a little wet, wrapped in cotton paper. As he turns to the firelight, I see the blooming rosettes of blood on the wrapping. I watch with interest as he unwraps the thing, and reveals a good-sized lizard. It is about the same length and width as his forearm and has already been butchered. The headless, organless creature gets pinned onto a pair of metal skewers and suspended over the flames. It drips juices into the fire that hiss and sizzle. I feel-hear Icarus's stomach rumbling.

Judging by the dry crevice they're huddling in, and the lizard they're about to eat, I extrapolate that they must be in the desert that fades into the edges of the slums. I know that there are lizard catchers who sell their wares to the poor who can't afford factory food. I've even seen tables of insects and other creatures in the marketplaces. I've never eaten lizard, however, but it seems like I'm about to, albeit secondhand. It's a strange, dislocating sense of being. I can experience what Icarus's body is experiencing, but am unable to affect it in any way. Much like a regular dream, I suppose. I wonder for a moment if all dreams are connecting us to another person, in another place, ones with different laws of nature than here. A glimpse into life-after-life.

I'm brought out of my ponderings by the tangy taste of hot meat upon Icarus's tongue. It burns his fingertips, and mouth, but he and Pollux both strip the flesh from the lizard's bones in record time, gulping it down. It is an interesting texture, chewy, but the flavor is inoffensive.

The clawing hunger in Icarus's stomach subsides, and he grins at Pollux. They communicate silently for a few moments, and the world begins to lighten with the first hints of dawn. The stark black outlines of the rocks against the sky soften and the stars fade out of view.

I wonder what they plan to do. If they're traveling somewhere, or just hiding out, fearful they're being tracked down. Pollux licks the corner of his mouth, snakelike, and they begin to sort through their rough camp, about to move on. That answers that question. Pollux disappears behind a rock to take care of necessities, and in a few minutes they're ready to go. They've been doing this for a while, maybe for the full time since the Institute fell. Months.

As they begin walking, I see that the rocks are an earthy reddish gray, and look crumbled and soft. Their feet dig into dust, creating a thick cloud that settles onto their legs and shoes. I'm startled when Icarus halts abruptly; he gropes at his hip for something, and I feel his hand close around the hilt of a knife. He draws it, a smooth and predatory movement. I can't make out what he is reacting to, even though I can feel the trembling tension in his muscles. I see the threat at the moment Icarus's arm streaks out, the knife flying as a silver blur before thudding into the meaty body of a snake, on a rock shelf at waist height. The shock of the impact seems to throw me out of him, and I spiral through the blackness, wondering if I have left Cassandra behind. I hope I have. Let her son carry her.

I wake with a shudder, clawing at myself. It takes me a few moments to be convinced my mind is back where it belongs, and I have control over myself. My hip thuds into something unexpected, and with confusion, I realize I'm not lying in my bed; there's no sound of Alyssa's soft snore or visible square of light from the vent above the door.

Heart pounding, I spin around, banging into something, and a glow lights up the area abruptly. My breath comes in little pants, and I realize it's the light from a computer monitor. I'm in a large room, the lights off and the door closed. I'm close to panicking as I back into a corner, and then with a thump of relief I realize where I am. The ARC control room looks different at night. This room is used for meetings and organization. The staff who are working right now will be in the smaller operations room. I'm alone, inside a room that should be locked down securely. Shakily, I tiptoe toward the computer and hesitantly draw up the file log. My heart shudders in fear as I see the list unfurling. During the last four hours, around a hundred files have been opened and viewed. To my relief nothing seems to have been edited. Cassandra is so quiet in my head for a moment I can't feel her at all. Then I get a faint sense of her and the feeling is wound through with a smug sense of success.

I squeak in distress, backing away from the incriminating evidence of my nighttime excursion. It must have been me. Or rather, her, through me. But bad enough. Thoughts streak across my mind. I could go now and speak to India, get him to read my dreams and try to make sense of what is happening to me. But if I do that, and they find out that Cassandra is locked inside me, I don't know what they would do. I know what I would do. I would put a bullet in this brain to make sure she never gets out to inflict her own special sort of misery on the world again. Maybe that's what I should do.

Gathering myself, I head back to the monitor. Clicking through the firewalls by reading the residual presence in the area, and using those invisible fingerprints, I figure out the password, I delete the footprints on the machine, thankful for the ARC technology classes that covered this exact situation. The air feels heavy as I sneak to the doorway, hoping that no one decides to check the video feeds from the control room this evening, and let myself out with trembling hands.

I make it back to my room without bumping into anyone, and slip through the door. To my relief, Alyssa lies sprawled out in her customary sleeping position, half on her side with her arm flung off the bed and her fingertips just grazing the cold floor. I slide into bed and spend a sleepless hour tossing and turning before I decide to just head to the gym if I'm not going to get any rest.

It takes me two hours of vicious exercise before I even begin to shake the lingering feelings of dread and quell the sick fear in my guts. I'm sweating and wrung out when Ria saunters over and asks if I fancy going over to the shooting range. Despite feeling like a wet cloth, I agree.

Ria's an excellent shot, and she agreeably thinks "aloud" what she is doing as she positions herself and aims. I mimic her process and manage to hit the target consistently. I'm still not used to the heavier, strange guns that ARC uses. The same as the Watch, they send a blast of concussive energy out. They don't have a great effective range and are ridiculously loud but have the benefits of being difficult to block psionically and never need reloading, just recharging. We also can't fire someone else's without reprogramming the chips they contain. Some operatives carry traditional projectile firing guns as well, but ammunition is expensive so they're much less common.

We spend an hour practicing, and by then I'm so hungry I have to excuse myself and head to the canteen, only stopping for a brief dry shower, leaving me reddened and raw-feeling on the outside to match my heart.

Toby is sitting at one of the long tables, gesticulating as he explains something to Alyssa and Serena. The brown-skinned girl is grinning at him, following his every elaborate move, while Serena looks less impressed and is clearly distracted, folding some piece of paper over and over itself. I grab a tray and slide into place. My brother grins at me.

"Morning, twin. You're up late!" I blink at him, allowing the rolling happiness he's exuding to drive back the last of the cold that's taken up residence in my bones.

Alyssa nudges him with a bare elbow and rolls her eyes. "Thea's been up since dawn, lazybones. I bet she's been in the gym?" She looks to me, with a smile. I grin back, enjoying the slight pout on my brother's face.

"Yep, two hours in the gym and an hour on the shooting range. Not all of us sleep till—" I glance at the digital clock on the wall and subtract five minutes. "—nine thirty."

Toby grins. He's beautiful when he smiles, which might be a strange thing to think about your brother, but is the only way to describe the wide openness of him. He's so unsullied. Pure.

"Actually, Serena and I just got back. So there!" He pokes his tongue out, and Serena smirks.

"Well, even though you weren't sleeping in, Tobes, you could do with a trip to the weights. You're looking a bit soft."

Alyssa joins in the teasing, gleefully. "Well, he is sort of out of shape now. Too much time in the labs and not enough in the gym!"

Serena nods seriously, not even giving Toby a chance to respond, even though his mouth is open in indignation. "That's true. All his muscles are turning to goop. He's relying on his telekinesis too much."

Toby finally twigs that they're joking, and wrinkles his nose at us all. "I'd show you my rock-hard stomach if I didn't think it'd put you off your food with jealousy!" He smirks at Serena.

She thwaps him in said "rock-hard stomach" making him *oof*, and I snicker. "It'd be the "gay" that puts me off your hairy, gross stomach, loser." She laughs at him, swiping his last piece of bread substitute off the edge of his plate, but he yanks it back with his power and stuffs it straight in his mouth, making his cheeks puff out.

"Oh please, you think I'm totally sexy," he grunts through his food, cracking Alyssa up so much she can't breathe, but she manages to pant out.

"Oh yeah, you're gorgeous. Who doesn't love a man with a mouthful of half masticated dough? It's the sexiest." I burst out laughing at the look on Toby's face, causing Serena to fall into hysterics as well.

Darcy arrives at that moment, plopping her tray on the table and looking around at our laughing faces with confusion.

Toby points at his mouth, where he's trying to swallow a mouthful of dry bread and not choke with laughter. Darcy just raises an eyebrow and starts cutting up her food.

It takes a few moments for Toby to manage to clear his mouth, which just makes us all laugh harder. He's bright red in the face by the time he forces it down, and he collapses onto the table with a sigh. "I could have died!" setting me off again at his weak gasping.

Serena manages to get herself under control and leans over to plant a smacking kiss on Darcy's cheek.

"Breakfast is the funniest meal of the day!" she announces seriously, and Alyssa chokes on her water at Darcy's confused expression. The artist meets my eyes and makes a questioning face at me, and I grin back, shrugging a shoulder.

"I think there's something in the eggs."

She nods wisely, scooping up some eggs with her fork and waving them at me. "Well, I'd best get on the train, then. If you can't beat 'em, join 'em, right?"

Serena snickers and thumps Alyssa on the back gently. "Or beat 'em and join 'em. Join 'em and beat 'em. Not that you'd ever beat me."

Darcy smirks and raises an eyebrow at her, holding her gaze until Serena's cheeks flush red. Toby blinks stupidly at them, and then the tips of his ears darken and he looks down at his plate with a smirk and a thought-shape I can't miss. *Oh.* I'm never gonna be able to look Serena in the eye again.

Darcy smiles at me, smug, taking another bite of her eggs before stating matter-of-factly, "The trick is to know your audience. And never let them forget anything."

The mention of forgetting reminds me of my illegal sojourn and sobers me up, so I finish my breakfast and then place my cutlery together at the side of my tray, before sliding out of my seat.

"I'll see you all later. I need to speak to Kion before he hits the sack." I glance at the clock and make a face. Kion will have been out all night. I know he was scheduled to knock off at nine a.m. I always know when everyone is scheduled. He should be done returning his kit but might have already gone to bed. I'll have to hurry if I want to catch him.

The group waves me off with a few calls of "See ya later" as I return my tray to the stacks for one of the shift workers to deal with. Toby's managed to wangle his way onto a lab shift, along with Alyssa, so they don't have to do manual labor, but I have a week of evening shifts coming up next week.

I walk with a bounce in my step toward the barracks. It pleases me how strong I feel. I used to get trembles in my legs if I had to walk at a fast pace for more than a few minutes, and now I could run all the way to the building. In fact, as soon as I step into the sunlight, I do. I break into a light jog and lope across the gravel pathway toward the building that has been converted into a barracks for the Operatives.

Most of the ARC personnel live here, in bare-bones rooms. Serena and Darcy have their own apartment in the regular housing, and the rest of us are lumped in with the kids in dorms for another two years. Luckily, I share with Alyssa now, which is a vast improvement on the grumpy girl I shared with, at first. Toby's still sharing with Jake. There's also a quiet, dark-skinned boy who has the last bunk, but he's so introverted we only know his name because it's written on his locker. Andrea. I used to call him Delta-19. Darcy says he's a promising artist; she teaches the art and design classes to everyone under seventeen. There aren't that many teenagers on base, so the classes are small. I don't think he'll become an Operative, since he could have already taken the course if he wanted. Officially, I'm working up to attempting the Arena, but it just doesn't seem that important. I've been an Operative in my own way for most of my life. So far it doesn't seem like anyone is going to argue that point.

I slow to a walk as I approach the barracks building, my feet skidding in the loose stones. I grin at the soldier lounging outside and gesture at the building.

"Is Kion in yet?"

"Nah, Alon and Tal just got back, but so far they're the only ones." He rubs a hand across his face blearily. He probably had a late shift last night and got up early. I don't recognize him, so I sit on the bench, folding my feet up under me.

"I'm Thea. Toby's twin." I always introduce myself this way. Everyone likes Toby, and by deliberately drawing that association with him, it makes people more willing to forget that I'm also the freak from the Institute who remembers everything.

He nods, sucks his lip for a moment, and leans his head against the sun-warmed stone. The transal here is placed in a sort of huge half sphere above the whole area, filtering the sun's rays, but invisible unless someone focuses on looking for the joins between the plates.

"I'm Domas." He has sleepy, blue eyes, and a few scraggly beard hairs on his chin. "Toby's a good kid."

I snort before I can stop myself, which surprises me in itself. I've been so controlled for so long. I'm changing. "How old are you? You look about twelve, except for the beard." I keep my tone light, trying a joke, which Darcy says puts people at ease. I must have done it wrong, because he looks affronted and sits up straighter.

"I'm eighteen."

I wonder when he passed the Arena, but I don't want to ask. Toby beat Serena to become the youngest ever, by a month or so. He likes to tease her about that. She says he wouldn't have passed if he hadn't cheated, but she looks proud when she says it. Turning invisible is kind of like cheating. Well, a lot like cheating, really, but then I guess everything we can do is "cheating" compared to most people. Anyway, it's still cool that he's the best at something. There's around 325,000 people living inside the Wall, about double that outside, and just over 400 people living on the ARC base. I think about 150 are Operatives, and maybe 100 are kids. Everyone else is sort of "support" or "research and development." Lots of scientists around here.

The silence stretches awkwardly, and when a crunch of gravel makes me look up from my hands, I'm pleased to see Kion, walking with his arm slung under Ria's, helping her walk. I dash over, grabbing his kit bag out of his other hand, and look worriedly at Ria's face, which is lined with pain. She's limping heavily. It takes another minute for Domas to get to his feet and try to help her, but she bats him away in irritation, and he just hovers awkwardly. Kion gives me a look which means "Wait here; I'll be back; don't worry."

I set Kion's kit bag down and wait by the door. I play with my datapad so it's not as awkward, as Domas retakes his seat, marking Kion and Ria off as returned and messaging for a medic. There's a little clinic set up in the barracks, but it's not manned full time. Sure enough, Doc Grey ambles out of the main building and saunters over to the barracks, going straight in without acknowledging us. I guess even if he's not that worried about Ria, he's distracted. Usually he's quite nice to me.

I enjoy the warmth of the sun, and try not to think about Ria until Kion comes out, looking exhausted. The rest of the night shift have straggled in in twos and threes while we've been waiting, and Domas disappeared without a word, presumably to count Zaps, or something equally important.

Kion sits next to me on the bench, resting his strong hands on his knees, worrying at a tear in the worn fabric for a moment, before stilling.

"Torn tendon. Six weeks." I smile at his familiar laconicism. I want to tell him about waking up in the control room, but I'm too scared. He reads that something is wrong and twists a little to look at me. The crow's feet around his eyes crinkle in silent question.

"I want to go to Second City." I blurt out.

He narrows his eyes at me curiously, waiting for me to explain.

"I think... I think that we need to know what the Institute is doing, and I think the best person to find out is me." My voice catches with tension, and Kion picks up my hand from where I have been gripping the stone bench so hard my fingers are cold and stiff. He pats it and sets it down in my lap.

"Why?" I meet his questioning eyes, trying to show how serious I am.

"I'm worried they're doing something, getting ready to do something. I can hide from them; I did it for years, and you don't have a stronger Reader on staff here. I can parse more information than anyone else. I can read them without them even realizing."

"You haven't passed. They'll never approve it." I swallow convulsively, balling my bloodless hands into fists.

"I'll go anyway. I'm not a prisoner. I'll go anyway and..." The rest doesn't have to be spoken. With no equipment and the tube not running, I'd die in the desert. But I can't just stay here, hiding away while the Institute plans Google knows what, and wait for them to make a move. I'd love to, I would, but I'm too scared. I'm scared that Cassandra will come out of me, that she has some plan for me. I'm even scared that going to Second City is her idea. But more than that, I'm scared that if I stay here I'll do something horrible and destroy the fragile balance ARC is trying to create.

Kion sighs, and his head thumps against the wall of the barracks. He nudges his shoulder against mine, in a companionable fashion, and wipes a hand across his face.

"Aright. I'll ask. Later."

I sniff, and lean my head against his broad shoulder for a moment, then slide off the bench.

"Go to bed." I manage a weak smile at him, and he snorts faintly, unfurling from the bench with enviable grace.

"Yup."

I walk away from him without looking back. I know that if he persuades Mr. Jacobs, then it'll be him that comes with me. There's no one better equipped to deal with the desert. There's also no one I feel safer with, not even Toby. Kion knows what it is to do evil to survive. I trust him in a way I've never trusted anyone. I don't need to look inside him to know who he is. To know he sees me.

If he says he'll ask, the chances are I'll get to go. Which means I have a little groundwork to do.

Chapter Four

TOBY

A noise catches my attention and I look up from my datapad, which is resting on my knees as I sit cross-legged on a pillow, leaning my shoulders against the padded wall. Darcy is resting a hand against the doorframe. Her lips twitch in amusement as she takes in my disheveled hair, and then Thea slips into the room, footsteps soft against the tiling, barefoot, as she usually is.

I know something's wrong before my twin sits down. She's twisting her hand in the edge of her sweater, a newly developed tell of discomfort that I'm pretty sure she adopted from Jake without even realizing it. Darcy gives me a look loaded with a mix of emotions I can't seem to decipher. I wish I could read people better. Not even psionically, just in general. The corners of her mouth pucker in a half smile, devoid of amusement, and then she catches Thea's attention, sending her something that helps her untwist her fingers, and half turn to face me. Darcy disappears down the corridor.

She swallows, and I set my datapad to one side, cracking my neck and shifting position so my arms are hooked round my legs, my feet flat on the floor. I've been sitting for too long, my muscles tight and sore.

"You okay?" She's clearly not okay, but I don't know how to ask her to tell me why.

She shifts, blue eyes darting to me, and away, glancing around the room.

"I'm going... I have a mission. I'm leaving this evening."

My mouth opens a little in surprise, and I lick my lips. "What mission? You don't have clearance." My voice sounds strange. I can see from Epsilon's... Thea's eyes, that she can feel my confusion mixed in with a little fear and hurt.

She chews her lip and leans her shoulder against the wall. "Kion and I are going to Second City to try to gather some intelligence. I may not have ARC clearance, but this is what I've been doing my whole life. They're not asking me to do anything I'm not trained for."

Protectiveness surges through me, and her eyes soften sympathetically. I look away, not wanting her to look right through me at this moment, even though a lack of eye contact won't help. "They shouldn't be asking you to do anything. You've done enough."

She snorts softly, then sighs, reaching out and resting a hand against the back of my neck. Physical contact feels very natural between us. We may not have grown up side by side as we were meant to, but the experience we shared in the Institute's cell, and the merging of our consciousness has left us with few barriers. "They're not asking, I am."

I take a moment to digest the words, and let my head fall back with a thunk against the wall. The silence stretches, and Thea's fingers twitch like she's stopping herself from fidgeting. They're cold on my skin. Unlike with most people, skin-on-skin contact doesn't increase our connection. It hums permanently between us since the event, regardless of distance, if we focus on it. She feels me deciding that if she must go, then I must go with her. I owe her that. We've "talked" at great length about the fact that I'm not responsible for her childhood, or for her happiness, but living her life with her has left me heavy with guilt, and that guilt has channeled into a desire to make sure she never, ever gets hurt again.

She shakes her head gently, and a bead of blood wells up on her lip from how hard she's worrying at it with her teeth. I frown a little seeing it, and she swipes at her mouth with the back of her hand, smearing it. "You can't come, Toby. ARC needs you here."

"Bollocks to ARC!" *Thanks, Serena, for the continued urge to swear in obscure colonies slang.* "You need me." She smiles a little, shuffling round to sit next to me, hands in her lap now.

"Yes, I need you, Toby. But not for this. This is... This is mine to do."

Hot anger boils through me at the unfairness of asking her to put herself in danger from the same people who kidnapped and tortured her. My stomach churns and I pull my knees into my chest, knotting my hands together while I try to sort through my feelings.

She leans her head against my shoulder and opens our connection a little, so I can feel what she's feeling. I usually have a sense of her emotions, the immediate reactionary ones, but I can't go deeper unless she lets me. The way our powers are aligned doesn't allow for more than that. But now, the helplessness and constant state of apprehension I've never understood from her becomes crystal in a moment. I feel how ragged she feels, inside. How raw with fear, waiting for everything to come crashing down on her. I understand her need to control her terror. I understand, and I sigh. An aching sigh, something inside me fissuring in sympathy.

Her breath tickles my neck, and I wriggle, wrapping an arm over her shoulder, and try to accept that she has the right to make her own decisions, that by trying to stop her I would be hurting her myself. We sit for a long time, emotions crashing through me, until I think I have a handle on how I'm feeling. Thea moves moments before I do, in sync as always. She manages a shaky smile as she untangles herself and gets to her feet. Her eyes are a little red-rimmed. I realize, with a start, my face is wet with tears. I don't know if they're hers or mine.

"Hitting stuff helps. With the knots." She pats her stomach through her stab-proof vest, the nanofibers glinting a little as they move. I scrub my face with both hands and nod. She slips out, shutting the door behind her before I have to struggle for a reply. It would be eerie how well she knows me, if it didn't feel so right, and so ordinary.

I listen to angry music for at least an hour, ignoring the beeps from my comms, and the knock on the door. It's a study room. I'm studying how not to accidentally be a dick to my twin by letting my fears override her need. So, what if I'm supposed to be in class, then in training? Screw it. If I saw any of the board right now, I'd probably try to punch them, and I can't see a good outcome for that. Especially if it was Kion. I might be 'stronger' than him, but I'm pretty sure he'd break my arms and legs before I landed a blow, telekinetic or otherwise. Taking Thea out into the desert and then into the heart of enemy territory... I guess he might let me hit him once. He's a pretty fair guy.

After growling and pacing has worn a little thin, I head back to my dorm and switch my light sneakers for heavy boots, planning on heading to the gym and working off a little steam. Just before I'm out the front door, I hear Serena calling me.

"Tobes, yo, wait up!" She skids to a halt next to me, brushing her wild hair back off her face and looking up at me with a weird expression.

"How're you doing?" There's an edge of something in her voice, but it takes me a minute to figure out what it is. Guilt. I narrow my eyes at her.

"You knew!" A beat passes, and she squirms uncomfortably. "You helped...?" The hurt is stark in my voice. Brittle. She looks up at me through her eyelashes and shrugs awkwardly.

"Not really. I mean, I thought it was a shitty plan, and my dad asked me what I thought, and I was gonna say that, but Darcy..." She really does look upset, but the anger is hot in my guts, and my fists are clenched against my sides.

"So, you sold Thea to ARC so your girlfriend wouldn't be mad at you?" My throat is so tight the words sound strangled.

"No. NO! Come on, Tobes. It wasn't like that. She wants to go, and we're flying blind here. I volunteered us for guard duty, but my dad shot it down. He reckons a small crew is the best chance to stay undetected, and that...well. That you'd be a liability."

Something burning and raw bursts through me, and for a moment, I think my power is about to smash out of me, into her. Part of me wants it to. I back away. I'm out the door before she shouts after me, and I run flat out for the gates. I pull my power around me and disappear before she can see which way I turn.

I run like it's all there is, lungs burning, legs strong and solid beneath me. It feels good, and I stop paying attention to where I'm going, what people might think of the footsteps thumping past them with nobody there. I weave around the people on the streets; there's too many for me. I want to run with no one in my way, run until I puke and fall and get this feeling out of me. I reach the Wall without meaning to, and then I realize I want to be out in the slums. Unshielded roads mean few people will be around, thanks to the beating sun. My UV proof shirt has a high collar and long sleeves. I wish I'd swapped it out for one with cooling threads running through it, but my sweat will have to do.

Invisible, I dodge the guards on the gate, propelling myself up in the air, over their heads. One of them turns a gun on me, a Reader. I'm past too fast for her to get a shot off. I'm not sure, but I think it was Grace. I get lost between the buildings, feet hitting the packed dirt and broken concrete with a rhythm that helps me think only of that.

I run until I can't anymore, collapsing in the shade of a broken wall, throat throbbing and dry with the dust. I'm soaked. I didn't bring any water, and my head is pounding viciously, like my brain is trying to escape from my skull. I can feel Thea searching for me, pushing for our connection, and I cut her off for the first time. I slam my shield into place as forcefully as I can, coat it in slippery memories of other places, and will myself to be Blank, to be alone. I left my comm on my bed.

I need water; my body is shaking from exertion and my sweat has evaporated in just the few minutes it took for me to get my breath back. I take a moment to figure out where I am. I can still see the top of the Wall, maybe three miles distant. The sun's to my left, which makes that the west. There are four wells in the townships, and assuming I'm not totally off, positioning wise, the nearest one should be about a mile east of here. I get to my feet, realizing I haven't held my power up for a while. I wonder when I dropped out of invisibility, and if anyone saw. They probably thought they were hallucinating, if they did.

Wearily, I trudge toward the well, hoping against hope there won't be a gang on it. As soon as I'm down the street from the square I think holds the well, I know I'm out of luck. I try to whisk my power up around me, but I can feel it failing. I don't think I've exhausted my strength. I think I'm just too tired and angry to concentrate enough. Leaning against a convenient ancient lamppost, twisted at a strange angle and with a rope tied round the head, looking creepily like a noose, I consider my options. I scrape my sweat-soaked hair off my forehead and look down at myself. Good boots, good clothes, but no pockets. They do not, as a rule, accept chip credit transfer in the slums. I snort to myself. I have a bracelet on I could trade. Although, if anyone sees me, they won't care if I do have trade, they'll try to take my stuff. I crack my neck and yawn. I could just head back to the city, but if I scan my thumb, then Serena'll track me down in minutes. I'm surprised I don't have a GPS chip embedded in my neck, all things considered. I don't want to be found just yet, and I doubt that she'll leave me alone. Best friend she may be, persistent she definitely is. I sigh, trying to figure out a solution. A man appears at the end of the alley and I duck out of sight before I even mean to. I guess I've learned my stealth lessons at least a bit.

He goes past me with a plastic bottle full of water. We don't make plastic anymore, just recycle the millions of tons already out there. The far end of the slums backs onto an old landfill, which is how a lot of the people living out here make a living. I don't have anything to put water in.

Making a decision fast, I step out of the shadow of the alley, and the man spins to face me. I hold my hands out to show I don't have a weapon and smile reassuringly.

"Hey, friend. I didn't mean to make you jump." He has a black eye, and a few missing teeth, but they don't look that fresh. He eyes me skittishly, ready to run.

I relax, leaning on a wall, trying to be unthreatening.

"I want to trade for your water. I have a leather bracelet. I'm gonna show you, okay?" I pull my sleeve up and show him my bracelet. It's woven leather, with an old-fashioned coin held onto the surface with cunning knots. It's worth about five credits. The water he's carrying isn't even worth one. His eyes light up, and I grin.

"You can trade it off for more, right, but if I go up to the well, then the runners will beat me up and take all my stuff."

He grins slyly, showing the gaps in his teeth.

"Yeah, they'll take all your stuff. Like, if I shout for 'em." He opens his mouth to yell, and I leap forward, smashing my fist into his jaw before he makes a sound. The blow knocks him down, and his water bottle goes flying. I throw the bracelet down the street, and he scrambles after it wildly, trying to keep an eye on me at the same time, but I'm already scooping up the water bottle and sprinting out of sight. Hopefully, he won't bother getting the gangs to look for me. They'd just cut him out of any profits anyway. Silence follows me, so I assume he's reached the same conclusion and slide to a halt in a triangle of shade between two shanties. I pry open the water bottle and gulp it down eagerly, then upend some over my head, but just a little.

I'm gonna have to head back to the city when I get really hungry, but the water will hold me for a while. I don't have anything else to "trade," and I won't just take stuff from the poor out here. With a groan, I straighten up, realizing even if the guy I saw doesn't send anyone after me, I'm still a sitting duck in my city gear. I wish I'd thought ahead and changed my clothes, but I didn't. They're dusty enough now that at first glance I'm not too noticeable, but if anyone bothers to look at me, I won't pass in the slightest. A grin comes to my lips at how much I've learned, how much I have changed since the first day I went outside the Wall. Then, I had no idea what it was like out here. Now I'm pretty comfortable in the twisting streets, trusting my knowledge and instincts.

I take another swallow of water, then swipe the droplets from my lip. I need to shave, I note. Serena made it very clear that until I can grow an actual, proper beard, she will tease me mercilessly should I grow a sad little moustache. I pop the cap back on the crackling water bottle. It's so old the plastic is soft and creased, but it's clean. I have nowhere to carry it, so I hook it on my fingers, where it swings as I walk. Without a real plan, I amble forward. I feel a lot calmer, more in control than I did earlier, but I still want some space to think without people bothering me. I'm immeasurably sad that Thea feels like she has to do this, but I can understand why. I wish she'd let me go with her, but I think even if David Jacobs said I could, she'd ask me not to. The way I felt when Serena explained her part in it scared me. My power is still a little unpredictable, and I don't want to put myself in a volatile situation with emotions running high for Thea, it affects me too much.

I walk, and I think. Eventually I decide that I'm not angry at Serena so much as generally angry, with her as a convenient target. I'm so distracted by my thoughts I don't pay as much attention to my surroundings as I should, and I run into someone. Moving around them, I mumble an apology, and try to put distance between us, but my neck starts tingling, and I look around. Shit. So much for congratulating myself on being so clever now. There are four guys ahead of me, standing across the narrow alley in an obvious block. I spin, and there's two more behind me. I crack my neck, squaring my shoulders, and pop the lid of my water, taking an unhurried gulp.

"Howzit?" I copy Serena's casual arrogance and try to embody myself with the "I don't give a damn" essence she exudes so well.

The leader seems a little taken by surprise and looks me up and down, chewing on a stick of plastic. Something about his teeth is familiar, and in a flashing moment I realize I know this guy.

I laugh incredulously, and he eyes me, squinting in the sunlight. He doesn't seem to twig, and so I hold up my left hand, the one missing most of a finger, and his eyes settle on it, then widen.

I smirk in what I hope is a dangerous manner. "Now, CJ, isn't it? I owe you, big time. But if you turn around and walk away, I'll forget all about you taking my finger. A'ight?" I'd dropped the street, cant in my surprise, but he knows I'm a city kid anyway. I wonder if his boys are the same as last time, if they recognize me. I try to spread my awareness around me, cursing my lousy reading skills and tingling with anticipation of a fight. I'm not scared, not this time. I could bounce them all off the walls and onto their heads before they could move.

CJ sees it in me—the lack of fear—and he curls his lip. He's afraid of me. I can almost smell it. I turn a little, so I'm close to the wall, and gesture at him, as though to offer him an exit. His jaw clenches, and I can't help smirking just a little more. The turning of the tables feels good. He should be afraid of me. I wonder if I could fight my way out without even using my powers. The boys are spread out, and it's only CJ and another lad in front of me. I could probably barrel my way through, kick him in the balls for good measure, and leg it. I know the streets now, and I'm a damn sight better fighter than I used to be. I roll my shoulders, anticipating the explosion of violence. He can back down, or I'll make him back down.

CJ steps back, just a little, but enough. I step forward, toward him. "G'wan, get." I'm taunting him. Although I'm not proud of it, I feel good. Strong, tough. Like I could smash them all down if they make me. The scuff of movement behind me doesn't warn me in time. I turn and thrust my power out a moment later, but then lightning explodes in my eye, scarlet and green, and the floor hits me in the knees out of nowhere. I try to shield myself, to throw my power outward, but it's recalcitrant, and it's too late. The second blow knocks me face-first into the concrete, and everything fades out, sound stringing like sticky toffee behind me and into the blackness.

MY HEAD POUNDS, my body is curled on something cold. I retch, puking up the water I drank. It takes a while to recover, and the foul taste in my mouth burns. I groan.

"Whast uben...?" The words stick in my throat like they're made of wax, coming out garbled and incomprehensible. Something hits me in the shin, and I flinch back. Reaching up to scrub my face doesn't work. My wrists are tied behind me. Squirming in the dust doesn't help but does bring another blow to my lower leg. I lie still, trying to make sense of what is happening.

It takes a good few minutes to get my eyes open; there's a crust sticking one together, and the other is swollen half shut. When I manage it, I'm not even sure I have for several moments, as it is as dark with them open as it was with them closed. I groan again and am rewarded with another kick in the shins.

"Shut up, kweed." This hissing, urgent voice doesn't sound cruel, more desperate. Every inch of me throbs with pain, even parts I didn't know could hurt, like my armpits. Agonizingly slow, my battered eyes adjust, and I get to grips with my surroundings. I'm lying on a rough concrete floor. The only light coming into my prison is pushing its way through a chink way above my head. There are other people in the room with me, one of whom, a young lad with a bruised, narrow face and a shaved head, is the person who's been kicking me in the legs. He's sitting, his back against the wall, with his hands tied behind him. The knots securing his ankles are run through an old iron ring set into the concrete. He narrows his eyes at me, then jerks his chin toward the ceiling, looking up dramatically.

I get it. There are people up there, listening for any noise. Clumsily, I maneuver myself around, inch by inch, until my constrained hands are touching the wall, and I can see the whole room. I have puke in my hair, and my face feels like raw meat. The other figures—to my confused brain it looks like there are two more of them— appear to be either asleep or unconscious. Satisfied there is no immediate danger, I take a minute to catalog my injuries. I don't think anything is broken, although my whole body is protesting rough treatment. I take a deep breath and settle myself, checking my shields over and then sigh.

The Psionic shout I send out is weaker than it would be if I was at full strength, but the day's activity has taken a toll on me, as well as the distracting demands from my bruised flesh. However, Thea clocks me immediately. Her concern and distress are apparent over our connection, and I concentrate on sending out a constant signal, letting my friends know where I am.

I'm bored stiff by the time the cavalry arrives. The awake boy has been eyeing me with curiosity, probably wondering why I'm not panicking, and how I managed to get my ropes off. It took a while, the delicate concentration needed for unpicking tight knots is more controlled than my power likes to be. In the end, I force my Talent between the ropes and my skin, pushing it outward with so much pressure it stretches enough for me to wriggle my fingers through.

I'm massaging the feeling back into my hands when a series of *whumps* from above makes me grin, albeit weakly. It also wakes the other two figures up. A girl and a boy, a bit older than me, I'd say.

"Hey, hey!" I'm getting to my feet with some difficulty when the pointy boy gets my attention. He raises his eyebrows at me and waggles his feet. "Share the love, eh?"

I snort and nod, limping over and squatting down, wishing I had a knife.

"There's a blade in me boot. Idiots didn't search me." I stop trying to make sense of the snaking ropes and, instead, wrangle the blade out of his boot heel. It takes only a few seconds to slice through his bonds and set him free. His gaze is glued to my missing finger. I realize with a start, that I've been using telekinesis to compensate for the loss. It must look strange, but it's clear he doesn't know why. While he's trying to get feeling back into his wrenched shoulders, I free the other two captives, who are wild eyed and terrified. I grin reassuringly, but they scoot back against the wall, shaking.

I shrug and leave them to it, tiptoeing ungracefully to a set of stairs that lead to a hatch in the roof. Listening at the hinges, I can hear muffled shouts, and a crunching noise. I don't want to stay down here like a kid, but I know I must look at least as bad as I feel, if not worse. I scrub some of the dried blood from my face, but the vomit in my hair is a lost cause without water.

"Stay here." I hiss at the narrow-faced boy, and he squints at me like he's trying to figure me out, but then his mouth quirks, and he jerks his head, once.

"Leave the 'atch open."

I pull a face but put my hand on the hatch and then duck as an extra loud thump comes from above. Zap shot, for sure. Nothing else is that loud. My head ringing, I wait a few seconds and then push the hatch open. It's bolted, but I use my telekinesis to force the screws out of the wood, and it jerks upward. It pushes too far, and then falls abruptly. I was unprepared. It nearly smacks me in the top of the head, and I curse but push it up again more carefully. There's shouting, audible with it open, and no one in the room I emerge into. A table is flipped on its side, and there are cards scattered across the floor.

Greedily, I spy a water jug and grab it, swishing a few mouthfuls around my mouth and then emptying some over my head. The boy from the cellar pops up through the hatch like a meercat, grins at me wickedly, and scarpers, clambering up a shelf and through a window so thin I have no idea how he could have managed it. He throws out a "Thanks for the assist, brah!" in his wake.

I open my mouth to say something, then shrug and carefully finger poke my eye and try not to throw up again. I'm sitting on a lopsided chair facing the door, with my hands up ready, when Serena busts through it, gun first. I see her finger jerk on the trigger in reaction to seeing me, but thankfully, her reactions are fast enough, and she stops herself from shooting. I breathe a disbelieving sigh of relief and try to grin at her, but it hurts my head. Marty is right behind her, his back to us as he watches the outer room. He glances around when Serena starts yelling.

"Toby, you are a..." She is lost for words, finishing with an incomprehensible growl that manages to sound furious, exasperated and affectionate all at once, and beckons me to the door.

"You okay?" Maybe a little worried too. "You're in an organ farm, you know that, right? They could have butchered you like a pig before you even woke up. I should kick your ass." She helps me to my feet with kind hands, belying the anger in her voice.

"My ass is already plenty kicked, thanks." My voice is croaky and hoarse still, and Serena growls again, escorting me to the exit with a firm grip on my bicep. I refrain from telling her she's poking me in the bruises and keep a sheepish silence as we join the team who've come to pull me out. There are four bodies in the room, heaps of wet meat on the floor. I shudder and remember the other kids in the cellar.

"There's people being held down in the hatch there." I jerk my thumb back toward the room and Marty ducks through the door. Johan gives me a disapproving glare, which softens when he takes in the miserable state of me. I must smell pretty bad too from the delicate sniff he gives the room. I hang my head, embarrassed.

"Can everyone yell at me later, when my head stops exploding in slow motion?" I say meekly, and Serena hums irritatedly but hustles me out the door without waiting for Johan's reply. I'm glad Thea's not here to see me, although she can feel the state I'm in. I guess she didn't make the cut for active team today.

Serena doesn't talk to me all the way home, but my head is throbbing so hard it's a relief. She drops me at the medical rooms, sits me on a bed with cursory attention paid to my aches and pains, then leans over me.

I wilt. She might be miniature, but I swear she is the scariest person I have ever met. Her eyebrows are furrowed, and her fists are clenched.

"If you ever do something that stupid *ever* again, I'm going to get your operative status stripped. As your commanding officer, I can do that. I swear... And then I'm gonna kick your ass and get Thea to tell me the most embarrassing thing you've ever done, and I'm going to print out FLYERS and stick them everywhere so everyone knows how idiotic you are. Get some sleep. Everyone else is going to come to yell at you, and you're gonna need your strength." She's red in the face and her eyes are flashing fury at me, so I nod hard enough that my stiff neck muscles complain.

"I'm—" She cuts me off before I can apologize.

"Shut up." Then, to my surprise, she gives me a fierce hug, squashing my bruised face against her collarbones. "Idiot." This time, her voice sounds more upset than mad, so I tentatively hug her back. After a few minutes, she pulls back, sniffs once, points at me like she's going to yell some more, then sighs and turns on her heel and stalks out.

The nurse, who had been waiting discreetly in the corner, gives me a sympathetic grin as she starts poking and prodding me. I sigh. Shitty day.

Chapter Five

E17

I leave without going to see my brother, and since he's on lockdown in medical he's easy to avoid. David Jacobs gave Kion permission to sign out whatever equipment we want, and so we're pretty well set up when we head out to get in the chopper.

Serena, Darcy, and Jake come to wave us off. Serena, looking pale and grim, tells me "Don't you dare get caught," and I promise to do my best. We climb into the chopper, the hop step to get in is easy, and I can't help but grin, thinking about the last time I did this, and then my mood turns slightly somber as my thoughts switch to the team I was with. I wonder where they are, and what happened to them when ARC destroyed the Institute base. It hurts to know they're probably dead. They were never bad people, just…misinformed, perhaps. Or reprogrammed to forget the atrocities dealt out by the company they worked for.

Kion sits down next to me, and I scoot over a little to make room for his shoulders. He gives me a wry, lopsided grin. We settle back against the uncomfortable metal seats and strap ourselves in. The plan is to fly to the end of the chopper's range and hike overland. No chance of taking the tube, as our spies have reported that the other end has been blockaded, and even if it was open, I assume it would be monitored.

The helichopper engines roar to life, making conversation impossible, and I lean my shoulder against Kion's comfortably. He starts flicking through pages on his datapad and I look out the open sides of the machine lifting us up into the painfully blue sky. Garfield, the pilot, grins over his shoulder at me, and the chopper tilts queasily and then accelerates forward into the sprawling desert.

It's too bright to look at the outside world, and I squint to shade my eyes, and then I remember we've packed goggles for the desert. I nudge Kion and mime covering my eyes with something. He jerks his chin and efficiently locates the item in our packs. I put them on and smile as the glare is cut to a comfortable level, and I can make out much more detail. Behind us, the blackened, crumbling remains the Great War left in its wake sprawl westward in the far distance. The ravines on the damaged ground are vein-like, eerie. Deadland. I look away, taking in the magnificent vista of the mountains in the distance and then shuffle closer to the door, pulling against my harness. The straps digging into my chest and shoulders don't detract from the magnificence of the City from above. The gleaming buildings, invisible transal shields, and the vastness of the Wall. Even the slums look pretty neat from this distance.

The City recedes, and soon we're flying over the featureless expanse of dusty, arid plains that separate the cities. The tube line is visible, a glinting snake, undulating gently below. Second City is visible only as a shining speck on the horizon. We'll be dropped about twenty klicks out from the edge of the slums, which should take us about six hours, Kion thinks. We're aiming to land in the cool of evening and get to the City several hours after nightfall, to maximize our chances of sneaking in unnoticed.

I get bored of looking around, after an hour or so, but Kion is relaxed against the seat back with his eyes closed, enviably comfortable-looking. My butt is numb, and my body is bored, making me squirm. The harness is chafing my neck where my skin is bared, and I wish I'd thought to have my datapad handy. I realize with a start how much I have changed even in the few short months since I was freed. I'm *bored*. I'm considering "accidentally" waking Kion from his impromptu nap, just to entertain me. I notice his datapad clipped onto the side of his pack, maybe juuuuuust within reach, if I stretch. As stealthily as I can, I lean forward and manage to hook my fingertips around the carabiner holding the shockproof case of the datapad. Awkwardly, I fumble at the clasp, trying not to knock into Kion's legs.

Suddenly, so suddenly I can't even work out how it happened, I'm slammed back against the seat with a muscled forearm wedged over my throat so tightly I can't breathe, Kion's face filling my vision. I see the glazed confusion drain from his eyes, and he releases me immediately. I cough, more surprised than hurt. Kion's mouth falls open in shock, a look of distress clouding his face. I pat his knee, killing the urge to rub my sore throat as it would just make him feel worse.

"Hey, I'm sorry I made you jump." My voice isn't even raspy, and he relaxes a little, but still frowning, pressing his lips together in the way that means "I feel bad and uncomfortable," in Kion-face. He clears his throat, obviously about to fumble through something awkward, and I thump my knee into his gently. "Can I borrow your datapad? I'm boooored." I whine, joking around. He rolls his eyes at me, finally convinced I'm none the worse for wear, and unhooks his datapad deftly, handing it to me, before settling back into his comfy position.

I smile to myself, pleased he's not upset anymore and tap my way into his book folder. I find something with an interesting title, and I squirm, managing to get my feet up under my butt, which is more comfortable. I get lost in a fictional world of space travel and aliens, snickering at the funny parts, but trying to stifle my laughter so I don't wake my jumpy companion. By the time I finish the book, I can see Second City looming in the distance, like a blister of sparkles against the beige of the desert. The noise of the helichopper changes pitch and I realize we're hovering, instead of moving forward. I glance at Kion, wondering if I should wake him, but he's already opened his eyes. Clearly, he's super sensitive to changes around him, and I pout a little. I wish I could fall asleep wherever I want, safe in the knowledge that I'll wake if anything happens!

The chopper drops gradually, wind from the blades spinning up a cyclone of dust that fills the air. We rise again, and Garfield levels off, speaking into his headset and sounding tinny through the speaker next to my ear.

"All right, kids, you're gonna have to drop out. Hope you had a nice trip." He flashes me a grin over his shoulder, and Kion checks his gear before unclipping and pulling himself hand over hand toward the rappelling equipment. He sets up his harness, then throws one pack out of the chopper and keeps the other in between his feet as I unclip and shuffle over. He helps me get into the harness and checks me over and then grins, shouting to be heard over the *whump whump* filling our heads. "You got it? I'll grab you if you need." He taps his temple and maneuvers me to the edge, my heels sticking out into open space. Adrenaline buzzes through me as I give a whoop and jump out, rope whistling through the metal rings and then catching, letting me choose my own descent speed with the angle of my hand. I'm happy I took those abseiling lessons back at base.

I land without much difficulty, stumbling as my feet sink into the soft sand. I clip free and move back to wriggle out of my harness. Kion thumps down as I finish and is out of his kit before I've moved back over. He clips our harnesses back on and taps his wrist comm to signal Garfield. The ropes start winching back up and then the helichopper heels and pulls away, only stirring the dust up a little. Kion grins at me and fishes out his own sun goggles. They block peripheral vision a little, but the glare should be gone in an hour or so and there's no one out here in the desert except the traders, and they should give us a wide berth. I'm a strong enough Reader that it's unlikely anyone will get the jump on us.

Kion checks me over, making sure my trousers are tucked into my boots, and my collar is up, scarf over my head and tucked over my lower face. Then I return the favor, and we smear sunblock over the small amount of exposed skin remaining. We even have thin gloves to pull on when we're finished. Kion hoists the big pack up onto one broad shoulder, his faded brown, irregularly striped shirt blending in with the scenery behind him. Like if I saw him out of the corner of my eye, he'd have an invisible torso. I pick up the small pack and squint up at the position of the sun, and then I point in the direction I think Second City is in. Kion tugs my wrist around a few degrees and gives me a big grin. I mock frown. A few degrees isn't a huge amount to be out, but walking for five hours in even the slightest wrong direction would mean we miss the City entirely. Ugh, deserts. A movement on the floor catches my eye, and I realize it's a lizard skittering away from us. I flash back to my dream, wondering if Icarus is out here. A chill drips down my spine, and I try to shake it off. We both take a few gulps of brackish water from our hip bladders, and then we start walking, me ahead of Kion.

It's hard going. The sand sucks my feet down, making walking difficult, my calves soon burning with the unfamiliar gait necessary to stay on my feet. The sun might be close to setting, but I feel like it's broiling me as I trudge through the sand. We stop every twenty minutes for a slug of water and to check in with each other. The walking is too difficult for conversation, not that Kion is a chatty kind of guy, even if we'd just been out for a stroll. This walk would take us about three hours under different conditions.

My feet feel like the boots I'm wearing are made of fire, and my exposed skin—the sliver below my goggles— is stinging. I tap Kion and pause, attempting to stuff my scarf up under the goggle seal to protect the tender skin. Kion shuffles closer and takes over, gentle fingers tugging the covering into place. I can just make out his eyes through the tinted transal of his goggles, and I see them crinkle in a grin. I grin back. If I look half as silly as him, it's worth a smile. I feel like an alien.

Gradually, the sun disappears over the horizon, and with it, the oppressive heat, although the sand below our feet is still burning hot. The sweat that's soaked through my kit chills as the wind picks up, and I'm relieved when we stop in the lee of a sand dune and Kion yanks open the big pack. We shrug on jackets and change the position of our scarves to get drier material over our faces. We're ready to go again in a few minutes, and it's easier to keep a decent pace now it's getting cold. In fact, every time we stop for water, it's only a minute before I'm shivering, so we pick up our speed. The City materializes in front of us as we crest a hill, previously just a glow in the sky from the electric lights, now a looming darkness under that halo, with a few sparkles visible nearer in the slums.

The sight rejuvenates us and we jog for the final half an hour, our feet sinking into the soft sand. We slow when we're close enough to make out the lines of the shanty roofs, sloping, dangerously sharp edges. Kion squats down, so I mimic him, and after a moment with the datapad, he tugs his scarf down and grins at me, then uses his power to shift sand out of the way, digging a hole. It takes a while, the loose sand slipping into the hole as he digs, but eventually he seems satisfied and sits back on his heels. I keep my awareness of our surroundings on high as he sorts between one pack and the other.

Eventually, he quests toward my awareness, and I nod, shucking off my desert-appropriate clothing to yank on the rags he has set out for me. I feel his shock echoing through our connection at my sudden lack of covering, and I freeze, grabbing the slum clothes and pulling them on as fast as I can. It's so easy to forget that things are different now, that I'm not just a tool to be used as efficiently as possible. Not that anyone would ever have looked or touched me, but even the fact I'm afforded privacy now is strange and unwieldy. My skin is hot, even through the vicious chill lying next to my bones, and I'm awkward, fumbling as I fold my discarded shirt and trousers. Kion had turned away as fast as he could, and now he's changing, swift movements in my peripheral vision. I don't look.

The tension passes, and I smile tentatively when he lets me know he's finished. We hide the packs we'll leave out here in the hole and cover it with sand. When we return, we'll find the spot with a combination of technology and my reading skills.

I give Kion a once-over, checking no one can see his comm unit strapped to his upper arm, and that he doesn't look too neat and tidy. I snort at the thought. The trek through the desert has left dust etched into our skin, our eyes are reddened, even with the goggles' protection, and Kion's hair is staticky and wild. He grins back at me and jerks his head in the direction of the City. His beard seems to have thickened since we left, though it could just be the dust that is already caked into it.

We approach in silence, Kion letting me read his observations and intentions. He is treating this a little like a training exercise, but I appreciate it. The stench hits me first—rot, sweat, human excrement, and miscellaneous other smells weave together to create a miasma of discomfort. I don't choke, even though the air becomes thick in my throat as we move in. Kion lets me know we're passing the garbage dump on the outside of the slums, where dwellers pick through the waste of the rich and try to scavenge useful items. He tells me to slump, sending me an image of slum kids walking. Shoulders up, brows down, uncomfortable flicking eyes. I do my best to settle into this character, tension filling my spine. I'm out of my element here, and I need Kion's reassuring presence by my side, solid and unwavering.

He looks like he belongs, in some unknowable way. His surroundings don't affect him, as such. Nothing about his presentation, his body language, has changed, but he fits. Slotting into place. I get a faint impression of another time, a younger Kion walking in places similar to this and calling them home. I glance at him, his face shadowed and sharp in the low light. He flashes a grin at me, teeth glinting. If anyone gets close, I should remember not to smile: our teeth are whole and white, marking us out from the dwells.

We've walked for maybe twenty minutes in a seemingly meandering way. I'm not sure where we are, but I don't need to know. If anything goes wrong and I can get out, I'll just home in on our abandoned kit and try to make it back through the desert to the pick-up rendezvous. In all honesty, if Kion isn't with me, my chances of making it aren't that high. I'm pretty sure I couldn't even carry the water I would need, for a start. I assume we'll have to find more before we leave, as we finished what we had with us before we left our kit.

A sharp whistle interrupts my musing, and I jump, startled as a figure drops out of the shadows above my head. He lands silently in front of us, invisible to my Psionic senses. I have my hand on my knife hilt, the blade half out of the sheath, when Kion reassures me.

It's okay. He's ours.

I blink, my chest juddering in shock. I suddenly feel unprepared and panicked. Kion's hand is on my shoulder, calming me. He's not able to read my thoughts, but he knows panic when he sees it. I force myself to relax, and Kion pushes me gently, urging me to follow the person, who I can just make out as a scruffy-haired, lanky boy. We move through the slums at a quick pace, passing groups of rough-looking people gathered around fires contained in metal bins. There's a night market, noise and delicious smells curling out and filling my body; there's a group of ragged men waiting in a line for what must be a brothel. One of them eyes me wolfishly as we pass, and Kion moves between us. He doesn't say or do anything, except meet the man's eyes, but the fellow collapses against the wall like he's been pushed. He doesn't look at me again. I eye Kion when we're out of hearing, and the corner of his mouth puckers in amusement.

It's a very distinctive sort of look. You'd have to practice for years.

I draw a whisper of Toby's power, distant though it is, it still comes easily. *Will you teach me?*

He smirks at me, turning a corner so fast I have to trot to catch up. *Maybe. Would you use the power only for good?*

I laugh inside my head and then we're ducking through a gap that doesn't look like it could be a door but turns into some sort of low-lit corridor between two shanties. Somehow, it manages to be welcoming and even, thank Google, warm.

I trail my hand along the material and furrow my brows in a silent question. *How did they get graphene into the slums, and why hasn't it been stripped?*

Kion rolls his neck, and it crackles, the sound loud in the still quiet. *The King of the slums keeps a nice palace.*

I drop my hand, looking around eagerly as we filter into a wider room, softly lit by glowing boxes in each corner. A large, angry-looking man pushes off the wall and stalks toward us. The boy who brought us here slides between Kion and the bodyguard, hands up in a placating gesture. I shift ready to grab my knife, on edge.

'S'alright, Beom Su, we're expected." The giant narrows slanted eyes at us, a harsh once-over, then jerks his head toward a dark doorway behind him. I follow Kion past the intimidating man into the pitch-black passage. Resisting the urge to put my hand out and hold onto Kion's shirttails is difficult, but I manage. Blindly, we walk forward. I read our surroundings, my feet sure on the uneven ground. Kion and our guide are silent in the darkness, eerily so. Only my scuffing steps are audible. Self-conscious, I try to mute them.

The black starts to thin; we've taken several turns around unseen corners. I'm following Kion with my mind, Google only knows how he is following the Blank boy. Mysterious soldier talent, I expect. Now I can see light leaking around a closed door in front of us, and the presence of dozens of people beyond it. The boy raps sharply, a staccato, deliberate rhythm. Passcode. Automatically, I memorize it.

The door pushes open after a few heartbeats, and I slink after Kion, unsure what to expect.

The sight that greets me is so far outside of my experience it takes me a minute to figure out what is happening. Haphazard tables built out of a variety of materials, men and women crowding, raucous shouts. The smell of food reaches me, and my stomach cramps with a sudden, extreme demand. Kion hovers next to me, and the boy who led us here turns and grins.

"Welcome to the Dented Drum!" He has to raise his voice to be heard over the layers of noise. Someone is playing some sort of instrument, and Kion rakes his hair off his forehead, looking around and grinning faintly.

"Looks a bit different from how I remember it." The boy snickers, flashing an evil-looking grin. He's both tanned and grimy, with a sort of sly charm about him, delicate Asian features and a wicked expression. His wild hair is matted into thick, greasy spikes, and his clothes are so nondescript it must be deliberate. He performs an elaborate bow, gesturing at an empty table crushed against the wall, out of the main crowd of the room. There is a piece of metal perched on it, with a picture of a drum punched onto the surface.

"Have a seat, I'll getcha beer, some grub, and the man." He slips into the crowd, out of sight before I finish blinking. I turn to Kion, creasing my face in question, and he smirks slightly, striding to the table and pulling it to a better angle. We both slip into the seats, and I feast my eyes on the exciting and busy room.

"That's Leaf. He's...well. Just himself. My cousins' cousin. Good man to know." He leans forward and uses his thumb to swipe something out of my hairline. I duck my head and ruffle it, miscellaneous debris dropping out of my cropped hair. Kion props his ankle on his opposing knee and leans his thick shoulder against the wall, undeniably at ease. I try to relax. A few eyes are on us, appraising. A gorgeous young man with deep ebony skin and incredible, beautiful cheekbones gives me a slow smile. I try not to blush. He lifts an elegant finger and beckons to me; his mental presence is alluring; I'm half out of my seat before I realize. I shake my head rapidly, a combination of refusal and trying to shake off his influence, sitting back down with a thump. He tilts his head to one side and lifts a shoulder, graceful shrugging that says, "your loss." I'm inclined to agree, and then Kion leans forward and flicks me in the forehead, making me flinch and whatever hold the man had on me disappears like a bubble popping. Noise rises again in my ears, and this time I do blush, full force, looking embarrassedly at Kion. I can't believe I got suckered by a siren.

Kion laughs, a deep belly laugh that rumbles through the table and settles in my chest. Leaf dances back through the roiling crowd and sets down a laden tray. I'm impressed that it arrived unspilled. I eagerly reach for a plate and spoon, a fragrant aroma teasing my hunger, so it sits upright and begs like a dog. Kion snags his own food but takes a huge drink from the newly arrived tumbler first, burping and smacking his lips. I smirk at him and dig into my food. Leaf pulls up a stool made from an old metal hubcap balanced on spindly metal sticks that look like they might have been golf clubs, once. He perches on it cross-legged and starts fiddling with something.

We devour our dinners, and Leaf places something on the table. I tilt my head to look at it and let out a surprised bark of laughter. He's made a small metal sculpture of Kion's head and shoulders. It's one piece of wire, bent to create a silhouette, but it is unmistakably Kion. Leaf grins at my openmouthed delight and pushes it toward me.

"'Appy birthday!" It's not my birthday. I know that for a fact, one of the surprise perks of having a twin, but I reach out and close my hand around the wire.

"Thanks. That's uh... It's really nice." Kion rolls his eyes and takes another drink from his tumbler, then picks up mine and sniffs it, raising an eyebrow at Leaf but putting it down for me anyway. I take a tentative sip and cough in surprise. It is not delicious.

Leaf cackles and folds himself up, crossing his hands around his knees. "So, you're pretty young ta be doin' this."

I look up from the sculpture, raising an eyebrow. He looks younger than me. There is only a hint of shadow on his chin. Kion huffs and finishes his tankard.

"Leaf's twenty. I've known him since he was a little gi..." he trails off awkwardly and then rephrases. "Since he was little."

I quirk my mouth, confused at the verbal gymnastics, and Leaf liquidly slides off his stool. "Since I was a little girl." He throws over his shoulder as he slinks into the crowd again. I can see the tension he's carrying in his back, shoulders stiff as he slides past people. I scrape my spoon around the bottom of my bowl, looking where Leaf disappeared from view.

Kion clears his throat. "Yeah." He drops his guard a little so I can read the embarrassment and guilt. I can feel how he didn't mean to spill Leaf's secret, and that he's worried I'll be shocked or disgusted. I don't know how to find the words to explain that when you've lived in other's heads, as I have, for so long, the concept of gender is nebulous, at best. I can't read Leaf, but I don't need to. He's so unmistakably male. "Huh." I shrug, chewing the side of my lip in thought. I finish my meal and take another cautious sip from my tankard. It is still unpleasant, but a comforting warmth begins to spread through my chest, relaxing me.

By the time Leaf returns I've finished and moved my stool so I can lean against the wall, watching the room with interest. The rowdiness of the place is reflected in the mental projections, and I have shut down my sense to the bare minimum to keep me aware of who is present. The siren continues to tickle at the edge of my awareness, and I have to work hard to avoid looking in his direction. I try to catch Leaf's eye, to let him know with a smile that I don't care. Couldn't care less, actually. What business is it of mine? He's helping us, and that's all I need to know.

He looks up at me, and after a brief moment of eye contact, where I try to communicate that I don't think differently of him, his face relaxes into a smile and then he bends down, exchanges a few words with the fellows at the table next to ours. After a moment, grumbling, they move their table away from us, closer to the standing crowd who are gathered around a musician playing a jaunty tune on some kind of stringed instrument. The air is thick and ripe with smells of sweat and food.

A man walks through the crowd and the noise level drops, people moving out of his way. Leaf drags a heavy chair from a nearby table and pushes it next to Kion. The newcomer drops into it, flicking wild hair out of his face with long, bejeweled fingers. My mouth falls open a little. The man is lean, whipcord muscles showing in his brown arms, but what surprises me is the intricate tattooing covering his face and hands, every inch of skin I can see marked with whorls and dots.

The patterned man gives a wolfish grin. One of his incisors glints, covered in, or made of silver. He has a string of carved wooden beads around his neck. A sure sign of importance and wealth, as though the parting of the rowdy people hadn't already proved that. Behind him is a tall, lean woman, her hair shaved into two distinct strips, each lined up with one eyebrow. Metal sparkles on her lips and ears, nose, and one eyebrow. A sword tattoo starts above her right eye and slashes over her eye socket and cheekbone, adding to her already striking features. The cross guard sits just above her unpierced eyebrow. She has a large, dramatic laser pistol on one hip. Her wary eyes and stance humming with energy mark her as a bodyguard. She sees me looking and gives me a slow, appraising once-over. I can't tell if she is checking me for weapons, or flirting with me, but I meet her eyes until the corner of her mouth lifts, and she blows me a kiss before scanning the room. Hitting on me, then.

I turn my attention back to the table: Kion and the man are finishing what looks like an elaborate greeting ritual, or some sort of seated dance. Leaf perches back on his stool. After they finish slamming their shoulders together and slapping their chests, the man turns to me and offers his hand. I take it and he swoops it up to his mouth, planting a smacking kiss on the back of it. I'm so surprised I let out an undignified squeak and snatch my hand back like it's on fire. Kion barks a laugh, and I slide my hands back around my empty tankard just for something to do with them. To my surprise, a hand closes around the tankard from over my shoulder, making me jump again. I realize that the bodyguard woman has a brimming cup for me, and she slides the empty one out of my tight grip. I gratefully accept the replacement, and bury my face in it for a moment, ears burning. My shields are locked down tight; the sort of thoughts rolling around this room are not the kind I want to eavesdrop on, but it's making it easy to surprise me.

"Dent, Thea. King of the Slums, meet protégé." Kion calling me his protégé does nothing to alleviate my embarrassment, and I gulp half of the bitter liquid down before I feel comfortable enough to resurface. A tingling sensation spreads from my stomach, and my legs feel strange. Kion reaches out and puts his hand over the top of my mug, looking at me for a moment before removing it. The unspoken message "Take it easy" is loud and clear, but the King of the Slums snickers and pushes Kion's hand back across the table, holding onto it for a long moment. They're clearly very friendly. Physically intimate, even.

"She's safe 'ere. Let 'er 'ave a little fun. She looks like she needs it. We can talk business without 'er well enough, less she wants to look at maps with us. Leaf, take the lassie and remove some of them shadows from 'er eyes. Go an' 'ave a dance or a game." His voice is soft but carries a command, and Leaf slides to his feet, hooking sharp fingers round the crook of my arm and prompting me upward. I stumble for a second before finding my balance, and Leaf deftly procures my mug, upending it into his mouth and grins at me, wiping his upper lip on his shoulder and giving me a gentle tug. I look helplessly at Kion, and he gives me a reassuring smile, then returns his attention to the strange man who is unrolling something on the table. The glimpse I get shows me a map of the City. No wonder the table of men was asked to move. Something like that is valuable. The bodyguard is scanning the room on high alert but spares a moment to flash me a lascivious grin. I fall over a stool as I take a step backward, and only Leaf's hold on my arm stops me from taking a tumble.

So embarrassed I just want to curl up under a table, I shoot a helpless glance at Leaf, and he laughs, soft and kind, before turning me around and sliding his hand down to my wrist. We weave through the crowd and toward the music. People at the back are standing around, chatting and bouncing to the rhythm. We snake through the bustling, sweaty people. I'm glad I'm not carrying my drink as I rebound off arms and trip over awkwardly placed feet. Apparently one of the lessons I've never learned is "how to move through crowds." Leaf seems to not even brush shoulders with anyone as I reel and bounce off various intimidating people. I fix a nervous smile on my face and try to look apologetic. Leaf maneuvers me to a spot where the floor is raised, and I have a view of the room. There must be two hundred people milling around. What I thought was one musician is actually a group of three, and now I'm closer, I can hear the singing. Several people are spinning around in a mad dance just in front of the group, and I can see servers pushing through the heaving masses to drop off drinks and food. Leaf lifts his hand and flicks a finger at the ceiling, catching the attention of the closest one. He makes a "two" sign at her, and I shake my head.

"I don't think I need another." The words feel a little heavy in my mouth, like the shapes I make with my lips need to be more deliberate than usual. Leaf laughs delightedly.

"I'll say. Yer sloshed! S'alright, loosen up a bit. Ya look like the weight of the world's on you alone." He finishes more seriously. "It ain't, ya know. Yer not on yer own." My gaze flicks to Kion, who is stabbing a large finger at the map and gesturing with his other hand. The wild hair of the man with him is bobbing in agreement. Leaf catches my look and grins.

I sigh and lift a shoulder. What the hells. We might die tomorrow. Leaf crows in delight and swipes the two tankards from the approaching server. Agreeably, I clink mine against his and lift it to my lips. The music settles in the base of my spine, and I tap my foot as the somehow less-unpleasant-now liquid cools my throat.

I'm giggling and dancing, two things I would not have described myself as likely to do, by the time Kion shoulders through the crowd and finds us. He rolls his eyes with a grin on his face, and then we're all dancing together, and the King of the Slums joins us, a pretty, redheaded woman with him. He spins her and crows, throwing his head back so the sound rattles against the roof. A chorus of replies answers him, and when he does it again, I lift my chin and join in. My drink is long gone, but I have a flask of water slung over my arm from somewhere, and Leaf sneaks it off my wrist to take a gulp. The King's bodyguard has her arms raised to the ceiling, eyes closed, lost in the music. The pulse and heat of the crowd surrounds me, and I grin and grab Leaf's hand, spinning under it and laughing in delight.

Chapter Six

TOBY

Serena's still mad at me, and I'm still mad at her, but in the way we get mad with people who are going to stay in our life. Where it's going to pass, but the emotions kind of need to be given some space before we figure it out. I feel...betrayed, because she sided with Darcy and helped get Thea's mission passed, but I also know Serena well enough that deep down I believe it can't have been the only reason. Or, at least, I do once Alyssa points it out.

"Do you seriously believe she'd have sent Thea off if she didn't think it was for the best?" Aly moves the glowing marble that represents the knight on the chessboard, smoothly taking out a pawn I'd been hoping to convert.

I grumble in response, both to my lost piece and her comment. Unphased by my attitude, she pokes me in the arm as I fiddle with her captured bishop, reevaluating my strategy.

"Even if it took Darcy pointing it out, and Darcy's a better Reader *and* more intuitive than either of you, Serena wouldn't have supported it if she didn't actually, you know, support it."

She's right. I know it, but it still grates. The part of me that carries Thea's past and remembers every awful thing she's experienced, seen and *done,* aches to make it stop. I don't want her to know anything but peace. And since we're still at war, that's a pipedream. "Yeah, I know." I give it up, and move my queen into a stronger position, threatening her remaining knight and repressing the grin that twitches in the corner of my mouth when she sees my plan. I *never* beat Alyssa at chess, but boy, do I wish I did.

She smirks, seeing something I've missed, and moves a pawn without taking much time to think it through. "We all...we all know how protective you are, Toby." Alyssa sounds like she's being careful, picking her words. It makes me itchy, and I shift defensively. I know I still project my thoughts and feelings to all and sundry, that my shields slip and fail and my power bursts out wherever it wants, but I'm working on it. I'm working on it every day, and it's unfair to use that against me. It's rude. Like, reading my diary even if I left it open.

I take Alyssa's knight with more aggression than necessary, rolling the ball down its channel until it hits the knight. Her mouth moves silently, like she's trying to say something and can't quite find the words. Protective. I've always been that, but there's no way for any of them to *know* like I do, what Thea has been through. What I could have been through if not for a twist of fate that left everyone believing I was a Blank. They would have killed me, if they hadn't invested so much into making me. Instead, they tried to turn me into a different kind of weapon, a blindly trusting patriot who'd be untouchable by Psionic means. A leader the people would love. It makes me feel sick.

"It's not a bad thing, but you have to give her some space. She's been *alone* her entire life..."

"I know!" I snap, because I do, I know more than anyone how isolated she's been, how the only contact she ever had with people who didn't own her was through dreams of me or on missions, and therefore fabricated. "I just want...to fix it," I finish miserably, my stomach clenching.

It takes her a minute to reply, and she squeezes my wrist gently. "Some things can't be fixed." She catches my gaze, her expression serious and weighted, her dark eyes gentle. I nod, blinking to clear the stinging threat of tears. She nods back, and then releases my wrist. I miss the warmth immediately.

A plonking sound grabs my attention away, and I groan as her castle takes my queen, lighting the board up in red and informing me I'm in checkmate. The seriousness of the moment broken, I push the board away, getting to my feet and stretching, rolling my shoulders. I'm stiff from running my feelings out, and I wrinkle my nose as the soreness in my muscles lets me know they're still mad at me. I need some space, so I turn away and pull my shirt off, grabbing a clean tank from the shelf. "I'm gonna go to the gym," I inform Alyssa, without looking back over, feeling off-balance and exposed.

"Sure, Tobes. Hey, swing by the lab later. I want to show you something." She lets me go without saying anything, but she stays sprawled on my utilitarian bunk as I head out, itching to focus some of my juddering energy on something physical.

I find Serena at the weights, lifting more than she should be able to, using telekinesis to supplement. It's good for our Psionic muscles to work them out as well, but Serena's the only person I know who lifts like this, trains with her muscles packed full of Psionic energy. She finishes her set while I stretch. When she catches my eye, I jerk my head at the mats.

The matting bounces under my feet, sticky and smeared with sweat in a few places, blood in a few more. The gym always smells like old socks, catching in the back of my throat like paint fumes, but it's easy to tune out after a while. We get used to it. I run through a kata to warm my muscles, turning and bending and holding just so, the now-familiar shapes flowing through my body in something that always feels akin to meditation to me, like I'm dragging my power inside myself as I move, spinning around my own axis, jumping, slamming my fists into the air with enough force the nothing impact rocks up my arms.

"Looking good," Serena eyes me critically, sends a wisp of power at my left foot as I balance, holding my arms at right angles to my sides. The nudge of telekinesis makes me push down a little farther, squat into the position, and my thigh twinges in protest, but I hold it for the required five count before returning to "ready" position.

Serena squares off in front of me, fists up, and I turn to present her with my side, ducking behind my guard and shifting my weight back and forth.

She comes at me with telekinesis and fists both, like being attacked by a tornado. I'm nowhere near fast enough to block them individually, so I just throw a wall of power around myself, absorbing all the energy an inch or so away from my skin. Most people can't shield like that, but I always have power to spare, compared to the average person, and she'll wear out on attacks before I will on defense.

She frowns, trying to trick me into shifting my power in the wrong direction, and I send out a tendril, yanking at her knee and then switching to a push when she blocks. The bluff works and she stumbles, dropping into a roll and regaining her footing before I have time to push the advantage. It goes on like that, neither of us landing much until Serena starts pushing her martial advantage. She's been training since she was small, and even though I can block her, when she starts locking my limbs and twisting them against themselves, I go down again and again, saved only from broken joints by my own power cushioning my fall and her hold.

I'm bruised and sweaty and calmer by the time she pins me on the floor, hand in a blade at the base of my throat. I tap the mat and she climbs off me, offering a hand to yank me to her feet. I accept it gratefully, and she nudges her shoulder into my side as we start for the changing rooms. I clap her on the shoulder, so she knows I've mostly forgiven her, not that she probably hasn't heard it from my stupid loud brain already.

I shower off in peace; everyone else seems to be out and about, no one else using the men's changing room, and I wonder where everyone is as I amble back through the lush grounds of the mansion, looking somewhat worse for wear now the water supply has been rerouted for more useful purposes.

The only person in the meditation room is Jake, and I slide into a spot quietly so as not to disturb him. The kid's hovering off the ground, like always, and I marvel at him while he can't see me, always amazed by the way his telekinesis works. He cracks an eye and grunts, "Stop thinking so loudly." And I sigh, attempting to do so as I settle into my own meditative state.

At first, my mind keeps slipping to Thea, to worrying about what she's doing, and as I concentrate harder and spend more energy on wrapping my power in, I get a vague sense of security, even happiness down the connection ever present between us. I don't think she feels me trying to reach out though, which is strange, but maybe she's distracted. It seems like there's...music? Apparently there definitely *is* music, at least in my head, because Jake kicks me to tell me to stop humming. Chastened, I let the connection to Thea slip into dormancy and concentrate on my body and power instead.

When I'm done being able to focus, I check my datapad to see if anything's come through for me, but I haven't been assigned anywhere. Jake has left the room sometime while I was focusing, so he isn't around to entertain me, and I decide to swing by the labs and see what Alyssa wanted to show me.

I find her, lab coat clad and sorting slide samples. She's apprenticing to one of the biologists, and I guess they're something gross or dangerous, so I stand around and wait for her to notice me. She's fun to watch, dexterous hands and swift movements, confident, and with a little hint of pleasure crinkling the corner of her mouth.

She sees me after about five minutes and greets me with a gloved-hand wave. I can see a sliver of her wrist between her white latex glove and the lab coat she's wearing, and I remember how narrow her wrists used to be, how you could see every tendon and the curve of the bone. She's not underfed anymore, though, her cheeks filling out and muscle starting to build soft over her skeleton. I grin. "Hello, doctor."

An eye roll is the only reaction, and she carefully puts her slide box away on a shelf before shrugging her coat off and disposing of her gloves. "C'mere." She beckons me over and grabs herself a wheely chair, rolling it over to a computer screen and waggling the mouse. It boots to a main screen, and she clicks through a few things.

"Is this what I'm here to see?" I lean my hands on the back of her chair, ducking down so I can see the screen properly.

"Sure is, check this out." She pulls up a bunch of images, genetic coding by the looks of things, all marked with various colors and numbers. I don't know enough about genetics to make much sense of it. "So, you know how they've been trying to pin down a genetic component to Psionic power, and haven't done so well localizing it?"

I nod, humming agreement and waiting for her to carry on explaining.

She points at the screen. "Okay, this is you, and this is Thea, and this is a Blank, and this is a no-Tal," she uses ARC slang like she was born here, and I grin as I follow her hand to the various images. "They've been sequencing Psionics for a long time, and no-Tals as well, easy to get hold of, but they've never had anyone with as strongly weighted Talent as you and Thea before, and Viromi thinks they might have found the mutation that identifies Talent *and*"—the excitement is clear in her voice—"if she's right, then the theory about all Blanks being protected Talents could be right! And it could mean we're able to unlock Blanks."

I blink, shocked at the idea that all Blanks could be like me. It makes sense, I suppose, because of what happened to me that day, but it's surprising still that that occurrence could maybe be replicated. And then I wonder if, like me, Blanks would need to believe they were in mortal danger before they could access their powers past their shields. I shift, uncomfortable.

"Isn't this...a bit like what the Institute was doing?" I try to strain the distaste out of my voice, phantom memories of drills and saws and needles hovering at the top of my spine.

Alyssa twists her mouth sympathetically, reaches behind her to pat my hand where I've rested it on the back of her chair. "It's a theory, and ARC have been looking into Psionics and the science behind you since they were first formed. And everyone here is happy with them, aren't they?"

"I guess," I agree, but I can't help thinking that the people working for the Institute on the outside were happy, too, after years of subjugation and torture, just wiped away and replaced with happier, more wholesome lies.

Aly squeezes my hand and returns to the keyboard. I miss the warmth of her immediately and flex my fingers without thought. She types a few things in and pulls up some files, pressing play on a video. An unemotional voice informs us this is test twelve of twenty on candidate Jacobs, S., before the screen flicks from blackness and I see Serena, young and skinny but unmistakably Serena, giggling as telekinesis-powered balls fly at her from across the room. She ducks and dodges, using her own—paltry at this time—power to deflect what she can't avoid and is eventually nailed in the forehead with a beanbag, crossing her eyes and sticking her tongue out. She looks happy.

"It's not the same," Aly reiterates and then closes the video. "I promise."

Even though she's just a trainee tech, powerless, at that, I trust her. I nod, grateful, and she smiles at me before pushing her chair back a little so it forces me to step back out of the way so she can get up. She stretches, stiff from a day of work, and then gestures toward the door.

The mess is pretty quiet, but we track down Darcy and Serena and join them for dinner, and afterward when they suggest a movie, I agree easily, not having anything to do until tomorrow when I have a packed schedule: morning patrol followed by two classes I have to take, and one I have to teach. I jump at the opportunity to maximize my downtime with my favorite people, in the hopes it will keep me distracted from Thea.

We find a small media room and get settled; Darcy even has some puffed corn snacks, and we grab handfuls to munch on through the movie. It's pretty good, some action comedy sort of affair, and I'm laughing when Serena stiffens in her seat, cocking her head to one side and hitting me hard in the thigh. Knowing what that means, adrenaline spikes in my bloodstream, shallowing my breathing and quickening my heartbeat. I slide out of my chair and gesture to Alyssa and Darcy to stay still as I check the door, listening for I don't know what. An Institute invasion?

I have no idea what's going on, but the door seems clear, and I shove some power at a couch to shift it in front of the doorway, providing some cover and giving us a line of defense. Alyssa and Darcy are whispering frantically, but Serena has her hand out toward them, trying to mute their questions. I check the windows, seal them with some threads of power that I'll have to keep attached to me, since I have no better options for blocking them, and then grab the civilians by the hands and tug them into a corner, gesturing at them to get down before I run back over to Serena and take her hand, using the skin-contact to hitch a ride on what she's feeling or hearing.

I can't make sense of it. There's a slippery feeling at the corner of her consciousness, and I don't have any idea what it is until she throws a memory at me—a memory of me vanishing into nothingness as I pull my perception warm around myself and the oily sense of wrongness it leaves behind—*there's someone here.* She sends me, as quietly and softly as I've ever felt.

Where? I don't even try to read the room, the corridors and myriad floors above and below us. I'm way too untalented in that regard. Instead, I pull my power to me, making ready, loading my hands and legs with humming energy.

I don't know. Frustration and a little fear are staining her inner voice, and that frightens me. *Stay with them.*

No! I refuse, then acquiesce immediately as she flashes reason and purpose at me—*you can't read; we don't know what it is; I need to check, but someone has to look after the civs and message Dad; I mean, command*—she's still my superior, and I trust that she knows what she's doing, but it's hard to watch her inch to the door, hop over the couch and push the door beyond open soundlessly.

I project after her, *Stay safe,* but I don't know if she caught it. I pull the door closed with Talent and sneak across to Alyssa and Darcy, who are holding hands, with their backs against the wall. Alyssa's face is drawn and hard, but Darcy just looks afraid. I position myself in front of them and then notice that Alyssa has a chair leg in her hand. I have no idea how she managed to detach one in the few moments I was with Serena, but my heart warms to see her with a weapon. She may not be Talented, but she'll hit any son of a slitch who tries anything with her.

"It's okay. Serena's checking it out; she just noticed something a little weird," I whisper, trying to sound reassuring, while grabbing my datapad and typing out a quick message to David Jacobs that reads, "In media room 2J, w Jacobs and 2x civ; suspicious movement outside; send readers meet w Jacobs corridor J, Reynolds." It still feels weird every time I have to use surnames, but that's the military way and the way ARC runs.

A message response comes through immediately, "Support en route; stay put."

Satisfied I've done what I can, I crouch down, hands extended and power tingling in the tips of my fingers. "Darcy, you're a stronger Reader than me; can you sense anything?"

"Nothing," she murmurs back, fear painting her words. "What's going on?"

"I don't know. Backup's coming, though. And whatever it is isn't here, I don't think. It's outside."

A hand curls, soft and warm around my ankle through my sweats, and for a minute, I think it's Darcy, reaching out for comfort, but then I realize it's Alyssa. I can't read her, not at all, but I think if I could, all I would get is determination and expectancy.

We wait in throbbing, anxious silence until the door swings open, and I straighten up, power rushing out of me in a wall. A wall I only just manage to stop in time, when I see a white-faced Serena in the doorway, three soldiers behind her.

"Toby, c'mon!" She yells, and I run for her, the urgency in her tone overriding the instinct to stay with the girls. The soldiers open to let me vault over the couch, and then we're running together.

She takes my hand midstride as I use my power to brace me, bouncing off the wall to turn in the direction she's now dragging me, our footsteps syncing as she uses her power to bounce herself forward to match my longer legs. *Cover me.* She's full of potent rage and thick, seeping fear, and I catch the impression she gives me of someone-me-not-me-almost-Toby-not-Toby running down the corridor ahead of us. The power shielding them is so similar to mine that Serena can't tell the difference, except I'm by her side, and we're chasing down whoever is in front of us, our muscles stretching and warming.

I feel her send out a telekinetic grab, trying to settle tendrils of power around this interloper—no one else at ARC can do what I do, so it's someone different, someone *new*—but they slide off like water hitting glass, like an optical illusion where I can feel her power more than I can feel the person ahead of us. *Power's no good,* I send. *Faster.* We both lengthen our strides. I'm using telekinesis to push out of my feet now, as well. We're careening at an unsafe speed, dodging furniture and people and all I can see is the blurry impression of shocked faces as we knock into them. I'm only on my feet by dint of Serena's reading, sending the wireframe of the world to me, and telekinetic pegs I can slam into the floor, the ceiling, the walls, to keep myself from succumbing to gravity or ricochet.

We leap down a flight of stairs in a single bound, sending someone sprawling, but there's no time to stop and help and apologize. Whoever this is who's wearing a cloak of power more efficiently than I have ever managed to do is heading out of the building. They're fast, fast with telekinesis powering their feet, invisible, with power coating them, but they don't know the route.

At Serena's lightning-fast thought-request, I take a door off its hinges, and we barrel through, disturbing a classroom full of teenagers without a second's thought.

She boosts me, letting go of my hand, and I slam through the window, power busting the transal out of its frame a millisecond before my flying body impacts it. I catch her as she follows me, my power grabbing her, slowing her, steadying her, and then we seize each other's hands to reopen our connection as we leg it down a corridor and burst out in front of...nothing.

The hallway is empty, both to my mundane senses and Serena's reading. Aggravated and afraid, I send a barrel of telekinesis down the entire width of the corridor, just in case.

Nothing.

Chapter Seven

E17

Something's prodding me, and for a moment, everything is confusing and blurry and then my head starts to throb. I groan, my throat dry, and I realize my mouth tastes terrible. The prodding desists, and something cold plops onto my forehead, shocking me and making me jerk, but immediately becoming appreciated. I manage to flop my hand onto the cold thing, holding it tighter against my head. It takes a second, but I figure out it is a wet cloth.

I drag it down to my eyes for a moment, and then my energy abandons me. Pitiful, I whimper, and a kind hand pets my head for a moment.

"Open yer mouth." It's not Kion. I pry open one eye to investigate. An indistinct shape hovering over me comes into focus. It's Leaf, a shit-eating grin plastered on his face. He holds his hand up, something small and white between his finger and thumb. I let my mouth fall open, and he drops the pill into the back of my throat.

"Am I dying?" I gasp out after swallowing the medicine. I must have come down with some awful plague. Maybe something from this city that I've never been immunized against. "Is Kion okay?"

Leaf snorts. "Big man's fine; he can 'old 'is liquor. Yeah, on the other 'and, threw up on my best shoes. My *only* shoes." Oh. Liquor. This must be my first hangover.

It's awful. My insides are rebelling against even the medicine, and I'm worried I'm going to vomit again.

Leaf doesn't sound mad, and I struggle upright, half sitting so I can reach out to pat his knee in apology, and bile rises in my throat. Leaf reacts fast; I'm dangled over the side of the pallet with my face in a bucket before I even start puking. It feels like I vomit for hours, but Leaf holds me up, pets the back of my sweaty neck with the cloth, and supports my limp and useless body.

When I'm done, he maneuvers me into a leaning position and helps me drink some water. I moan and push it away when I'm done. He snickers and sits on the end of my bed for a moment. Belatedly, I realize the other side of the large sleeping area is wrinkled and obviously slept in. Then it becomes apparent that I'm clad only in shorts and a thin shirt that aren't mine. I look around wildly, causing my head to pound even more viciously.

Leaf notices my face and shakes his head at me with what looks like mild indignation painting his features. "Ya puked on yer things, and Kion was off havin' a nice time. Not the sort've time ya want ta interrupt, if ya follow. I borrowed ya some clothes an' my friend Jess sorted ya out with a place ta kip. No worries."

Oh. Embarrassed, I wipe the now warm cloth over my face, grateful for the wall behind me. Irrationally, I feel like I might start to cry, and Leaf's face softens. He reaches down onto the floor, and hooks up a tray, balancing it on my lap he pats my hand.

"Try ta eat somethin', then go back ta sleep. You'll feel better. I'll come get ya in a while. Jessie might be in an' out; this is 'er room, but she'll try not ta wake ya."

I nod and pick up a piece of dry bread, nibble at it until I'm sure I won't puke it right back up.

The food settles my stomach a bit, and I snuggle back down under the covers, grateful for the low light in the room. Leaf pats my foot through the thin blanket, and I hear the door close behind him before I slip back into darkness.

The second time I wake up isn't as bad as the first, but my body feels strange: uncomfortable and lightheaded. There's a girl rummaging in a metal locker at the end of the bed, and she looks up when I stir.

"All right, petal? Those meanies got ya smashed, eh?" I don't really understand, but I nod anyway, and instantly regret it as my headache comes back. She makes a moue of sympathy and straightens. "Try another pill, eh? Leaf left ya one. 'Es a good boy." Her voice is soothing, and I look where she is gesturing. Sure enough, another white pill is waiting by the side of the bed, next to a tumbler of water. I sit up and gulp it down, water making me feel better.

"Do you know what time it is?" The light in the room has a golden quality now.

She smirks, flashing a deep dimple. "'S three and a quarter. Ya sure slept the day away." I groan. We've wasted a whole day, thanks to my inability to hold my alcohol. Wishing I could just go back to sleep, I drag myself upright and look around. Then I remember that Leaf said I threw up on my clothes and my shoulders fall.

Jess points at the end of the bed, and my eyes light on a pile of folded clothes. Mine! I recognize the top layer immediately. I picked it out just before we left. A brown coarse-woven material with several hidden pockets to secret things. I love hidden pockets. I brighten and shuffle down, stripping the shirt I'm wearing off, standing naked, rummaging in the pile for underwear.

The door bursts open, and Leaf catches sight of me immediately. He reddens and backpedals, slamming the door shut. I drag my clothes on. That's the second time I've embarrassed people with nudity. I have to get used to this "privacy" thing.

I slip out into the corridor, thanking a laughing Jess on my way and find Leaf leaning against the wall, one foot up behind him. He meets my eyes and wrinkles his nose at me. "Sorry, I should've knocked. I though' ya were still asleep."

I grin at him to let him know it's okay, and he kicks off the wall, striding down the corridor with loping steps.

"Kion's waitin' for us downstairs. I think you're all set for goin' in this evenin'." He smirks, mischief coloring his voice. "If yer feelin' up ta it, I guess."

I poke him in the shoulder, hard, and he cackles, bouncing a little as he walks. The smell of food once again wraps around me as soon as we enter the main room. I realize that I slept above it; there must be dozens of rooms up there. Then I realize that Jess is the server who plied me with liquor the night before and snort. Serves her right if she had to share her bed with me. I feel a lot better than I did earlier, and the scent of hot meat is making me ravenous. Kion's already seated, with an attractive, blonde woman who must be at least two inches taller than him. She has her hand on his knee. I slide into an empty stool a little awkwardly, and Kion grins at me.

"Morning, sunshine!" There's a little laugh in his voice, and I poke my tongue out at him, in a gesture completely stolen from Toby. His eyes crinkle and he motions at a server, pointing at his plate and then at me and Leaf.

Moments later, a plate of food is plopped in front of me, and I dig in, trying to be stealthy as I analyze the woman with Kion. I fail, not on top form this afternoon, and she catches me looking, raises a tattooed-on eyebrow at me and smiles. I smile back and Kion relaxes. Leaf bangs his knee into mine under the table, and we all eat in companionable silence.

The food is delicious. I'm pretty sure it's real meat, maybe pigeon, baked under a flakey layer of golden pastry. I get full pretty fast, but Leaf yanks my crusts onto his plate without asking, so nothing goes to waste. The woman sitting with Kion breaks the stretching silence. If Leaf didn't have his mouth full, I doubt it would be necessary.

"I'm Alejandra. It's good to meet you." She sounds cultured, for a dwell. I think she's around forty, gray streaks glinting at her temples. So, old for this world, as well. She must have had the cancer suppressors, else she'd be dead or on her way to it. That fact plus the educated tones make me think she's from inside the Wall. A Citizen. What's she doing here? I fiddle with my shirtsleeve.

"I'm Thea. Nice to meet you too." I fumble for something to say and look around the room. "Do you live here?" Why isn't Leaf talking? He's always talking.

She laughs, a musical tinkle that makes me smile. "It's actually my place. I own the Dented Drum. Or, I manage it, you could say. Dent is too busy to take any interest in the day-to-day tasks." I nod, not sure who this Dent is, and Leaf burps loudly, making Kion snort.

"You met Dent." Kion has his arm slung round the back of Alejandra's chair; she's leaning into the curve of his elbow. I'm interested in how comfortable they are together; it seems they've known each other for longer than just one night. Kion has never struck me as the relaxed kind of man he seems to be right now. Usually he thrums with energy, but here he's practically placid. Focusing on what he said, I realize he means the wild-haired man from yesterday, and I nod.

"Right, and he told Leaf to get me drunk." I say wryly, smiling so they know I'm just kidding.

Leaf smirks unrepentantly. "Gotta do what the boss tells ya!"

Kion flicks a bit of trash at him. I laugh as he bats it away. "Sure. Well, you took good care of me last night, so I guess I forgive you."

Kion's face stills for a moment, his eyes flicking from Leaf to me, and his eyebrows drop, indicating a possible explosion. Oh! He thinks... I hasten to explain before he breaks Leaf in half. "He found me a place to sleep in one of his friend's rooms. And this morning, when I was throwing up, he didn't let me drown in my own puke. So...that was pretty nice." With a narrowed eye glare at me, Kion subsides, and I try to hide a smile at his protectiveness, but apparently fail because his stern expression folds into a smirk, and he shoots me a quick wink as he settles back into his seat.

Someone arrives to clear the dishes, and I'm interested to see little metal chips being handed over as payment. Leaf sees my attention and holds one out in his pink palm. It's a small square of dark metal. I reach out to take it, and he closes his fist with a laugh, opening it again to show an empty hand. I gasp with surprise, and Kion smiles indulgently. Alejandra leans forward, reaches behind Leaf's ear, and produces the credit. My mouth falls open in delight and everyone at the table chortles.

"What, how did you do that?" Alejandra passes me the credit to inspect, and Kion snorts.

"You barely even blinked when we started showing you telekinesis... You'll accept Jake bouncing upside down along the ceiling, and...a simple bit of street magic flabbergasts you? You're a strange one."

I roll my eyes. I can *feel* telekinesis; it makes sense to me. This is different. I turn the credit in my hand. It is a flattened piece of what could be copper, thinner in the center. A series of dots is raised on the surface, almost invisible to the eye, but clear against the soft skin of my fingertips. I hold it up to look more closely, and I can't work out how it could just disappear, it's so solid.

"How did you make it vanish?" I demand eagerly, passing it back to Leaf.

He grins, a lopsided, cheeky grin that makes me want to flick his nose, and repeats the trick, clenching his fist around the credit and then unfurling his fingers. The credit is gone.

"A magician never reveals his tricks." He announces, with his nose in the air, and I growl. Kion twists to look at Alejandra.

"Got any cards with ya?" She widens her slanted eyes and purses her lips and then produces a pack of the kind of cards everyone plays games with back at ARC. Delicate, thin sheets of plastic marked with various patterns and pictures.

I'm entranced by the selection of tricks she and Leaf perform for my pleasure. They seem to enjoy having an audience and ham it up for my benefit. Kion relaxes and drinks some obnoxious smelling tea, watching us with amused tolerance.

The room has sporadic panes of translucent plastic which provide most of the low light, but as we play and they teach me a few tricks I'm excited to show off when we get back to ARC, the light changes and it gets darker. Soon, servers are flitting around lighting dangling globes that float in the air, looking like tiny suns. I can't see how they're suspended, but it must be on wires or something. No one would waste telekinesis concentrating on floating dozens of lights in a room.

Kion cracks his neck from side to side and looks up. He catches someone's eye in moments, and the dark-skinned woman he's looking at slides through the tables toward us. They slap hands, exchanging something smoothly between them. Leaf flutters the cards in his hands so they somehow fall back into an organized pile, and passes them back to Alejandra, who secretes them away up her sleeve with a flick of the wrist.

Leaf leans toward me a little and says, in hushed tones, "Be careful, okay? If ya get in trouble, draw this somewhere, then hide. I'll come and get ya." He pulls up his sleeve and shows me an elaborately tattooed image of an old-fashioned compass. North is marked by a star, East by a small flame, South by a fish, and West by a leaf. It's beautiful, and I turn his arm so I can see it better. He pulls his arm back, covering the tattoo on his wrist with his sleeve again. "Got it? I have people in the City; they'll lemme know ya need 'elp."

I nod, feeling the weight of our approaching mission again. Somehow, during this time, Cassandra has been quiescent within me, a shadow in the depths of my consciousness, but not shoving and pushing for space. I hope against hope that either the distance or the time that has passed is causing her hold to loosen. As if in response to the thought, she writhes and a shiver runs through me, hairs standing to attention. Once again, I worry that she wants me here. It's the only explanation I can think of for her restfulness.

Kion places a heavy hand on my shoulder and sends me a thought-form.

It's time.

I swing myself out of the chair, offering my hand to Alejandra. "Thanks for showing me those tricks."

She takes my hand in a soft grip and smiles at me. "See you when you get back, Thea."

I flush slightly, although I'm not sure why, and Leaf makes me jump by pinching my arm lightly. "Don't forget." I know he means the compass, but it seems like he doesn't want Kion to know, so I just smile at him with a tight jaw. It's a little forced, my mind already on our approaching evening.

"Let's go." Kion sounds confident and solid. I'm overcome with a rush of gratitude for the man, and I duck my head to hide my face as I spin on my heel.

"See ya." The flippant goodbye is the best I can do, and I follow Kion's broad back through the now bustling tavern. We exit in a new direction, and I match my steps to his, mind racing. It's tempting to reach out with my power, to look at what he is thinking as well as discover who is around us and search for threats, but I swallow the urge. I obey the rules of ARC now, and you never invade a person's privacy unless you are in immediate danger.

We emerge into a shadowy night, with dark smoke curling from various burning bins filling the air with an oily residue that catches in my throat and makes my eyes sting. Kion seems immune, but he reaches backward to take my hand, and I scurry to catch up. We probably look like he's paying for my company, I note, causing a pulse of amusement to skitter across our connection.

He uses the skin-on-skin contact to fill me in on the plan. His thoughts are orderly and easy to understand, without any underlying forms pushing to the surface. He's well-trained. He catches that thought, too, and mentally grins at me. Mind-to-mind information transfer is so efficient I'm all caught up in a few moments on what it took him and Dent an hour to iron out last night. It's pretty simple. We're taking the low roads I've heard so much about, and then we'll crawl through an abandoned sewage pipe that should be empty and should take us under the Wall. Kion has a cylindrical pack of supplies slung over his shoulder because the aim is to hole up and try to gather information. Kion's concern is that we don't have a tech with us, so we won't be able to monitor the local systems, leaving us reliant on our more esoteric skills.

The dwells leave us alone, and we make it to the low road without any difficulty, dropping into a pitch-black tunnel that freaks me out so much I seep my reading power out into my surroundings. Kion, of course, seems totally at home in the dark. One day I'll get the full story out of him. Well, in one-word bursts, probably. Or maybe I can get him to draw me a picture. I snort softly, and Kion squeezes my hand lightly, our connection muted but ready to flare up if something happens. Nothing does.

The wriggle through the pipes is not something I ever, ever want to do again. I have to block out everything and focus on Kion's reassuring solidness ahead of me. He knows I suffer in small spaces, and he babies me the whole time, sending warm thoughts that bathe me from head to toe and keep my burgeoning panic at bay. I wouldn't have made it ten meters without his protective thoughts surrounding me. By the time we emerge, coughing and filthy into an empty room full of disintegrating crates and debris, I feel like a robot, emotionless and empty. Like I used to feel in the Institute. It scares me a little. I shiver and miserably dust myself off as best I can, and Kion hands me a damp cloth to run over my face and hands. He flashes a kind smile at my discomfort and scrubs his own skin before taking a gulp of water and handing me the flask. While I drink, he checks the room. He's not even out of breath or uncomfortable-looking.

"It's not the nicest, but it's safer than any other route. You did a great job." I gratefully swish the water around my mouth before replying.

"It felt like it was getting tighter and tighter around me, and I'd get stuck there forever." I shift, uncomfortable with my weakness.

Kion laughs and gestures at himself. "Hey, if I can fit." I grin, nodding. He's probably three times as bulky as I am, and he was in front. Although if he'd gotten stuck, I would have had to reverse all the way back. I reckon we crawled over a kilometer. I shudder. Streaked with dirt and miscellaneous debris, he takes a look at me, and quirks his lips, then looks down at himself. Yeah, we're filthy. No way we'll pass muster if we're seen in the daytime. We'll be hauled in by the Watch before we can blink. I raise my ragged, dirty thumbnail to my lips to chew on it, and then realize how disgusting it is and pull a face.

"We could definitely use a bath."

Kion scratches his beard scruff thoughtfully, the stubble clogged with dust and grime even though he's tried to wipe himself off. He inspects his fingernails and shrugs a shoulder.

"Well, not a lot we can do. Try not to get too close to anyone. We probably smell pretty ripe as well."

I take another swipe at my face and neck, scrubbing till I feel the skin redden. Then I lean over and ruffle my short hair to clear it out. Kion snickers and then does the same, his long hair having caught far more than mine. It patters on the ground at his feet and I laugh. Our clothes are dark enough that the grime doesn't show too badly, and while we look a bit disheveled, it is nighttime, so hopefully we can remain undetected. Kion should be able to project distracting images if anyone looks at us too closely, as an extra deterrent.

The building we're in is a disused factory, but as we emerge, it's clear not everything in the area is abandoned. The building next to us is lit up from the inside, four stories of windows casting light out in bright coronas. We walk, as though we belong, down the street. Kion leads the way, and I follow a few paces behind, draping my awareness out lightly around us, ready to withdraw the gossamer threads of me if I catch someone powerful reading the area. I'm confident in my subtlety. I read people in the Institute for years without them pinning me down. I feel a pulse of anger from Cassandra but force her back so I can concentrate. I have to keep some concentration on her, worried that she might try to signal somehow, or distract me so we get caught. I feel people moving around us, bustling and busy. A Watch patrol of four stomps down the road in front of us. Kion turns into a side street and lengthens his stride to avoid them. I bustle after him.

When he was showing me the plan, it seemed like we were going to find somewhere to hide, but I don't understand why we wouldn't stay in the factory. I brush my hand against his to ask him, and he replies that we can't stay near the entrance to the tunnels. If we were caught there, the factory would be searched and the entrance would be found, endangering anyone who came through it. I nod, understanding, and then sense another group of people walking too determinedly to be anything but soldiers. Kion grips my hand, and we slip down another side street. The civilians who are around don't pay much attention to us, Kion's purposeful stride deflecting attention. I wish we had a Watch uniform for him, and then I would just look like a prisoner, and any disarray would be explained by a possible skirmish. He sends amusement, combing his hand through his hair and looking around. A sense of satisfaction comes through our connection, and he pulls me to the edge of the street. We wait there, as inconspicuous as we can be, until there is no one in the street. Kion points up, at a ladder I hadn't even noticed, and grabs me round the waist. With his help, I can reach it, and scamper up, Kion on my heels.

I belly over the ridge of the roof and scuttle out of his way as he hauls himself over, gesturing for me to be quiet. I hear boots in the street, and a whining, nasal voice. My delicate touch is much less likely to be noticed than Kion's mental presence, if they have someone with them who can read, so without being asked, I reach out tentatively with my power.

"Yes, sir. Just here. A big thug of a man and a slip of a girl, they looked quite surreptitious, if you know what I mean?"

A stern voice responds. "Thank you for bringing this to our attention, Yosep. We will look into it. You'll be paid if the tip pans out." She's the leader, shadows of military service medals and a penchant for whisky tangible in her thoughts. It's the next one who catches my attention, though; her thoughts feel...*red*, for lack of a better explanation. They echo the wrong way.

Kion's lips move in an unmistakable curse, and I slide my hand across the roof silently, so we can communicate.

No Readers down there, just four soldiers. Three women and a man. One of the women feels... I send him a summation of her mental presence: she reads like a sociopath, flat and sharp in the wrong places. I stave off a shudder, not wanting to make even the slightest rustle.

Kion is looking around; there's nothing to hide us on the roof. If they come up, we're sitting ducks. The slight rim around the edge of the flat roof offers us about ten inches of protection, not nearly enough. Down below, the soldiers are paired off, conducting a thorough grid search of the streets. I hope they will decide there's nothing to it, and then one of them calls out from just below us. "Team, there's a fire ladder here. I'm going up to check it out." He sounds bored, and his mind is flat and disinterested, Kion catches my eye and jerks his heads sideways.

Get out of the way. I'll take care of them.

A grating sound screeches out, the ladder being pulled down toward the street. My heart pounding, I shuffle, covered by the sound, as fast as I can toward the back of the roof. To my surprise, when I'm as far as I can go, pressed against the rim, I see another, lower roof that backs onto this one. Invisible from where we came up. Heart in my throat, I grab the first thing I think of, the metal credit from the bar, and throw it at Kion. My aim is good. He twists around as I slide over the small wall, off the roof. Moments later, he rolls over the edge, softening his fall with telekinesis, and then, a second later, we hear footsteps crunch on the rooftop we just abandoned.

Pressed against the four feet of brick that is the only thing between us and armed soldiers, I feel surprisingly calm. My hand is tucked against Kion's neck, we're squashed on our sides, as much of our bodies in the shadow of the small wall formed by the higher roof as possible. Above us, I hear the soldier call out, "There's no sign of anyone, but I'm gonna take a look at the connecting roofs. I'll rendezvous in ten."

Tentatively, I reach into his mind, trying to figure out if he is coming this way. I feel the tension thrumming in Kion, waiting for me to pass him information. Kion's not a weak Reader, but he doesn't have the finesse I do, and he's leaving it to me for now. I have to stifle a laugh when I figure out the soldier's intentions. I repeat them to Kion, just as the distinct smell of marijuana reaches us, across the roof. The soldier is sitting less than ten meters from us, enjoying a spliff. I wonder how he thinks his superiors won't smell it on him and try to ignore the cramping in my thigh.

We have to wait for fifteen minutes before he clambers down, awkward and mumbling to himself, and then we shift positions with gasps of relief. I stretch my leg out and dig my fingers into the muscles gratefully. Kion massages the blood back into a numb arm and smiles at me.

Looks like you found a good place for us to stay.

I nod, smiling, unable to project to him without direct contact, but not wanting to speak. We explore our new location quietly. There is a transal skylight in the middle we'll have to avoid, but we're still high enough off the ground that we shouldn't be seen as long as we avoid the very edges. There's a water reservoir, as there is on all buildings in the Cities, and it will provide an extra hiding spot if necessary, although I'm not sure Kion could force his large shoulders under it, I could wriggle out of sight.

While I peer over the rim of the roof after checking for people below, Kion sets us up something along the lines of a bare-bones camp. We're staying here, at least for the night, but at the same time we can't get too comfortable, in case anyone clocks us, and we have to run. When you're avoiding telepaths, you can't afford to leave a single object behind, especially somewhere like this, where no one else is likely to go and obscure our residue. Really, it would be better to find a building or somewhere we can be inside, and since we can't poke around too much, the best we can do for now is unroll a thin mattress and keep our ears and eyes open. Judging from the mental traces drifting about, we're close to a bank, a sports equipment store, a tech conglomerate and an elec-car rental place. The building we're on is a four-story apartment building, and from the unguarded thoughts of people passing below the skylight, I learn that we're above the staircase that leads all the way to the ground floor.

Just as I'm about to retreat back to Kion, a family of four hurries down the corridor toward the stairs. I can pick up scattered thoughts, and they're in a hurry, oh! And packed for a trip! This could be a perfect opportunity. Desperate for more information, I risk leaning over the skylight a little and see a balding man ushering two teens and a grown woman down the stairs. They're all carrying bags. The oldest kid, a teenaged boy, is grumbling internally about leaving behind his gaming system when he's in the middle of an important tournament. The dad has no patience, and clips him on the ear, speeding him up. I lose them as they clatter down the stairs inside the apartment building but catch wisps of them a few minutes later when they head out of the main door and into the street. To my great delight, I'm privy to the woman telling her kids it's only for a week, and that they should be pleased to get the chance to take a trip on the tube, and my skin tingles with excitement. It's ideal!

If we can break in through the skylight, get to their apartment and hole up in there, things will be a hell of a lot easier.

Chapter Eight

TOBY

"There's nothing on *any* of the scanners, and no one else noticed anything..." David Jacobs leans his hands on the table, watching Serena pace. I started the meeting standing upright, but after about twenty minutes of pointless conversation, I'm now leaning my hips against a cabinet, watching in mute frustration.

"I don't care what the scanner said, there was someone here!" Serena reiterates, her voice starting to husk from the amount of yelling she's been doing. "Maybe I'm the only one that noticed because I was the only one paying any nuking attention."

I wince at the expression on David's face and attempt to redirect some of the coming wave of anger. "Maybe you noticed because you're used to me." Well, now everyone is looking at me, perfect. I forge onward. "Think about it. Serena's with me, dropping in and out of cover, more than anyone. She's way more equipped to be sensitive to that if someone else can do it too."

David sighs, rubbing his hand across his forehead. He looks older than he did when we first met, worn down. "If that's the case, then we need to get you back in the labs, figure out how to get our scanners set off by you. And Serena, we'll need you to pass what you felt to the techs as well."

"So, when I tell you, you think I'm imagining things, and when Toby backs me up, you'll listen to him? I can't tell if this is sexism or reverse nepotism," Serena huffs, stalking out of the room and thrusting the door open with so much power it hits the wall hard and rebounds. I catch it with a puff of telekinesis before it slams closed.

"I'm gonna..." I jerk my head after her, and David nods, so I don't wait for anything else, just hasten after Serena. Her back is tight and tense, her hands in fists shoved into her jacket pockets. "It's not that he doesn't believe you," I start, cautiously in case she throws me into a wall. "It's that he doesn't want to believe you."

"What?" She snaps, enraged, but she turns down the corridor for the labs, so I breathe a sigh of relief.

"Think about it. If someone was here, cloaked, they got past all our security and we don't know how. They've gotta be Institute, which means there's a presence in the City we didn't know about, and they could have snagged nuke knows what kind of info. It'd be better for us if you *were* wrong." My attempts to sound conciliatory don't seem to have worked that well, judging from the look on Serena's face as she eyes me.

"If I was broken, you mean. Slipping early. That would be better." She growls it, slamming through another door with more power than her physical strength alone would allow. She must be buzzing with power, anger. I send out a mental call for Darcy, and Serena hits me in the arm before I can finish, hard enough that I flinch away, rubbing my arm, annoyance flashing through me.

"So, what, you don't believe me either and now you're calling my nuking girlfriend to come and force me to relax." My mind careens to the joke Darcy made about beating Serena at breakfast that time, and I shake my head to get rid of it, but not fast enough. She scowls at me and raises her fist, threatening another punch.

"Stop nuking hitting me," I complain, lifting my aching arm and stretching it out. "You know I can't hit you back." I see her face and roll my eyes. "No, not because you're a girl. ARC has beaten that latent sexism out of me, thank you very much, because I have very little control and I'm getting really mad at you and I might accidentally splat you, and as annoying as you are, we need you in this fight with all your limbs attached."

A soft throat clearing behind us stops any possible response from Serena, and I see the anger draining out of her as she turns. Darcy floats up beside her, wrapping a long arm around Serena's waist and pulling her in to her side. Serena goes easily, belying her irritation at me calling Darcy over. Darcy, meanwhile, just gives me a grin and a wink over Serena's shoulder.

"Alyssa got called down to the lab. And that seems to be where you're headed. Gonna fill me in?" she asks, her tone warm and relaxing. I feel the agitation draining out of my spine, as well. Darcy has that effect on people. She smiles, like she caught the thought, and takes my hand in her free one, Serena still curled into her side as we walk.

After a moment, it becomes clear that Serena isn't going to say anything, so I figure I should explain. "Serena felt someone, like you know, so we chased them but there's nothing...no sign of them anywhere in the building or gardens, and *nothing* on the scanners, so now they want me back in the lab for more tests on the cloaking stuff, and Serena so they can see what she's feeling when I cover us... I don't know, it doesn't sound like it's gonna help much."

"Well, if someone was able to get in here without any evidence, that needs to be looked into by any angle possible," Darcy says calmly, gesturing for me to open the door with my free hand so she doesn't have to let go of either of us.

I oblige, and we enter the main lab. It used to just be storage, so it's still a little rough around the edges, but there's lots of shiny equipment, and a harried-looking tech heads over to us. "Jacobs, Reynolds, let's get you hooked up." David must have messaged down. I untangle my hand from Darcy and follow the tech, to give Serena a moment of calm before she has to go through the equipment hookups.

She clips the monitor onto my head, brushing my long fringe back with fingers that feel judgmental. I wonder if they'd prefer us to have our heads shaved for ease of access, like the Institute, and both Serena and Darcy glare at me from across the room, where they're stood pressed together. I wrinkle my nose in apology and make an effort to tamp down a little harder so my thoughts stop popping out.

We're knee-deep in tests when the alarm goes, blaring through the room at agonizing decibels, coupled with a bright-red light flashing from the corners of the room.

I bound to my feet, heart skipping as adrenaline spikes through my system, setting me buzzing. I yank the sensors off my head, because there's no point in being attached to the computers if something is going down, and sprint for the door to the small test room, yanking it open.

The techs look focused, already on their datapads and doing whatever it is they're supposed to. I scoop mine off my pile of clothes and look for instructions on the screen, but Serena pounds a thought at me from across the room.

Institute, in the City. The first whistling sound of an incoming rocket punctuates her thought-form, and I get the impression she doesn't mean to send: a wall falling in the East offices.

I run for the door, barefoot and clad in sweats and ready to go and fight the incoming army in just that, until Serena grabs my hand and yanks me toward the barracks. A hot flash of the kiss she just got from Darcy jacks my nervous system for a moment before she gets ahold of herself—it's *be safe, take care, I love you, come back, go fight, you're everything, I understand,* and my heart aches with it for a beat before it's washed away by the bellowing alarm and the singing in my blood that says I will *not* let them come here and hurt us. I will *not* stand by and watch anyone die. I toss a thought back to Darcy in my wake: *I'm with her,* and then I lose myself in the slapping pounding of my naked feet on tile.

The barracks is full to the brim with soldiers gearing up, shirts off and battle suits on, underpowered Projectors pulling heavy mech suits on that will allow them to stand up better to telekinetic blows, falling rubble, Zaps and guns, and debris that will fly through the air ready to take us apart.

I'm breathing heavily, blood pumping through my veins so hard I feel it in every millimeter, every cell in my body. I feel lit up, and like I'm gonna shit my pants at the same time. This is my first real firefight, and it sounds bad. I can hear distant yelling, booms, sounds that distort the air. I can smell cordite already, thin and acrid, greasing my tongue, although I don't think it's really that strong. Yet.

Serena's dressed before me, years of practice speeding her hands and quickening her fingers. She helps me yank on my body armor, sleeveless reinforced plates instead of the lay on, gel kind. That's for when you have *time*. There's no time.

People sprint out of the barracks, breaking off into groups. I can feel James directing but I can't get enough of him, even projecting at his loudest, purest, to know what I should do. But I'm a Projector; that's not my job: to listen. My job is to respond.

I clip up the second to last buckle with clumsy fingers, my missing digit slowing me by maybe a full second, and Serena growls her impatience, grabs me by the belt, and yanks me into her with inhuman force. She grabs the straps and secures me with what would be an echoing click if it wasn't drowned by the sudden, booming crash that reverberates through the room and sends me to my knees.

My power is up before I impact the floor, catching the weight of the crumbling ceiling, holding it up. I have most of the room shielded, another Projector in the corner holding up maybe a fifth of the falling concrete and Serena is already grabbing people, throwing them out of the disintegrating room. The floor slips under me, making me lose my concentration as I start sliding. Serena falls, crashing into a bunkbed before she can catch herself. I throw out hooks of telekinesis to try to anchor myself onto the plane of teetering concrete, anchor her to me, and run lines of power through the building, through the walls, wrapping around the support beams and holding them tight.

I scream; it's so heavy; it's so much, but there are people here, our army is here, and if they die, we all die, so I bare my teeth and scream with the weight of it, and then Serena inches across the floor and slaps her hand into mine where it's scraped and bleeding, pressed flat against the floor I'm trying to hold and our power surges together.

She reads; I react, and she throws her Projector strength behind me to bolster my brute force. I slam spikes of power, hard as iron, crumbling concrete out of my way as I pin the pieces together, and she follows, follows, threading them with her more delicate touch and weaving a web around the sliding pieces that escape me.

It feels like forever, there's dust in every inhale, my face is wet and my forehead stings where something's hit me. I cling to the slanted floor like an insect on a sliding leaf, not able to spare the concentration to get myself out, get us out. If I lose my grip for even a millisecond, the whole barracks will be down around us and everyone left in the building will die.

Forty-two people, Serena tells me, and I don't know if she's somehow found the attention to count, or if someone's sending to her, but it doesn't matter because every muscle in my body is screaming like my bones and sinew are holding the building together, and her face is purple with effort, and both of us will die under here if we so much as *blink*.

Thirty-seven. My heart strains in my chest; I feel like it might explode; my power is everywhere, everywhere, everywhere; everything is me; I'm bricks and mortar and collapsing iron.

Nineteen. Almost there, almost there, nineteen people left. It could be Ria, could be Daine, could be Marty, could be any single one of the people who live and work and train here. Could be me. My lungs stop working, and somehow Serena finds the space to slap me in the face. I slip, losing it for a second and everything shifts and creaks; there's a scream below me, and I find strength left in the soles of my feet, in the palms of my hand, in the hairs on the back of my neck that are stood fierce like trees. Rebar hits me in the shoulder, jarring through me with enough energy to push my physical body inches down. The concrete groans.

Eleven. I can't. I can't. I can't.

Two. I hold. I hold on. I can't see anything but red. Serena pushes a little more power into my spine and braces and then groans: *Take us out, Toby,* with what sounds like the last possible ounce of energy in her.

I don't have the power to control anything, to hold onto anything. She shows me the nearest gap, and I grab onto the trees outside and yank us through it with the last dregs of power that make me sick, makes me throw up dust and bile even as we shoot out into the clear air. Behind us the building smashes down with a sound like the world ending. I black out before we hit the ground.

Chapter Nine

E17

The dust on the roof eases my passage as I worm back over to Kion, who is pulling out food packs, all while crouching down to make sure he's not seen from the ground, or from the windows looking down onto the roof from nearby buildings. I realize that tomorrow, when people are at work, we'll be visible if anyone should glance in our direction and am doubly sure that my idea is a good one.

Kion's wrist is warm and strong under my fingers as I curl them around his forearm, and he cocks his head, listening. I play back the thoughts of the people leaving town and show him an image of the skylight. He scratches his nose with his thumb, gazing into the middle distance, absorbing what I have to show him. I know the room number. I know the combination for the alarm—it had still been floating on the father's consciousness while he was leaving, the classic "Did I remember to set the alarm?" tangled in with the code itself—and after a moment, Kion nods. He's thinking about whether to go through the skylight and drop down, or head down the fire escape and use the front door.

After a long moment, his agile brain scanning through options and thoughts that I dance along with, the corner of his mouth curls in a minute grin, and we wriggle across the smooth surface together. He feels around the frame of the skylight, a sheet of transal as long across as I am, while I keep an "ear" on the activity below. It's late enough that the lucid thoughts drifting around are few, most people dreaming. I tune out the sleepers, something about the way their thoughts feel—soft and malleable—makes it easy to sort them from the people who are still awake. A man leans over a datapad, analyzing financial information with angry, tired determination. A woman sits on a soft couch, cursing in a low voice over the phone at someone, talking about something technical I don't know enough about to understand.

Somewhere down the hall a child is waking from a nightmare, thoughts full of fear and loneliness. I watch Kion with my real eyes, breaking and entering not being something I know a lot about, aside from a bit of lock picking and how to use the fancy equipment that cuts through glass. Satisfied nothing is happening below we need to be concerned about, I let a part of me monitor for any changes or approaching persons, splitting my attention.

The stocky soldier lines his face up millimeters away from the transparent surface, peering through the glass and then lays gloved palms down over the frame. I note that he's avoiding touching anything with his skin, to confuse any Readers trying to trace him. Good. There's a sharp snapping sound, and the window drops inward, making me jump. The movement of the glass is aborted before it's moved even six inches, and Kion, with a frown of concentration on his face, uses a piece of string to tie in physical place what his telekinetic powers were holding. Ah, he's broken the latch, so the window swung down, and now he's lashing it off so we can clamber through. I assume he'll then force it back into place and trap it there somehow. Unless someone comes to open it, our entrance should remain unobserved. Without needing him to ask, I widen my awareness, looking for any sign of trouble.

While I stand guard, so to speak, lying on my belly with my hands tucked in my sleeves and something sharp digging into my left kneecap, Kion swiftly packs the bags we've brought onto his broad back, and then looks at me with a sharp gaze. I give him a reassuring smile, and he winks at me as he, with enviable ease, swings the transal pane out of his way telekinetically, and rolls through the open space. His hands grip onto the frame tightly, supporting his whole—not small—body weight, muscles in his forearms and biceps bulging even through the fabric of his shirt. He looks like a gymnast as he lowers his body forward in a roll, head down, and then using his stomach muscles to hold his legs as he straightens. It looks impossible, and I'm sure he's anchoring himself with telekinesis, but when I read him, there's no trace of the sparkle of energy that would show bolstered muscles. Wow. I hope I'm not expected to do that. He drops through the window frame, a muted thud as his feet hit the carpeted floor the only thing to hear.

With a gulp, I look at him, wide-eyed, and his face crinkles into a soft expression, before he holds up a hand for me to wait. I duck out of sight and he pads down the corridor, casing the route and opening the door to our chosen hiding spot. The night air feels thick and constricting as I wait, not able to pick up on even a tendril of thought from him. The dangling skylight makes me feel exposed and obvious, and sweat prickles my upper lip as I gaze at the stars, keeping my mind as open as possible.

His communication, when it comes, makes me jump. *Thea. Come.* Even his mental speech is short and to the point. I wriggle onto my belly, and peek through the window frame. Kion stands in shadow, against the wall, with no sign of our bags. He must have dropped them in our new rooms. Unable to project to him, I hold up my hands, point at the frame and try to indicate the roll he did, then shake my head wildly. He gives a snort so faint I feel it in my mind, instead of hearing it out loud, and holds up his arms in an unmistakable gesture. Oh. Screwing my courage up into a tight ball, I squirm into a sitting position, sliding my legs over the frame. Below me, Kion looks small and far away, and I close my eyes to steady my nerves. He'll catch me; I know it. Won't he? Before I can chicken out, I shift forward and then I'm falling. Air rushes past as I drop, but before I have time to panic, Kion's power, and then his hands, are wrapped around my waist, and I land lightly, remembering *just* in time to bend my knees. We both stagger a little, and then Kion shoos me down the corridor, and I manage a jittery walk to the cracked door of apartment 16B.

I assume Kion is dealing with the skylight, and I take a moment to lean against the wall just inside the door and take a shaky breath. I didn't like that at all, and I've never had a problem with heights or the dark before. It's strange, and it takes me a few minutes to put my finger on it. Trust. That entrance was nothing to do with me, really; all I had to do was not scream and trust Kion not to let me fall. And for someone like me, that doesn't come easy.

Knowing what the problem is helps me calm the adrenaline pinging through my shaky limbs, and I make myself useful. Grabbing two glasses of water from the dispenser in the corner and leaving one on the side, I take a minute to pad through the apartment. It's a four-bedroom affair, large and comfortable. The carpeting is plush under my boots. I wish I could take them off, but we still need to avoid touching anything directly if possible.

I'm safer than most, with my close to zero projection capabilities. Even the average, ungifted person on the street leaves what looks like a screaming blur of color and shape compared to my faint wisps, but a talented Reader would recognize me from my traces and maybe even be able to pull out some information about the resistance. I try not to think about the rebellion as I wander through the rooms.

I feel Kion come in and shut the door behind him and leave off my exploration to check in with him. He sits on the couch, and I grin at the sight he makes. Messy hair, stubble—he looks like a soldier even though he's dressed in civilian garb. It's like seeing a tiger in a city park. The plush furnishings and shiny surfaces make him look dangerous and wild. He quirks an eyebrow at me, and I realize I'm grinning. I don't really know how to explain what I'm amused by, so I just shrug a shoulder and join him on the couch, swiping the glass from the table on the way and handing it over.

He drains it gratefully and smirks at me. "Ta. You could use a shower."

Oooh, I *could*. That sounds divine. "Is it safe?" I mean, will it seem off to the neighbors if the shower is running, and no one is supposed to be here.

"Ah, I reckon so. No lights, though." He sets his glass down on the table with a clunk, ignoring the coaster that's set right next to it.

I give him a look that I hope says "I'm not an idiot" and rub a hand across my face. "Which bedroom do you want?" We should use as few rooms as possible to minimize our tracks, just in case anyone discovers we've been here

The couch shifts under me as I get up, and Kion waves a hand dismissively. "Whatever. Use the main bathroom. Pick a bed."

My nod reminds me how tired I am, the hangover from yesterday still tugging at my bones, and a face-cracking yawn explodes out of me. We're deep in enemy territory, and the constant nerves have taken their toll on me today. I lift a hand in acknowledgement and slope off to get clean.

THE BATHROOM IS spacious, but with no lights on, it feels small and unwelcoming. A single, translucent window covered in some kind of pattern provides a little illumination, filtering the strip lights from the street. A soft, plush rug hits my feet as I inch forward, relying on a read of the room to bolster the poor visuals. The ceramic tiling of the bath is set low into the floor, and after yanking my clothes off, I barely have to step up to climb in. There's a transal sheet that unfolds once I'm in, and a small panel on the wall beside me flickers to life, making me jump. It's creepy in here, the dark and my nakedness reminding me of the Tank.

Gooseflesh springs up on my chilled skin, and I click the temperature display to a nice, hot level before selecting "On" and bracing myself for the spray. It's freezing for a split second as the pipes clear, and I can't help letting out a slight squeak, but it rapidly warms to a deluxe heat that permeates my skin, feeling like it is rinsing the chill off my very bones. I can't figure out which bottle of liquid is which, so I guess, lathering my body with something bubbly.

The luxury of the actions makes me grin, alone in the dark. I can count the number of wet showers I've had in my life on one hand, and it is a simple, direct sort of pleasure. But I'm mindful that the pipe noise may draw attention, so I shut off the shower as soon as I'm clean. I was so filthy that I can make out the waterline on the base of the bath, a faint rim of scum so clear that even in the dark it's visible now my eyes have adjusted. Self-conscious, I drag my foot around to scuff it away before climbing out. A soft towel is waiting for me, on a rack that would usually be heated, but has been turned off by the house's occupants. Shame.

Wrapping myself in the fabric, pinning it over my chest with my forearm, I scoop my clothing off the floor with one hand and exit the bathroom, leaving the door open for Kion. I find a bedroom to the left at the end of the short corridor that is stamped all over with teenage boy. The kid whining about his video games, it must be. He looked around my height, and so with my shirt wrapped round my hand, I poke through his clothes until I find some cozy sweatpants and a long-sleeved T-shirt to pull on. We'll launder everything we touch before we leave for good, or at worst, set the whole place on fire, but I'd rather not leave more traces than necessary, so having sleeves that can cover my hand is a good idea. I take a moment to steal a mouth-cleaning capsule from beside the bed before sliding in. The airy duvet and cool pillow nearly send me into a paroxysm of delight. This is bought with blood money, built on the backs of the poor who are trapped outside the City, with plastic bags for bedding, but right now I don't have the energy for disgust. I just relax, letting the comfort cradle me into sleep.

THE NIGHT AIR is still and heavy, the tang of fresh blood scalding my nostrils. My hand holds the knife with easy competence, slicing down the pale, insipid belly of the sand lizard, and I watch as the guts spill out, livid against my dirty skin. The edges of my nails are ragged and grimy, torn with teeth. My fingers are long and strong, somehow delicate as they manipulate the corpse that will make our dinner, slicing off the head. The hands of a surgeon, or artist. I don't recognize them, even as they work.

Icarus.

The thought comes to me from far away, but it is jarring, and for a second the confident movement of shoving a stick into the open wound of the lizard's neck halts. Just for a second. My-his head shakes, as though to clear fog from our thoughts, but then our dinner preparations continue. The stick makes a slick path through the meat, and then I prop it against a rock, leaning the body over the burning coals heating my thigh. A movement to the left catches my attention, and I shift to look, hands spinning the knife around of their own volition. I'm holding it in a guard I don't recognize, blade pressed down against the thin skin of my-his wrist, but ready to flash out in an instant. But the noisemaker doesn't need to be attacked. It's Pollux, shuffling down the rocks, looking wan and exhausted. My fingers twitch, as though I'm typing, and I blink the sensation away. Then an echoey voice sounds from somewhere down the gorge we are hidden away in. *Thea.*

Icarus-me looks, and so does Pollux, both twitching to attention. Icarus shifts fluidly so we are balanced on the balls of his feet, ready to attack, or to run. *Thea.* The voice is more insistent, but I can't see where, or who is calling. The name feels familiar, but I can't place it, and then

Epsilon Seventeen cuts the air in half, iron in the tone, and I remember. I remember who I am, who I'm not, and where I should be. The connection between my mind and Icarus snaps like a metal wire, springing me back into my body, dashing my mind against a rock wall that has been built there in my absence. There's no way in. No way back into my own self!

For a moment I scrabble, helpless, trapped in the nothing world between bodies, a liquid substance without a vessel, pouring away into the cracks between molecules. I *feel* myself disappearing. Then a brutal pain bursts across my whole face, and I explode back into my body, lungs, beautiful lungs pumping like bellows, arms and hands and eyes and skin, wonderful skin separating me from nothingness, and I cry for the joy of it, big, sacred sobs. The tears scald my lovely eyes, the marvelous burning pain in my cheek throbs with my heartbeat, and around my body, *my body,* I can feel strong arms. Cassandra screeches in frustration, relinquishing the last of her hold on my flesh and retreating into the space in my mind that she calls home.

Kion holds me as I cry. I can feel his confusion as palpable as heat against my skin. I feel his strength, and his fear. I never want to stop crying, because I know when I do, I'll have to talk. To tell him. But between sobs the tears spangle my vision into green stars, and I realize that the light in the dark room is coming from my lap. Coming from a datapad that isn't mine, dropped on my thighs. My eyes clear with a kind of inevitability, and I groan deep in my chest at what is on the screen. A message. Our address, the address of our hiding hole, and a number that I don't recognize flashing at the top of the screen. Blinking on the page a pop-up warning. *This message has no subject, are you sure you wish to send*? With an unsteady hand, I slam my thumb down onto the cancel button and then hurl the datapad away from me. I squirm away from the arms around me, pushing at Kion until he lets me go, and then I run.

The bathroom offers sanctuary, and I slam the door behind me as soon as I'm through. In the mirror opposite the doorway, I don't recognize myself. A ghost watches me, with hollow eyes and fear etched into every pore of their face. My lip trembles as I inch across the floor, watching my reflection. All I can think of is what I'm not. Not free, not strong, not safe, not a slave, but not a master, not a girl like other girls, but not a boy like other boys either. Just nothing. Just between and nothing and never complete. A gentle tap on the door jerks me out of my reverie, and Kion's voice is the same as it always is, gruff and kind and safe, calling my name. My new name, and I press my hand against the mirror, covering the reflection of my face before I answer his next call.

"Thea. Talk to me Thea." I can't detect a note of fear or rage in his voice.

"I'm sorry." I choke on my own apology, snot thickening my words.

"What happened to you?" The lack of judgement in his voice folds around me like a blanket, and I finally pull my hand away from the cold glass, but I don't look at myself again, just turn around and wrap my arms across my chest, trying to feel warm.

"It's...Icarus." *Cassandra*, my thoughts correct, but I can't. I can't tell him she lives in me. The words stick and pull in my throat. They'd never let me stay, if they knew. They'd send me away if they knew she was in me. Was here, always. *Coward.* I taunt myself, wishing for the courage to tell him. I'm a danger to ARC, a danger to everyone, and I can't make myself tell them. I'm the worst kind of coward, a lying coward. But I can't lie to myself. "When I sleep, sometimes...I dream of him. And then when I wake up, I'm not where I'm supposed to be, or doing what I'm supposed to do. He gets in my dreams, Kion. He's doing things to me."

There's silence, pressing in my temples like the barrel of a gun, then a soft sound like he's pressed his face against the material separating us. "How long?"

Always. I don't say it, can't. Instead I softly tell only part of the truth. How can I trust him, how can I trust anyone? People aren't safe, no matter what they tell you, no matter how they feel. People are selfish, and scared, and you can't trust them. I've been in too many minds not to know that. "Twice. This time, and once at ARC. I was in the control room. That's why I had to leave. I have to know what they did to me. Why this is happening." It doesn't sound like my own voice. I can feel the partial lies, like snakes, weaving in and out of my words. I can feel them in my throat.

"Okay. We'll take care of it. Come on, we need to sleep." That's it? I blink, sickness crawling in my stomach. "Thea. Come out. It's going to be okay." He puts a little Talent into his words, not forcing me to come out, but showing me his belief, his trust. The emotion settles in my chest soothing my ragged nerves.

Exhaustion pushes down on me so and I stumble a little. My feet carry me across the room, and I clench the door handle too hard before I twist it open. I'm convinced he's going to put me down as soon as I exit, neutralize the threat I clearly present, but let's face it, a door isn't going to stop him if that's his plan, and the dark bathroom is creepy and cold. He's not even outside the door as I exit, and I shuffle down to the room I chose. As soon as I'm in the doorway, I realize Kion is laid out on the floor, kit placed to one side. He gestures to the bed. "Now you'll tread on me if you go on any more excursions. Problem solved." He forces lightness into his words, but the memory of his swift reactions in the helichopper remind me that he's a light sleeper, and as I settle under the cold duvet, I try to convince myself he'll wake if I move. I don't believe it, and am sure I'll lie there awake for hours, but sleep drags me down into a black hole. When I wake, Kion's gone, but my dreams were clear.

I'M NERVOUS AS I enter the open-plan space of kitchen and living area, Kion is balanced on the back of a chair that leans against a wall. He's reaching up, pressing something into the seam where the ceiling meets the wall, and then he grunts in satisfaction and springs off the chair, landing without making a sound. He spares me a slight grin before sliding the chair across the wall, into the next corner and climbs back up. He repeats his actions, and glancing around the room, I realize that there are black rectangles around the length of my index finger, pressed into every corner. I narrow my eyes, but can't figure out what they are, and traipse into the kitchen for some water before asking, my voice throaty with sleep and stress. But if he's not gonna bring what happened in the night up, neither am I.

"What're you doing?" The water is cool and refreshing, clearing the fog from my morning brain.

"Camera. Bombs." He holds his hand out toward me, and the tap springs to life again, making me jump. A glass that had been resting in the sink bottom fills, and the tap snaps off. He gestures with his forefinger and the glass flies across the room, water not spilling out, even though the angles and force demand it should. It slaps into his open hand without losing a drop, and he drains it in two gulps.

My brain chews over his words as I sip my own drink, and then I nod in understanding. A camera to watch for anyone coming into the apartment, and bombs to clear any evidence we've left behind when we clear out. My guts shift as I wonder what would happen if a cleaning lady came in while we were out, or the family returned home unexpectedly, but I don't ask. I have enough guilt weighing on me.

Kion's voice makes me jump, lost in thought as I was, and I slop water onto my hand, wiping it clean on my sweatpants. "Ready to go in twenty minutes."

I hum agreement and rummage through the cupboards, turning out some cereal which we scarf down dry, the fridge not having a milk tap set up. Splashing water on my face combined with the food rouses me properly, the cobwebs of exhaustion blowing away, and I walk back down to the teen's room. His clothes are all black and dark, with band logos and symbols I don't recognize marring them. I yank on an undershirt, followed by long sleeves and a hoody, a pair of black jeans and boots I have to stuff socks into the ends of to make fit. I catch a glimpse of myself in the full-length mirror in the bedroom and do a double take. With my short hair and lean body, I look like a young boy. I narrow my eyes at myself and lift my lip in a snarl. Surprisingly pleased with my appearance, I slope back down the corridor, trying to minimize the natural sway of my hips and swagger a bit.

Kion looks up from where he's sprawled on a couch and snorts faintly. A grin tugs at his lips as he flows upright. He's found a nondescript suit somewhere, which sits awkwardly on him. I assume it belongs to the father, who was around the same height as Kion but with a belly and narrow frame. The sleeves and legs fit the soldier well, but it tugs too tight over his broad shoulders and is baggy round the middle.

"You can talk." I jerk my chin at his outfit, and he rolls his eyes.

"I think we pass. C'mon, we have things to pick up." He heads for the door without looking at me again, and I hasten after him.

"We do? What things?" I shove my hands in the pockets of my baggy hoody, looking down at the thick carpeting. It's still early, but I can "hear" people bustling around in the apartments near us, and I keep my mental ears open for any sign that people are going to head out into the corridor. No one bothers us as we shuffle down the stairs and out into the streets, and Kion doesn't reply.

We hurry down the main street, Kion leading the way with confident strides although I'm *sure* he's never been here before. We take several turns down the square-cornered streets, and after a while, I give up on trying to keep track of where we are. If I lose Kion I might not be able to find my way back, but I give myself the cold comfort of running through scenarios wherein I've been separated from Kion, and all of them are so awful that I doubt I'd be headed back to the apartment. Shaking off the paranoid thoughts of being hauled in by the local Institute, because I'm hardly equipped to defend myself, although my personal knife rests against my spine, under my shirts just in case, I concentrate on the gradually filling streets.

Kion leads us out of the busy areas fast, and I nudge him whenever I sense a patrol approaching so we take a long, convoluted route that doubles back on itself a few times and confuses me thoroughly. My mouth is dry by the time we saunter into a storefront that advertises sportswear and camping gear in faded, peeling letters on the window. Kion lazily peruses a wall of air rifles and rubber-handled hatchets, while I amuse myself looking at a turning display of colorful helmets. I watch Kion from the corner of my eye and see him point out a neon-orange axe to the man behind the desk, who has shown very little interest in us so far.

"Pass me that sunset orange one, please." He sounds disinterested and unconcerned. The man scurries over and looks at Kion obsequiously.

"Are you sure you wouldn't rather see the military-grade, black hatchet, sir, a big man like you?"

"Quite sure. That's my favorite color, and I like the angle of the blade."

The weaselly shop owner flicks his eye from side to side and then nods, shuffling around the desk and pulling a shade down over the window. Belatedly, I realize this must be the drop, and presumably, rather than sunset orange actually being Kion's favorite color, the short conversation was an exchange of code words. The shopkeeper glances at me nervously but leads us both through a small door and then straightens up, looking less like a rodent. The room is dingy, a single bare bulb the only source of light, and black shelves lining every inch of the room, covered in bags and boxes. My hackles are up, the place has a creepy, dark feel to it, and I can sense the shadows of anger and violence in the small space.

"Case number?" He opens a small book on the large desk dominating the empty space, and Kion, seeming to be completely relaxed, reels off a twenty-digit number without hesitation.

"Mmm, good. Here we are. Delivered this morning at first light." He runs a grubby finger down the ledger and then turns to the shelves, peering at what I can now see are small labels affixed to the black metal. He finds what he's looking for, what we've come for, and tries to heave it down from the head-high shelf it's resting on. It tumbles out, and I'm just starting to move forward to help when Kion grabs it off him. At the exact same moment it thumps into the soldier's chest, a red light illuminates the room in an angry glare, and the shopkeeper swears under his breath. "Watch patrol. Out through the back, quickly, quickly!"

I barely have time to get my feet under me before I'm ushered out of a hidden door and into a narrow street. The ground is cracked, dirty concrete and the smell is ripe and rotting. Kion grabs my bicep and we run together, feet sliding on the rough ground and Kion so weighed down by the enormous bag that he can barely see over it. My chest is tight with fear, were the patrol after us? Were they raiding the drop point or just stopping by? I spread my power out delicately, draping the people within 300 meters of us with a quick thread to read their thoughts.

There's a Watch Patrol, indeed. Six men and four women thundering down the street we entered the shop by. They run right past it, not even pausing. I can't find any suspicion of us in their minds, but that doesn't mean much... I'm distracted by the need to stay upright and can't look too deeply at them in case they have a Reader. My thundering heart feels like it's going to burst right through my breastbone when Kion slides to a stop. He looks around wildly, pressing me back against a brick wall. I drag in air gratefully, closing my eyes to keep focus on the patrol, but flinch and open them when I hear the sound of breaking transal. Kion has his hands pressed flat to a pane that comes out in two pieces when he pulls back. He lays them gently on the floor and throws the bag in through the newly made space. I dive after it without him needing to hurry me, and he thuds through behind me. He's already fitting the sheets of transal back into the frame, sticking it there with some sort of tape when I finish checking the building for presence.

"Just us." My whisper is steady, unshaken, although ragged with my heavy breathing. Kion crouches down next to the window, closing his eyes. He's reading the street, listening for pursuers. Gravel shifts under my feet as I creep back to him, squatting on my haunches and taking the hand he proffers to me.

I don't think they were after us, but we should change fast and get out of here. Go to the bag, find your clothes and tools. I'll watch the road.

I nod in agreement and hook the bag with my spare hand and then realize I can't lift it, and scraping it over the floor will make a noise. Kion catches my thoughts and telekinetically raises the bag, sending it spinning through the air to land with a quiet thump and puff of dust on the other side of the room. *Go.*

The place we're in is abandoned, the wiring hangs loose from the ceiling and the space is dusty and worn-looking. It could have been a storage room, or something, when it was in use. I trip over a vicious length of wire sticking out from the concrete floor, but instead of falling, I catch myself with my new reflexes and muscle resistance. My heart is still hammering with nerves as I get to the bag, and I feel like it must be audible, thrumming in my ears like a drumbeat, leading our pursuit toward us. Shaking off the sensation, I force myself to concentrate, unzipping the bag and sorting out what's for me and what's for Kion. There's no sign of the soldier patrol as we change and organize ourselves.

Chapter Ten

TOBY

The beeping drags me out of a warm slumber into a place I wish I wasn't. My whole body hurts, a slow, seeping ache that feels like my bones are made of glass and my muscles of fire. The sound I make isn't a word, I'm not totally sure what words are, but someone must hear because a warm hand touches my shoulder.

"Toby?"

I blink my eyes open. It's bright and white, like lightning being applied directly to my eyelids, so I slam them shut again, groaning.

The groan sets off a chain of bodily responses, and my stomach cramps before attempting to empty itself. Unfortunately, there appears to be nothing in me, and I cough miserably, trying not to choke on my own saliva.

"Here, I've got you." It's Aly, I realize, and this time when I peel my eyes open it's not quite as awful, although it still feels like I've been kicked in the head full force by Kion.

"Aly," I garble her name, and she smiles at me. It's bleary 'cause my eyes are gummy and gross feeling, but I see it. She doesn't look like everyone died.

"Hey, Shockfactor." Affection is thick in her tone. I wonder where she heard Sam's old nickname for me, but I'm too wiped to ask. Not important. "Can you have some water?"

I can, as it transpires, but not gracefully or without needing her to hold the glass, and my head. I still end up damp by the end of a few sips. Someone's put me in hospital whites, I realize, my clothes gone.

"Serena? The soldiers?" My voice is scratchy, harsh. Like someone's taken a sander to my vocal chords.

"Serena's okay; she's on her feet, helping with the cleanup. We lost sixteen soldiers and nine civilians from here. Google knows what the death count in the City is. Everyone got out of the barracks though."

"The last two?" The two we were waiting for. They were still in when we couldn't do it, couldn't keep our power up and get out alive.

Aly laughs, there's humor in it, but not much. "That was you guys. Everyone was out. You held an entire building up for long enough to evacuate."

And then passed out and did exactly nothing of any good in the actual fight. I try to sit up; my head spins and wheels, and I collapse back to the bed with no objection, when Aly's soft hand guides me down. "Stay, Toby. You have to rest."

"Is it over?" I moan, feeble, my body shaking, and I feel cold all over, like I'll never be warm again.

"It's over. ARC was able to repel them. We even took one of their helis. Marty jumped clean through the window out of a building and took the pilot out."

"Okay." I subside, curling up painfully under the blanket, trying to huddle down so I can be warmer.

She drapes another blanket over me. I feel it flutter down and then hear her footsteps, and then blessed silence except for the beeping, beeping of the heart rate monitor.

THE NEXT TIME I wake up, I'm alone. The monitor is still clipped to me, and I notice an IV next to my bed, empty now. A corresponding dot of blood on a cotton ball in the soft crook of my elbow confirms that the IV was for me.

I feel a little steadier than I did the first time, and I look around for a datapad to message someone, to find out what's going on. But there's no tech in sight, save for the medical equipment, and I get bored fast. This is not the hospital wing; there's no other beds or patients. Presumably they ran out of room during the attack. I seem to be in some kind of office they've shoved a bed in.

It takes me a few tries to sit upright; my chest feels tight, like my ribcage has shrunk somehow, like it's not expanding to take in enough air, and I get lightheaded, grabbing on to the metal railing of the bedside to steady myself while white spots dance in front of my eyes, and my stomach tries to exit the building through my nose.

The dizziness passes quickly though, and my stomach, rather than settling into normalcy, informs me in no uncertain terms that I am *starving*, and if I don't eat immediately, there's going to be trouble.

"Hello?" I call, my voice weak but still echoing off the walls eerily. No one answers; no one comes, and after a few minutes, it becomes clear that no one is going to. That leaves me with two choices: try to scrape myself upright and find some food or stay here and hope that someone comes in the near future before my stomach finishes eating itself.

Not being the especially patient sort, I know as soon as I've thought about it that I'm going to be getting up, so I figure I may as well get on with it. I unclip my heart monitor and discard it on the bed, cracking my neck and wishing I hadn't as I swing my legs around and off the bed.

It takes me three attempts to stand, my knees buckling and the room swaying in my vision. I end up grabbing the IV pole to use as a walking aide. It scrapes and slides across the floor but helps me stay balanced, leaning my weight on the stand. The metal is cold and solid in my palm.

I stagger to the door, open it the normal way, because even the *idea* of looking for my power right now makes my whole body protest, cold sparks firing along my nerves.

The door opens easily, but there's no one conveniently in the corridor to come to fetch me, and I'm starting to reassess the sensibility of my plan to try to make it out on my own when my stomach sends a vicious cramp to remind me why I'm on my feet. Protein. I need protein, and fast. I must have burned through everything I have. It feels like I might have lost weight, even, somehow, like my hands are bonier than they were just a day ago.

I step forward, and again, the tile is cold and firm under my feet, and I steady a little as I work my way down the hallway. The kitchens are the other side of the building from the makeshift hospital I was in.

All I can think of is food, and I'm almost right past the big windows in the open corridor before I glance outside.

It's...destruction. I can't even believe it. There's a huge cloud of black smoke boiling into the blue sky, staining everything it touches. It looks like it's over the tube station but it's impossible to tell. Closer, the walls around the garden are pocked and smeared with black, and in places, there are huge chunks missing like a giant has lost their temper and smashed massive fists through the brick.

The barracks, where I was changing when the attack caught up with us, is just a heap of rubble. People are running back and forth across the grounds, avoiding enormous holes littering the ground, mounds of earth and splintered trees and everything everywhere is littered with transal, broken into diamonds that catch the weak sunlight and partially obscure the bodies underneath them with the flashing white light.

Close to the building, close enough that I can make out details I don't want to see, a Projector is lifting a sheet of shattered transal off a person whose legs are bent at such extreme angles it makes me gag, my stomach swirling, and I slam my hand into the wall in an effort to stay upright, stars spangling my vision. I had to press my forehead against the cool tile to get my balance.

I had no idea. *None.*

I've seen vids, I've seen photos and images of the great wars. I've seen reenactments and documentaries. I've seen fights, between two people, between groups of people, between ARC and the Institute in a two-block radius.

I've never seen war.

Yesterday I walked over the green grass, soft under my feet, and today bodies are being piled up against a wall because there's no time to deal with them. The dead can wait, the living are screaming.

I've never been so glad to have null reading powers. I can't imagine what it would feel like to have these people pressed against my mind. I have to help. I push off from the wall, try to pull some power into me to steady my weak muscles, forgetting what left me feeling this way.

It's like trying to start a car that hasn't been charged overnight—there's a spark, something sputtering in my chest, but there's nothing there. I'm sliding down the wall in a sort of gray fugue when a hand grabs me around the bicep, making me jump.

"What are you doing?" Jake inquires as he helps steady me, slinging my arm over his shoulder. "You should be in bed. I was coming to see you."

"I gotta..." I wave at the window.

Jake gives me a supremely unimpressed look. "You gotta what? Learn to walk? You're like a wet kitten." He forces me around, and true to his words, I'm not strong enough to fight his grip, which kind of proves that I shouldn't be. "You need to eat, and sleep. You're no good to anyone like this."

At least he isn't making sarcastic comments about learning to control my powers this time, presumably understanding the circumstances kind of took that out of my hands. I let him half walk, half carry me back to the makeshift clinic, and he settles me into the bed with remarkable restraint.

"They won't let me help," he grumbles, flopping down in an office chair with wheels and scooting close enough to the bed to rest his feet on the mattress, shoes and all. I make an unsuccessful attempt to nudge them off with my own. He dodges easily, lifting them up and putting them back when I collapse.

"Yeah." I don't know what to say, because of course, they're not letting Jake help clean up dead bodies, he's barely twelve. But at the same time, he's being hunted just like all the rest of us, and he could have been one of those bodies out there. Asking him to sit back and wait is cruel. "Where's Damon?"

A flash of panic hits me in the chest, like I didn't realize until this exact, lightning moment that every one of those small bodies lying broken on the grass outside was someone I know. Could be Damon, could be Darcy. I only know Serena's safe because Alyssa told me. My chest refuses to suck in air, my ribcage is wrapped in hot metal wires that won't let me expand my lungs, just burn.

"Toby...dammit, Toby," Jake's voice sounds like it's coming down a well, and then a sharp pain in my upper arm flashes through my nerve endings and the panic loosens momentarily, letting me inhale. He pinches me again, small fingers sharp and strong.

He rubs my back with a warm hand until I stop shaking, and I curl forward, leaning my head on my knees and hiding my face.

"I know," he says, and it sounds too old to be coming out of his mouth.

The heavy, painful silence is broken by footsteps, and I scrape my tangled, dirty hair off my face and look up. Damon's hovering in the doorway, a tray balanced in his hands, wafting a smell of *food* right into my lizard brain, bypassing all critical thought. My mouth waters so I have to swipe my hand over my face to avoid drooling, and Jake huffs a weak little laugh.

Damon manages a shy smile as he hands me the tray, leaning his hip against Jake's chair. I listen with half an ear while the rest of me is occupied drinking the— thankfully not piping hot—soup straight from the bowl, ignoring the spoon completely.

"They've got civilians helping, 'cause we were the main target," Damon murmurs, "I heard them talking. They said there was a bomb come through the tube; they sent a bomb from the other City, and they were waiting in the desert and flew in when it went off."

Google, a bomb. That explains the black smoke hovering over the southeast of the City.

"They said they fought 'em off in the streets, that they don't know what's happening, but that it's all connected to the Watch being gone and the City being different."

I mop up the rest of my soup with a hunk of stale bread, not tasting anything, but still so hungry my stomach protests when I pause long enough to say, "Do you know who's dead?"

Because really, that's the only question that matters to me right now. Who we've lost. Who *I've* lost, and I'm sick with the knowledge that I'm hoping it's no one close to me, that I'd rather someone else carry the pain of it.

"No," Damon shifts awkwardly, and Jake curls his brown fingers around Damon's darker wrist, bolstering him enough to continue, "David Jacobs is in with Ria and a couple of others, but no one will talk to me, and Aly just said we should come and bring you something to eat and keep you company 'cause we couldn't help."

"Darcy?" I ask, because I can't not.

"She was with Serena, but she's helping in the hospital now," Jake replies, and I release a breath that had been trapped in my lungs like a lead balloon.

Of course, she was with Serena. I wish we were in together, Serena and I, sharing a room so we could have our people all around us together. But our people have to help. I see that.

"I bet medical could use an extra pair of runners, bringing food and water up for patients, stuff like that. Taking dirty linens out to burn. Did you try there or just outside?"

"Just outside," Jake says, letting go of Damon and sitting forward. "Do you think?"

"Yeah, I do. Talk to Darcy, I'm sure she'll give you something to do that will help her." I can see the itch in them both, the need to be moving, doing something. I feel it myself, but I'm also feeble enough that I won't be of any help unless I rest. "I need to sleep, anyway, guys."

"Okay." Jake is sold on the idea, and Damon will do whatever Jake suggests. "We'll bring you some more food later. Rest up, okay?" He slides out of the chair and races for the door, hovering just off the tiles when he spins to look at me again. "We need you."

I hate the look on his face. It's not fear; it's not anger; it's resignation or something similar. This situation isn't a surprise to him. He was raised underground, kept safe from people who hunted him. And now those people are coming back, but this time just to kill us all.

THE NEXT TIME I wake up, I feel better, stronger. My limbs aren't quite as hollow feeling. There's a plate of thick sandwiches on the small table by the bed, and I scoff them down eagerly, still hungry beyond reason. When I'm done, I take stock of myself. My power is still useless, small and fluttering in my chest. Johan mentioned this, in his lessons. I'm empty; it takes time for power to rebuild. Apparently, I hit my limits full force this time. The mere idea of trying to do anything telekinetically makes me cringe, my stomach lurching.

The old-fashioned way, then. I pull myself out of bed, test myself. I'm steady enough on my feet. Not strong enough to haul wreckage or bodies, but maybe enough to deliver medicine or clean up like I suggested the boys do. There's no way I can just sit here. Exhausted as I am there's an itch in me, bone deep. I have to do something, or I'll lose my mind thinking about what happened outside.

It takes a while for me to get to the hospital wing. There're harried people running back and forth, stretchers being delivered by soldiers. One of them shoves their burden at me, a groaning man with blood flowering shockingly red around his dark hair, his face untouched on the left. His right eye is gone, a crater of ooze surrounded by fresh, running blood. The bridge of his nose marks the start of the injury, which curls across the ruin of his eye socket and wraps into his hair.

I recognize him. Zeb. We trained together a few times. A good man, wicked fast with a knife. I'd always be striped in ink from his blunted blade after sparring with him. My hands have grabbed the stretcher, but I'm not moving, and the soldier who dropped him with me shoves it so it bats into my stomach; I stagger.

"Go," she says, sharply enough the command cuts through my frozen self.

I turn without replying and wheel the stretcher into the first room of the hospital.

"Urgent or not urgent?" A woman yells at me, harried, her clipboard in one hand and her other grabbing the stretcher to lean over.

"What?" I reply, stupidly, the words caught on my tongue. Of course, it's urgent, look at him, his face is wrecked, he's lost an eye.

"Is he dying? Internal injuries?" She doesn't even look at me, assuming medical training I don't have, but the man coughs and responds himself.

"Just my face. I'm okay," he wheezes, his head lolling sideways so all I can see is the canyon where his brown eye used to be.

"Down the corridor, third room." She points, moves on without waiting. Looks at the next person. We're already forgotten.

The corridor is long, and busy. People sprinting back and forth, people in wheelchairs, people strapped to stretchers. There's a spray of blood on the wall, likely where someone took the pressure off an arterial bleed, I think, surprising myself with my coolness in the face of it. Emergency mode, my dad always called it. Where there's no time to be upset, so you just push that all aside, and do what you can. Not everyone has it, but if you want to work in emergency situations, you need it.

The ward is small, twenty beds crammed into a space that's made for six. There's groaning and pained breathing and whimpering coming from every direction. It takes ten minutes to get Zeb out of his stretcher and onto the last, but one, bed. He can't help much, weak and loopy, and my muscles are shaky and worn.

"Just get me some pain killers, if they have some spare," Zeb mumbles. He's gray under his brown skin and I can't believe he's still awake.

"Yeah, of course." I leave him, squeezing his hand briefly because it seems like human contact might help, somehow. I find a tray unit of basic first aid supplies in the corner of the room. It has painkillers, and more importantly, some of the miracle cleaning spray Dr. Grey used on my hand, as well as gauze and bandages. If Zeb doesn't get his face wrapped up, he's gonna lose enough blood he could be in real danger. And just 'cause I can't stitch him up doesn't mean I can't help.

I take him the painkillers, willing my hands steady as I organize supplies on the top of the wheeled tray and pull on gloves. "I'm just gonna wrap you up," I say, trying to sound as reassuring and adult as I can.

"Okay," he mumbles, no fight in him. He screams when I wash his face off, though, screams like he's being tortured with a poker. And then he apologizes, and something in me feels like it's breaking.

Mechanically, I clean up the mess of his face, the cut goes right into his hairline but it's not as deep after whatever it was bounced off his eye socket. I can see bits of bone in the livid red. The cleaner has anesthetic in it, and the tension eases out of his bones as I work, internal and external painkillers united to provide some relief.

He breathes in little sipping gasps, as I press gauze into the wound as gently as possible, unrolling a bandage around his head until the gauze is secured and tight. It seeps red in a couple of spots but seems to be holding the blood back. I can't do anything else. I know how a staple gun works, but I wouldn't know where to start with the size of the injury.

Zeb squeezes my hand. "Thanks, Toby," he mutters, on the verge of passing out, and I manage a feeble smile for him, carefully lifting his head so I can turn his pillow and he doesn't have to lie in his own gore anymore. It looks better, now he's cleaned up and wrapped.

I'm half analyzing my handiwork and half wondering what to do next when a mumble from the next bed grabs my attention.

"Ribs," the middle-aged woman lying there moans. She's not someone I recognize, maybe a civ, red hair tied back and a huge scrape down her neck and bloodying her shoulder.

"Did you get painkillers?" I ask, wondering if I could trust the response, she might not remember right.

"Nah, we're not priorities. Just dumped us in here. Be a good boy and get me some morphex." She pats my hand

and I nod. Judging on how they sent me in here, that seems plausible. And she's in a lot of pain, drawn and pale with sweat beading on her upper lip. I help her take a dose of pills and then ease her back to the bed. I clean her shoulder graze off, too; it only takes a minute, and it was dirty and full of grime. She nods her thanks, and I move to the next bed.

Broken foot and ankle, not crushing, so not urgent. I provide painkillers and splint and wrap the foot, help her prop it onto some pillows so the weight is distributed more comfortably. It's all I can do.

I take debris out of the next man's back. It takes a long time, but I can't stop before I've finished. A doctor comes in as I'm leaning over, picking out a piece of transal as big as my thumb and wiping the blood away before applying a dressing.

"What are you doing in here?" The doctor asks, running professional eyes over my handiwork and then moving to the next bed.

"Trying to help?" I wish I sounded surer of myself, but everyone was so busy and there were things I knew how to do in here. So, I just did them. I'm not sure if that was the right thing to do.

"Write down what you give them, what you do," the doctor huffs, exasperated, and leaves the room.

I guess that means he approves? There are no charts, no pen and paper, so I finish with the debris-riddled guy, who grunts his thanks, and then head into the corridor. It takes a while to find pen and paper, but I hurry back, make notes on everything I've done and move to the next bed.

Painkillers, bandages, more painkillers, gauze, staple gun, broken arm, broken collarbone, gashes from flying transal, a narrow miss with a Zap—the injuries start blurring into one another, my mind shying away from the details. I work mechanically, steadily. When I've dealt with the room I brought Zeb to as best I can, knowing that I might have helped people fight off infection or at least rest in more comfort, lose less blood, I move to the next room.

Serena finds me passed out against a wall. I don't even remember sitting down. I'm in the third room of non-urgent patients, all of whom have just been put aside for now. The nurses and doctors have their hands full with the people who will die if they don't get immediate attention. We're not prepared for devastation on this scale.

We don't seem to have anything to say to each other, for once. She leans her knee against mine, her shoulder pressing against my own, and hands me a canteen box. I eat the chicken and rice without tasting anything. There's blood on my wrist; it's not mine, and I can't bring myself to care.

When we're done eating, Serena scrapes herself off the floor. She looks as exhausted as I feel. "You're doing good," she kicks my foot, offers me a hand. I take it, and she hauls me up, no Talent. I yank her off her feet and have to use the wall to catch myself. She gives me a wry grin, and I look at her, wordless. Struck mute by the things I've seen. I remember how quiet my twin was when she first was released from Johan's side. I wonder if it runs in the family. I'm beyond glad that she's not here, that we might get a veneer of safety back before she returns. She's seen enough.

There'll be time for self-pity later, though. I have work to do.

I stop only when I can't go any more. When I run out of side rooms—*sixty-five people*—I counted without meaning to, a doctor grabs me in the corridor and hands me off to a nurse. She gives me bedpans, and I begin a new, less dignified but equally vital task.

People I've known for weeks, months, look away in shame as I help them, or lift their chins proudly, or are too tired for either. It doesn't matter. I help anyway. Domas throws up on me, leans against my shoulder, and instead of flinching away in disgust at the hot liquid down my front, I hold his head while he weeps against my body.

I wonder if it's maturity or emptiness that means I don't mind.

And still it goes. It's endless, or so it seems, and then somehow there are more staff, clean and rested and unthreading my tired fingers from my cart. "C'mon now, kid. Time for a nap." A friendly, rotund man points me in the direction of the doors; won't let me turn back. We're all being relieved. I don't know where they found the staff, but I'm dead on my feet and don't have enough left to argue with.

I'm about to slide into my own bed for the first time in three days when something hooks into my chest and yanks.

Chapter Eleven

E17

We settle in, Kion rigs up technology that was stored in the bag until he has a pretty professional-looking setup, although using junk instead of a desk to support the equipment. I keep guard from just inside the broken window, ready to alert Kion if anyone is approaching. The street is quiet except for a few elec-vans and the occasional pedestrian. As a matter of course, I scan everyone in the area, and Kion keeps our gear organized apart from what he's using, so we're ready to bug out at a moment's notice. The air is thick with disuse, musty and dry feeling in my throat. I make myself take only small sips of water, though. Kion makes occasional small grunts while he works, which I think are sounds of satisfaction. I know he's looking for a place near a Watch station we can eavesdrop from, or better yet, an Institute team we can follow. For a moment the hopelessness of our mission breaks over me. What, I hope to just listen in on a few conversations and find out what they did to me, what they're planning? It's a childish dream, and I'm suddenly ashamed of making Kion come here, with me. I doubt we'll find anything out, and we might even get caught. The thought of that sobers me, and I clench my jaw, shaking off the brief spell of hopelessness. Any small piece of intel might help. We're cut off out in our City, and the underground factions here are more concerned with stealing and petty crime than revolution. Not that I blame them.

My thoughts drift to Leaf, and I think of the way he sculpted that piece of wire in a few swift movements. He's a slum kid but smart, from how he speaks and acts. I've always thought we can see some of a person's intelligence in their movements, the way they think and speak. So, a clever guy, but uneducated. I wonder who he'd be if his life had been soft and easy, like Toby's. I wonder who I'd be if I hadn't been fed on fear and lies as I was growing.

The hours drag past, my back stiffens and complains until I have to shift position, leaning against the wall. Concentrating isn't a problem. I'm well trained for this. I keep my sense open, searching, and use the time to chew over what I know, who I know. My thoughts are circular, spinning around on themselves and coming back to nothing of importance. The part of me that isn't watching the street, waiting and guarding us is asleep in the thick heat of the afternoon when Kion starts packing down the tech, disturbing me. A glance over at him gets a cycled finger gesture. We're ready to move. I get to my feet stiffly, stretching out tight limbs with relief. Sunlight spears through the room from small holes that used to hold wiring, and one large window that has a broken-out corner. I glance around, doing a last check for who knows what. I read the room, looking for traces we may have left. My power washes through the space, gathering faint impressions of electricity, a hint of "looking," the sense that someone here was searching for something, but no residue that may raise suspicion. Kion shoulders the bag, thick straps crossing his chest in an X, and raises an eyebrow at me. I nod, and then as he moves, a tingle of something more *him* shivers at me from the floor. Walking toward it gets me a questioning look, and I scan the ground, looking for the trace.

"Something little, but yours." It only takes me a second to hone in on it, a thread coiled around a broken nail protruding from a block of concrete. "Got it." I pick it up, coil it around my finger and stow it in my back pocket. Just a two-inch piece of synthetic cotton, but one that had been resting against his skin, picked up his sweat, his pheromones, and turned into a little slice of his thoughts and intentions. A piece of thread that probably would have passed unnoticed, even after this building was repossessed, but that could spell disaster if it got into the wrong hands. Kion gives me a half grin and looks down at his leg, twisting it around. A tiny snag is visible in the fabric, and I smirk. "I'm good at my job."

The half grin turns into an actual, honest-to-goodness smile. "So am I. C'mon." We find our way through the building and Kion breaks the lock on the main door. I can feel the weight of a tool belt around my waist, hidden under my fashionable jacket. My white shirt cuffs make my hands look dark. I hope our brief stay in the disused building hasn't mussed us up in a way I'm not seeing. Kion still looks fine to me, now dressed in an outfit that fits him, courtesy of the bag of tricks we picked up. We stroll down the quiet side street, and onto the main road, bustling with people and elec-cars. I assume Kion has found us a place to gather information, but I don't feel the need to ask. I've never known more than necessary before, and I trust he knows what he's doing. This is his playground, infiltration without passports that will get us past every barrier, without Shepherds gently touching their hip holsters and reminding recalcitrant Citizens of their duty to support and aid their government. Without a private army ready to swing by and force the world to their will. It's just me and Kion, out here. And the thought is both terrifying and exhilarating. My knife is strapped to my ankle now, and I can feel the comforting weight of it.

Kion leads me through the City, stopping at a few stores to buy trinkets, including a less military-looking bag which he fills with our gear in a public bathroom, to further our cover. We get closer and closer to the center of the City. I can feel it in the air. People walk with more and more purpose, apartments give way to skyscrapers holding offices and business centers. We've been walking for more than an hour when Kion leads me into a restaurant. The walls are floor to ceiling transal: giant windows tinted to block out a little of the sun's glare. Servers bustle between tables, waiting on patrons dressed in sharp suits, their pointed collars tipped with metals and jewels glinting over the top button. No one so much as glances at us until a smiling, plastic-looking man greets us.

"Welcome to the Central Cafe. Table for two?" He doesn't even wait for a response, just dances away through the crowded room and places us on a small table backed against the window. Kion discusses wine vintages with the man, while I open my menu, hiding my face. The food options are vast, more choice than I've ever seen in one place. I don't know where to start, but Kion catches my eye and winks at me, then taps my knee under the table. I take his hand so we can communicate faster than light. *I'll order for you; you concentrate. We're forty-five meters from an Institute entrance, as far as I can tell. This is also a major Watch route. Open your book. I'll work on my tablet so it doesn't look strange that we're not speaking. Turn your page every forty-five seconds.* I slide my hand back to the table surreptitiously. Kion hands me an e-reader, open to something fictional about a group of girls, judging by the cover.

I set the auto page turn to the time he suggested, having not the faintest idea how long it takes me to read a page. I would have guessed much faster than that, but it doesn't matter as long as it doesn't look suspicious. I want to crack my neck from side to side in the way the ARC soldiers do before closing with a new task but content myself with a quick glance around the room and a sip of the iced, lemon-flavored water that was already sweating on the table when we sat. The tablecloth tickles my knees, and I settle back in my chair, propping the book up in one hand. It takes a little time to tune myself in. I have to ignore all the myriad thoughts, petty concerns and everyday worries from my surroundings. I want the precise, organized thoughts of the Institute Shepherds, or the angry, focused minds of the Watch. The humdrum mental threads around me retreat as I block them out, push them away.

Time spent parsing through the Institute serves me well as I look for the minds that reflect those who imprisoned me. Inhuman. Too arranged and standardized. Grouped together in pairs or sets of four, with ties between them. Psionic ties. There's a team at the very edge of my awareness, over a mile away. I wouldn't be able to sort a normal mind from the crowds at this distance, but I can feel their connections to one another, a square of glass floating through a maelstrom of water-like thoughts, roaring and crashing around them. Nothing else is within my reach, but I also can't make out anything specific from this team; they're too far away. I drift around the area, trying to track down the door to the maw of the Institute, the sprawling underground facility must be below us right now, but iron-lined like ARC, keeping stray thoughts from escaping and locking me out as effectively as if they weren't there at all.

The team on my periphery flutters into focus as they make good time toward us. A woman, Rhino, I get her tag from one of her team, is the leader. She's strong, a Projector with a personality like the animal she's named for. With her are a gamma-strength Projector-Reader split who answers to Helo and another Projector named Royal. The last team member is Reader only, judging from the lack of information available to me. Shame, as Readers are more likely to know what's going on due to subconscious information sifting. I concentrate on the two supporting agents I can sense, Helo and Royal. I hope to follow their progress all the way back to the hidden entrance so that Kion and I can surveil the door and I can check anyone going in or out. If I'm lucky, I'll be able to trace threads of thoughts about specific projects and glean some keywords to scan for. I wish I was able to write down what I learn, and for a split second I miss the machinery that would be clipped to my head on information gathering missions. The patterns it would record for me would help me create a comprehensive report after I was back at base.

The information they're carrying is interesting but jumbled. Royal is by far the easiest to read. The team has been out on a mission; they even have a sheep with them. It seems they've already successfully completed their objective and are heading back to base. Somewhere back in a building on 5th Street four bodies are waiting for cleanup. Royal has only been a Shepherd for a few months; her loyalties are fuzzy at the edges and I know that she'll be sent down for a scrub and reprogramming session, a little brainwashing, when she's back. She needs her circuits stamped together, the Institute linked incontrovertibly to justice, freedom, equality and fairness. For now though, her thoughts are scattered, thinking about the dead face of one of the young people she left behind, blood soaking the carpet. The "terror attack" planned, in fact just an analysis of the stock markets, abandoned and useless on their now melted hard drives. Just college kids, out of their depth.

I use the cracks in her defenses caused by worry and distraction to worm into her mind and flick through the details she has of the events in Fourth City and what has been happening here since then. My real body watches pages turn, while my invisible fingers root through her brain, finding out what she knows. The dislocating sensation of being in two places at once is so familiar to me. I can still see Kion across the table, chewing thoughtfully on a meatball, overlaid by reams and reams of images that represent the thoughts and feelings of the agent I'm studying. Family, friends, work, training. Ah, here, the date Toby was brought in and the fury of ARC followed. All alarms raised, this base going into lockdown emergency protocol enacted. Seven Institute agents made it out of the ARC attack on their base and took up posts here. They watched the surveillance footage of the attack, and her thoughts are thick with someone else's mental stamp, edited to make the rescuers into the enemy, the kids that were saved into innocent victims. She's poisoned with hatred for ARC; she's excited about the attack that left... *Oh Google.* The attack... They've already hit ARC, while we we're here trying to gather info.

My heart does something strange, expands, contracts, rubbery in my chest like the cavity is too small. Her attention flickers and I think I've been noticed, but no, she's just stepped in something. The mundane action fires me back into reality, away from the details of the full-scale operation that flew out to destroy our home. Carefully, without releasing my hold on the Institute agent, still rattling her brain for more information, anything I can get, I slide my foot under the table and press it against Kion, so we're ankle to ankle.

The fabric inhibits my already pathetic Projector capabilities, but I pass him the message, he looks right at me, face stiffening into pale seriousness. He motions his hand toward his tablet, a minute gesture, and I nod and reply, *Yes, find out what happened. I'm looking for more.* Royal winces; I feel it in her inner thoughts; I'm pushing too hard, not letting her lead me from thought to thought, synapse firing to synapse firing. I'm forcing her to focus and the brutal headache she'll have later is starting to twinge. The others will notice if I keep going.

I snap out of her, leaving with the vague outlines. Something to do with the tube, the one they've shut that runs to our City. They've unblocked it, somehow without ARCs guard's noticing; they sent something through. Either she doesn't know what or a barricade has been erected around the thoughts, cutting me off. I drop out of her in the blink of an eye and dive into Helo, who's busy worrying about the crease between Royal's eyebrows. I'm treated to an unexpected and X-rated memory of the last time she saw that crease which was for an entirely different reason. I feel my cheeks heating automatically, privy to the flickering images of sex and lust tied up with some heavy emotional entanglement as Helo thinks about their last night together. She...oh, internally Helo refers to themselves in the third person, a gender neutral term, I correct my own internal narrative accordingly. *Xe*, in the singular, should keep it down, regardless of sexuality or gender identity, while fraternization among Shepherds is tacitly approved of, this level of feeling for a fellow operative, however, would be scrubbed out of xem with no compunction. Love is not a useful emotion.

I shove past the porn reel and scrabble for details about ARC, about the attack, looking for anything that might be useful to me. Kion's fingers are dancing over the keys of his tablet, and I know he is trying to contact the rebel forces, but I need more. Two blocks away Helo drops to xir knees, registering the invasion. I trust that I'm subtle enough not to be tracked, but the brute force invasion can't be helped. I need to know. More information spirals out of the struggling agent, codes, an authorization, project names.

Cassandra explodes in my head, in Helo's head, and in the restaurant, I feel wetness burst from my nose, spread onto my lips in a coppery flood. *Here, here, here.* She's screaming at the agents, Rhino, the leader, grabs Helo under the arm, shoves xem at the last member of the team, the secretive Reader I couldn't get a bead on. He seizes xir, threading his power into xir mind, looking for the invasion—*for me!* And then I recognize him. Angel. The man who once took me out to search for my brother, the leader of Smash's team. He gets a look at me, in my shock, and traces me back to my body, rivulets of power running over me and into the restaurant.

I snap back, dropping every ounce of Talent and shoving a shield up as brutally as I can. He's thrust out, but I can't do the same for Cassandra, who has decided to make up for her quiescence with an attempt to wrest control from me completely. In a fugue, my elbow slips on the table, e-reader dropping to the floor. "Run." I force the word out from numb lips. Kion's already on his feet and shoving past a server, getting his arm around me. His hand is hot in the small of my back as he half scoops me up and starts moving me past the bemused diners. Outside, I can feel the patrol approaching, and my attention is split in too many directions. I drag strength, emotional strength from Kion's closeness, the man like a wall between me and panic.

We burst out into the street, on the opposite side to the approaching Institute team, and all hell breaks loose. Zap shots explode into the wall next to us, their pressure sucking out the air, making little cyclones that drag at my loose shirt A Watch patrol has already opened fire on us, and the Institute team are closing in at our back. I stagger along, my brain dazed from snapping back and forth and Cassandra's attack, but she gives me time to gather myself. I don't think she's leaving thought breadcrumbs, but she doesn't have to, my blood drips thick and hot from my nose as Kion yanks me down a side street. My head clears and I clap my hand against my face, pinching my nostrils shut in an effort to stop the blood flow, but mostly just redirecting it down my throat. I try to swallow it like I was trained, but the salty taste makes me gag a little. They're so close behind us it barely matters; they don't need the blood when they have cameras and witnesses, but it's automatic. We careen around a corner and sprint down a road, Zap fire halted now as civilians scream and cower. The noise of engines approaching hums in the distance and I slide my hand into Kion's. I'm running full out, terror pulsing in my veins, but Kion is a calm presence next to me as he chooses the route. *Where?*

There's no time for extraneous thoughts and his mental sending is terse. *Don't know*. Away seems to be our only plan, and not a good one. They're too close on our tails to head for our safe house; we don't have time to check the map; all we can do is run and try to lose ourselves in the crowd. My lungs are straining a little, but I'm in good shape and we hurtle through the milling people, narrowly avoiding collision after collision. I keep my thoughts on the Watch and the Institute team; they've lost us for a moment but only that. Yanking my hand out of Kion's I run to a wall, grabbing the first thing I can think of to write with. My fingers drip with scarlet after I swipe them over my upper lip. Blood will give them a clear stamp of me, but Angel already knows who I am, and they're going to find us with or without a mark. We don't have a plan, so I think the worst they can get is that we have people to call on. They'll wipe it clear as soon as they've taken what information they can from it, but if one of Leaf's people sees it it will be worth the risk. I hope it doesn't tell our pursuers much as I scrawl a terrible reproduction of Leaf's compass on the stone wall. We need backup, fast.

Kion had gone on a pace or two without me and whirls around to reconnect. I reach out for him and our fingers slide together, lubricated by blood and sweat. He doesn't push for a reason I stopped, what I was doing, but I give it to him anyway, and he grunts as we thread our way through the myriad shoppers as fast as we can. But if Leaf is going to find us, we need a place to hide, and I'm drawing blank after blank. Off the streets is a must, somewhere we can escape from, and then I have a brainwave. *The tube*. The information I got, the clearing of the tunnel, the bomb. There must be a way through. If we can commandeer a maintenance vehicle, or a tube itself and then hack the electronics and run it, we'll be out of the City in moments, on our way home. We might be in time to help.

I pass all the information I can to Kion, rattling through what I have stored in the past, systems logs, timetables, maintenance manuals and other random pieces of information stored in me from a dozen missions. We can do it, and at least we know they won't be behind us if we back into the tunnel. Kion has weapons, explosives even; maybe we can collapse our route behind us and block off the inevitable pursuit if we have time. Kion's agreement is swift and to the point. He doesn't have a better plan, and neither do I. We run for the tube. It feels like the cameras swivel to follow us as we dive down alleys and around corners. The tube station we want is about three kilometers from us, a fifteen-minute run if we pace ourselves, but push.

People jump out of our way, sometimes with screams on their lips. We must look wild, blood smearing my lower face like a mask, Kion with his determined and violent expression as we wend our way out of the busier intersection, picking up speed on a more open straight road. My legs pump furiously, wind snatching at my short hair and ripping cold fingers down my throat while I gasp for air. I hope they don't have a huge guard on the tube station yet, but I can't think of any reason they would. According to the information I got earlier, it's closed for maintenance.

A Watch patrol bursts out of an alley mouth across the street, thirty meters away. Kion pulls something out of his pocket, without missing a stride, and throws it ahead of us. Pulse grenade. He throbs a command to close my eyes, and I squeeze them shut just as it explodes. My ears feel numb, sound disappearing in the wake of the flash-bang's ignition. Shaking my head to clear them I open my eyes to see the patrol staggering blindly ahead, clutching their faces. They'll be fine, I know. ARC tries not to use lethal force on innocents, but they won't hear or see for a while. We barge through them; I shoulder check a woman shorter than me and she hits the wall hard, breath squishing out of her, but I'm past before she can reach out a hand to try to stop me.

My ankle threatens to collapse under me as we hurtle around the corner, but I grit my teeth and force it to take my weight. We jink left, and finally turn onto the street that holds the tube entrance. We stop like we've hit a wall. A Watch patrol blocks the entire road, front row kneeling with riot shields protecting them, back row snugged between the shield gaps, Zaps pointing right at us. They're dressed in black shock gear, hard plates on their torsos and groins; there's twenty of them, and any second now, the patrol behind us will be on their feet. I catalogue all of this information in seconds, feeling Kion do the same through our skin-to-skin link. I read the order to open fire a split second before it happens, and Kion pulls the knowledge out of my flesh. He lets go of my hand, and I stand, all alone it feels, with an army facing me down.

But as the retort of Zapfire shatters the air, and I have a split second to be grateful they're not trying to take me alive, Kion moves. His broad palms clap together, creating a sound that is somehow loud enough to be heard over the brutal stuttering of guns. I feel the shockwave rush out of him. It blows forward like a hurricane—no—like the prow of a great boat, forcing the Zapfire sideways just enough, just enough that both sides of the street around us crack with the redirected energy. I feel the force drag at my skin, pulling hairs tight on the flesh of my arms. Kion's already running in the power's wake, and I scream something as I run after him. I don't know what I scream, but I know I won't let him fight alone.

Then we're in them, and I'm reading, reading, a Zap turned on my back, spin, grab the arm of a soldier, pull him across my body, spin again, back, forth, blow, duck, they're getting in one another's way, the sheer number of them blocking shots, and Kion is a war *machine*. I can feel him moving, silken, smashing these mere mortals into bloody, sagging pieces with telekinetic blows hammering their machinery into shards of useless plastic, hard palms bursting their noses and kidneys, every movement a precise, refined piece of destruction the likes of which I have never seen or felt before.

I can't let anyone get a clear shot at him, or we're both dead; my fists rain down on arm muscles, numbing them, throwing aims off and breaking wrists where I can with a sickening crack as I twist my hands around like butterflies. I take blows to the back and sides; a fist collides with my ear hard enough to stagger me, and I bloody my knees on the pavement but then twist myself up and under, just like in training, clipping my feet around a leg, turning over so the force drops the soldier like a stone. I see now how training, how reading the attacks over and over again, will save me, will make me better than they—unpowered—can hope to be. I know what will happen before it does. I move like water around blows, flow around hands and guns and feet and Kion mashes the team to shreds in my wake. And then we're through, somehow, we're through the wall of bodies, and Kion blasts the metal security grate out of our way, and my legs scream but I force myself up the stairs, aware they'll be behind us in seconds. I know the tube layouts, and I push at Kion's shoulder to make him turn, sprinting through the empty hall, ceiling towering far above our heads.

Everything is transal and white marble and I leave red footprints behind us, blood soaking my shoes from the slashes on my knees. Kion staggers, and I push myself an ounce farther, grabbing his hand and getting his feelings before he clamps down on them. He's done, empty, barely standing, having left the last of his Talent at the gate. When they're on us, it will be without his power, and he thinks we're going to die. But I'm buzzing with the fight; my face feels hot and swollen but I'm so alive I feel immortal. With that singing in my skin, I run faster, half dragging him now as he sags behind, weak and shaking. I lead us to the stairs that will take us to the tube line, and he trips over the bottom one, looking up at me with a split lip and wide eyes. *Go, I'll hold them.* I don't even bother to answer, forcing his arm over my shoulder. He's twice my weight, and I can't carry him, but I can help, and I push his shirt out of the way, find the naked skin of his hip with my hand, to share my feelings. Triumph roars in me, and Kion's feet steady slightly.

We stumble up the stairs, shouts behind us, and the sudden crack of Zap fire takes out the ceiling above us. Dust clouding down and thickening the air into flour, we have to force our way through, blind for a moment. The mouth of the tube gapes at us, and I know that all we have to do is get in—get in and we'll be safe. We can shatter it behind us, and we'll be okay. I force the factor of a three-day walk out of my mind, with demolitions experts and an army on our tails. Kion slips out of my hold and falls onto the tracks, hitting his palms hard and dropping the bag. Zaps fire again, but I don't see where they hit as I grab my friend by the most convenient grip, his hair and under his arm, and yank him up.

We're in the dark, open maw of the tube, the transal panels turned down to black so no light is coming through them, when I realize the bag is on the tracks behind us. The bag, with the explosives.

No time. I bully Kion forward, into the black, as far as I can before I have to drop him, my muscles screaming and shaking. Terror presses in on me like I'm drowning, like I'm back in the Tank, choking my throat closed. The soldiers are hanging back, setting up a cordon, scared we might have set a trap, as though we had time. My knees scream as I hit the ground next to Kion's limp body, desperately patting him down to see what, if anything, he has with him. An explosion above makes me yell and fling myself over him. The RPG shatters the ceiling, bringing down sheets of transal and twisted metal spars, light flooding in as we are buried under the falling world.

Toby's power is in my heart before I know what I'm doing, a gut reaction like covering my head while the ceiling collapses. I couldn't have controlled it if I tried. His Talent bursts out of me, raising a dome that glows a centimeter above my head, shimmering as it deflects blocks and debris. A city away, I feel my brother drop to the ground and shudder in muscular convulsions as his power races across hundreds of kilometers and fills me from head to toe. It doesn't feel like *his*; it feels like mine.

Chapter Twelve

TOBY

My knees smash into the floor, but I'm barely aware of it; there's screaming in my ears, and my body spasms against the hard tiles. The strip light on the ceiling above me expands until it fills my whole vision, and then everything goes black. A moment, or a lifetime later, everything smells like dust and blood. It paints my throat. I can't feel anything, and the world is a confusing mass, spears of light impaling gray clouds, filling the air; they should be filling my lungs, but I realize I'm not inhaling, not exhaling, and I try but nothing happens. A shout from my left makes me twist, and I see Thea, covered in grime and blood, crouching next to me.

Before I can open my mouth, she screams and stands, forcing a few tons of rubble upward and away, a telekinetic shield shoving the collapsed ceiling aside and letting the light in properly. The tendons in her neck are tight, and her teeth are bared as she spins toward me and falters for a moment, eyes meeting mine. "Toby?" I can't hear her, but I see my name on her lips.

What's happening? I think at her frantically, and she shakes her head as though to clear it, scattering sweat from her short hair. She looks from side to side, desperation sharpening her features into a fierce mask.

My question is ignored, and Thea brushes past me, her hand passing through my arm...my nonexistent arm. I can make out where my skin would be, a faint scattering of light in the exact shade of my Talent. As we touch, a flood of information rattles through me, every sense memory and event of the last hour, bringing her here to the tube entrance, with Kion. Kion... I look down, he's unconscious, scarlet blood leaking from his hairline and covering half his face. Thea pats him down, groaning when she encounters a spear of metal protruding from his stomach, her fingers wild but gentle as she probes the wound. She looks up at me, her thoughts and mine twist together. *We have to get out of here, into the tunnel.*

He won't survive the journey. She reads the response I didn't want to send, don't want to believe.

He will, if I have to hold him together myself the entire way. The thought is a snarl, a challenge. I've never seen her like this, but I nod, getting with the program.

In the distance, I feel a shock in my elbow, a sedative, probably. Good. ARC will keep my body safe while I help my twin. I ignore the whisper in my mind that threatens that I'll never go back, that I'll empty out here, into dead space. The whisper sounds like a woman, and Epsilon 17... No, why did I think of her like that? *Thea,* my twin, Thea, looks at me with horror on her face that I can't find a name for, but together we lift Kion. Somehow, my hands hold his flesh like they're real, like I exist in this dead tunnel. With his blood trapped under my twin's palm, as she forces it back into his body, makes a lid for his wound like telekinesis is second nature to her, like she understands it more than I ever could, we stumble over the broken ground into the mouth of hell waiting for us.

He's heavy, heavier than I expected he could be, being an inch shorter than me and only a little taller than Thea, who I remember weighs very little. We're struggling to move his deadweight, even with my telekinesis bolstering us both, but Thea is concentrating on his blood, his veins, the metal spar skewering his innards. My power trickles out through her finger tips, obeying her command.

She's holding him together with will, medical knowledge I didn't know she possessed, and my raw power. I have to concentrate just to stop his flesh from slipping right through me, which is definitely making things more difficult. I focus on putting one foot in front of the other, and I have a not-really-corporeal heart attack when brown hands pass through my stomach and fold around Kion, lifting his arm over the shoulder of a boy who is standing inside me. My non-body stumbles, as though I can still be clumsy and trip even when I'm not actually there, and it grabs Thea's attention. She blinks back to reality from the land of cells and arteries she's been inhabiting, and her eyes blow wide and spark with what looks like relief when she sees who has taken over my carrying duties.

"Leaf!" She chokes on her surprise.

"Got yer message. Although I was not expecting this level of a pickle. You've got mos' of the standin' army choked up in the tube station; gettin' through was a nightmare." He sounds quite cheery for someone who apparently just came through an army. I clear my throat, but although my twin's eyes flick to me, the boy doesn't react. Oh, right, I'm not really here? I don't understand this thing at all.

I take the opportunity to check out our new companion, not a threat by Thea's reaction. He's bowed under Kion's weight but looks to be a little shorter than me, thin faced with a sharp nose and slashing, dark eyebrows. His eyes are wicked and angled, teeth a little crooked, but white, and there's a sort of restless energy about him that rattles me. Or maybe everything is just rattling me. Behind us, welling out of the gloom, I can hear footsteps, stumbling over the jagged pieces we left behind. They must have night vision goggles, but the dust that still chokes the air might cover us a little longer. There's a bend in the tunnel approaching, and Thea and Leaf pick up speed, by apparently unspoken agreement. The boy pipes up again, breathless now with exertion.

"There's a service entrance jus' a kilometer down the line. If they don't 'ave people on it, we can get out there, head back to the slums."

There's no way they don't have that covered. My thoughts are echoed by Thea through gritted teeth, her feet sliding on the metal tracks. "Not an option. I can feel the soldiers; they've surrounded the tube; they're going to blow it ahead of us and send the crew in behind to mop us up. We're out of time." Experiencing panic without a body is bizarre, there's none of the physical sensation, just a bizarre lightness of thought and a feeling of nausea that leads me to believe someone holding my flesh back at ARC is being covered in very real vomit.

For a few moments, the only noise is the sound of Kion's feet dragging over the ground and the harsh breathing of the party members who are actually *present*. While they plod onward, heavily laden, I run forward, looking for something, anything that could help us. I don't know what I expect to find, but the back of a tube car isn't it. I run into it in the dark, the lights all off inside and out.

Hope flickers in my chest, and I throw the thought back to Thea. *A tube, hurry.* I read in her thoughts from before that she had a plan of getting a tube to run, and here's that chance. If she can make it before the soldiers behind her catch up and the ones in front of us blow the tracks, trapping us here for good. She feels my stress, my thoughts, even the ones I didn't project to her, and I realize how tied together we are when we share power like this. Because we *are* sharing. I felt the tube before I ran into it; my feet are confident in the dark, and I can tell where Thea and Kion are behind me. The boy must have gone...somewhere...for some reason. But as they stumble into sight, I see he's still there, still carrying Kion's weight and helping my twin. Although it feels like he's invisible, I can clearly see him. This must be what a Blank feels like to people who aren't as thought blind as me. I run back, gripping Kion by the waistband and chivvying them on. It's clear Leaf has no idea I'm present, as he looks startled, wide-eyed at Thea, nostrils flaring in shock.

"I didn't...know...you were a Projector." He grunts the words out as they lower Kion to the ground by the tube and starts to open a small hatch I hadn't even noticed next to the back door of the tube car. He's picking the lock before she can reply, nimble fingers twisting and manipulating the catch until the whole door shudders and puffs outward on a breath of air.

"Mmm." She avoids responding, and they manhandle Kion's limp body into the tube car. He looks dead. My twin's arms are bloody to the elbow, but she claps one hand back onto his torso, threading my power into him and to my shock, pulling a blade out of the back of her pants. "Do you think you can figure out a way to start this thing?" I can feel how torn she is, Kion will die if she doesn't help him, but they all might die, potentially including me as I have no idea what will happen to me if she dies when I'm here, tied to her through our mingled Talent. Leaf takes a moment to shut the subway door, looking down the tracks.

"I'll letcha know." He disappears out of the next door, making his way through the train. After a moment's indecision, I follow him. We have to start the engine, and I might be able to help.

I glance back one more time before leaving the carriage. Thea slices her wrist, the blood blooming up like a rose, growing, growing into a cylinder which she guides through the air, a perfect tube of telekinesis that dives into Kion's arm like a snake. A tremor passes over me at her sheer control, her power, but I force myself to leave them there. At least I don't have to pick the locks; my Talent-self just walks right through the doors, into the engine room. Leaf isn't there.

He's run off on us.

I'm so out of my depth, just reacting, and hoping somehow that we all survive this shit storm. The controls to this tube car don't look like anything I recognize, buttons and sliders and light arrays with no power. Right, power. That has to be first. I look for anything that could be a key slot, an ignition, but can't see anything.

I'm on the verge of ripping the cover off the dash and seeing if that makes more sense when a scuffing sound behind me makes me jump. Leaf clambers back in through the door, something gripped in his teeth. I'm taken aback by the amount of relief I feel, and then I realize why—my body, far off, strapped into a hospital bed. My body is shutting down. And I think I'm going to die.

Down the train, my twin's head snaps up, and she projects into my head, clear as Serena when we're holding hands for the connection. *You won't die. I won't let you.* There's a hard, frightening edge to her inner thoughts.

I get a glimpse of what she's doing, and my non-stomach lurches again. She's hauled the metal out of Kion; it lies on the floor of the tube next to her knee, in a pool of lurid cadmium. She's knuckle deep in his stomach cavity even as her blood spins out of her into him. In the engine room, Leaf is flicking switches with a look of abject concentration, but nothing seems to be happening. Thea looks out of my eyes and points me at a blue plastic, hinged thing. I focus on it, and it flicks upward, revealing a round keyhole. Leaf jumps, not starts, but jumps, up in the air, landing balanced on the seat of the chair, eyes flicking around the room. He looks so much like a cat, I laugh, but the sound doesn't penetrate reality.

Still, I've done what she wanted. He calms, spitting out the leather case he's had clamped between his teeth this whole time and makes short work of choosing lock picks out of it to attack the keyhole. The whole tube rocks, a cracking explosion sounding behind us. Zap fire? They must have finally caught up. Thea!

Leaving the engine to Leaf, who has somehow kept his balance and his picks in the hole, I sprint back through the tube. The engines catch just as I hurtle into the last carriage. Thea is collapsed against a bench chair, Kion's head in her lap. I think he's dead. I think they're both dead, but then she flicks her eyes open, catching me in an inescapable gaze. *Thank you, Toby. We're going to be okay. You can go now.* His torso is a mess of blood, but I can see the ugly wound has been sewn with something, jagged stitching sealing the red mouth of the wound together, puckered and hideous, but holding his insides where they should be. *Toby.* I look at her, her nose is weeping blood, and then I see-feel the tickle at her ears, and under her eyes. Blood, blood everywhere. Her eyes roll up in her head, and she slumps down, cradling Kion in her lap, and I hurtle back through space. My strained heart stops as I slam back into my meat body.

Chapter Thirteen

E17

"THEA!" The shout breaks through the veils of smoke and ash and blood that are wrapped around my head, drowning me in misery. Leaf's concerned face leans over me, eyes tight with worry. His mouth is soft and pink as he yells at me, crooked tooth pressing into his full lower lip so deeply there's a dent there. I feel drunk, again, my thoughts spreading out and spiraling uncomfortably, my body light and barely present.

The sound of his palm across my cheek reaches me a split second before the pain, and the world presses in on me, loud and bright and agonizing. I get my hand up in time to stop a second blow, but it doesn't come. He sits back on his heels and stares at me, hand hovering like he wants to gentle my cheek where he hit me. "You were freakin' out." He sounds scared, but I can't see into him to know what he saw, what I looked like. Judging from the expression on his face, I must be pretty rough. And he did come for me, all the way through the City, through the army at the tube.

"Sorry. I'm okay." The words are gritty and catch in my throat, which is brutalized by the dust. Kion's head is still in my lap, and I shift carefully, leaning over him and looking for signs of life. I feel his breath on my face like a benediction, a moment of grace. Reality catches up, and I press my hand to the cold floor, a small smile tugging at my lips as I feel the faint shuddering of movement under my palm.

Leaf grins broadly, pride in his words. "Yeah, I got her start', an' we're well on the way. Autopilot is on. Should be a few hours though. And I dunno what we're gonna do on the other side."

As he speaks, the world starts lightening. We're coming out of the tunnel and into the open desert. I wonder if they'll turn off the barrier and shoot at us. Not much we can do about it, though, except pray. Kion might have an idea, if he was awake.

I shift and feel the muscles strain in my back, knives digging into my spine and up into my head, the force of the sudden headache almost making me black out again. Leaf's strong hands catch me, seizing my shoulder and knee before I can collapse sideways. He helps me sit back up, lean against the side of the bench seat and then ignores my protests as he moves Kion out of my lap. Pins and needles sing in my legs and a groan chokes its way out of me. For a few moments, we just sit silently. I can feel his gaze on me, and it's making me a little uncomfortable, to be so watched. Just to break the sensation, I mumble, "How did you even find us? Not that I don't hugely appreciate it and owe you my life. Our lives." I look at him through half-closed, swollen eyes and he settles back on his haunches, hands on his knees.

"One of the boys saw yer symbol an' beeped me, not tha' yeh were subtle. I figured where ya were when the whole damn City Watch close' in on the tube entrance, so I took advantage of the service routes and popped up on the nex' platform over. Then I snuck through the smoke usin' my mad stealthy skills an' picked my way down the tunnel as fast as I could." He says everything so matter-of-factly it makes it sound ordinary, but I still don't understand how he could have even made it past the blockade. I could *feel* them setting it up, barriers erected and soldiers bustling everywhere. He's eyeing me shrewdly but grins when I open my mouth to ask how, cutting me off.

"I'm dead sneaky. It's my fines' skill. But yer the one who just walked this big lug down two kilometers of tunnel, and then performed surgery on him usin'…" He looks me up and down. "I'm guessin' a thread outta the hem of yer shirt an' sheer cussedness."

It startles a small smile back onto my face. Sheer cussedness. Yeah, I have that, I think. I can't bring myself to even try to explain what I did, what I used Toby for, and I can't explain how because I don't know myself. There's a thread between us; I understand that, but I don't know how I could pull *him* down it, not just the power. I'm starting to understand our Talent *isn't* separate, not like we thought. It's strung out between us, and it always has been. I think that's how I survived the Institute, and the wipes. But I also felt him collapse and know I could have killed him doing what I did here today. I shy away from the thought, focusing on my travel companion again.

"Sorry about your impromptu trip to Second City." I sound like I'm on the edge of tears, and I swallow, trying to squash the threatening sobs back into my chest. Leaf passes me a small metal flask with something swishing in it, and I crack it open, taking a swig.

"Ah, it's okay. I got friends over there an' I was due for a holibob. Sides, I hear you guys are Watch free. Sounds excitin'." He laughs as the liquor hits my tongue and makes me choke, eyes streaming from the burn, but it feels good running down my throat, and my hands steady instead of tremble, pressed against my thigh. He holds his hand out for the flask, delicate fingers brushing mine when I pass it over, and he wipes his mouth before taking a gulp.

"Are you always drinking, or do I just bring it out in you?" My tone is wry, and I tug idly at the fabric tears over my knee, inspecting the bloody grazes beneath.

His voice is laced with laughter, and he takes another gulp, offering me the flask again, but I shake my head. "Ah, well, the first time was a party, but this was 'cause you're talking *like this*." His voice turns into a broken, scratchy sounding rasp. "And I don't have any water, 'cause I didn't have time to prepare a snack bag before tryin' ta catch up with ya."

The bench seat is uncomfortable against my back, so I reach up and take the edge of it, hauling my protesting body upright and collapsing onto the chair. The cushioning helps, and I try to relax, pain still washing through me in waves. A gentle touch on my leg makes me start, opening my eyes, and I see Leaf has upended his flask onto a blue-spotted handkerchief he's magicked out of some pocket and is offering the wet fabric to me. I take it with a grim smile and begin to catalog my injuries. It's not as bad as I feared. My knees are sliced up like someone's been at them with a cheese grater; my wrists are bruised and hands banged up, the muscles protesting from going straight to impacts with no warmup. There's a slice from a knife curling around my left bicep, skin deep, that must have been from the whirlwind fight to get past the soldier barricade on the way into the tube station. Every muscle in my body hurts as though I've been stretched on a rack, and my chest and throat are sore from breathing in too much debris, but all in all I'm in close to working order. Down a few pints of blood, bruised and exhausted, but not about to die.

"Why don't ya get some sleep, miracle kid? I'll wake ya up when we start slowin' down. Or if ya start freaking out again." He's taking off his jacket, even as he speaks, folding it deftly into a pillow-like shape, and then offers it to me with one hand, nodding encouragement.

A wet sniff catches in my throat, reminding me of how much my nose bled, and I take the jacket and then use the damp handkerchief to clean my face a little. The whiskey stings in what must be small cuts on my chin, but I feel better for the weird little bath. "Thanks."

There's not much else to say, and I wedge the jacket behind my head, settling back as best I can. It's full daylight now, but I'm used to sleeping in the light; doesn't bother me after years below ground where everything was always on. Just before I fade into sleep, I hear him whisper, "You're welcome."

THE RUMBLE OF the tube car changes, and I'm awake before Leaf reaches out to touch my shoulder, which is good, because my first reaction is to grab him into a thumb lock. I abort the movement as soon as my brain registers who the blurry face leaning over me belongs to.

He's already got his hands up in a "no threat" by the time I'm fully back where we are. He's nuking quick; it's very impressive. Thankful for a respite from my creepy body jump dreams, I ease myself upward and grimace at the stiffness in my joints.

"Kion?" I inquire, pulling one arm across my chest and trying to stretch out the rigidity. My whole body is aching.

"Still breathin'," Leaf responds, looking at me with his head cocked to one side. He's ripped padding off the tube seats and made a little cushion for Kion's head, braced against a table leg. There's one under his hips as well, I see. Leaf follows my eyeline and has a butterfly knife in his hand before I can blink, swirling it in a silvery pattern in the air by way of explanation.

"How long have we been going?" On to stretching my neck. Really, I should stand and go through the harim ka stretches, but to be honest I'm not sure I'd be able to keep my footing...

It's bright out, still full day, the desert spooling out under our metal tube as it whirrs along. Apparently, they can't stop it from the main controls, or Leaf's done something to take it offline. I'm too tired to care that much. We're moving, so it's not a problem for now. Maybe for later. We have to figure out how to slow the thing down or stop it completely before we hit the wreckage of the bomb the Institute sent through.

Glimpses of what Toby saw—a building collapsing with him in it, a twitching hand covered in blood, the mangled, crimson-and-black crater where a man's eye used to be—assail me, and bile catches in my throat.

He's alive, though. I can feel it. I'd know like I'd know if my foot was cut off if something happened to him.

"Two hours, thereabouts." Leaf glances at the sun over the mountains, "so around two ta go. Can't see much, as i' is."

"Don't suppose you've had time to look for anything useful on board?"

Leaf blinks, and flushes, the color blooming under the golden skin of his cheeks, "D'ya know, I didn' even thin' ta look. Dent'll have my head!"

Snorting softly, I pull myself to my feet in a series of awkward, painful movements. I've stiffened up, and I'll be useless in a fight if it comes to it. Stretching as gently as I can, I spread myself through the tube car, or try to. The lack of information coming from Leaf is normal, standard; he's a Blank and I'll never feel him even if he's standing right behind me in an empty room. It's eerie, but I'm adjusting. The lack of information coming from Kion, on the other hand, is faintly terrifying. Either I'm drained out, or he's brain dead.

But there's nothing coming to me of traces from people leaving oils and sweat on the surface around me either, so hopefully it's the former.

Leaf also gets to his feet, heading to the engine room, moving silently. I feel like a clumsy, clunky mess in comparison. Even at the best of times, which this is decidedly not, I'd be a bear next to a deer. Which would make Toby an elephant. A faint grin tugs at the corner of my mouth as I inspect the tube car for anything we can use.

The first decent find is beyond obvious. An "in case of emergency, break transal" hammer in a plastic case. I unclip it from its covering and heft it in my hand. It's heavy. We can use it to make an extra exit for ourselves from midcar rather than going out the door, or as a weapon.

Leaf hollers something, and I hook the hammer onto my belt. Never leave a weapon behind. Someone else can pick it up and then they're armed and you're not. A lesson from the Institute but still applicable to my life.

"What?" I step over Kion's quiescent body, balancing myself with a hand on the table, and Leaf appears in the doorway of the driver's cab, beaming and holding up a white-and-red case. It takes me a second.

"A first aid kit!" That's huge. That's painkillers and clean gauze and maybe antibiotics? Do they keep antibiotics in first aid kits on tubes? Kion will die of infection if we can't get something into him soon. I did my best to filter the dust, the debris out of his wound, but I'm not a healer. I made a sieve out of my will and held what I could but there's no way I got everything, especially not the microbes and bacteria. I wouldn't even know how to start looking for those.

He throws it to me, snapping me out of my thoughts, and ducks back into the driver's cab, clearly expecting me to deal with Kion. Fair.

I try to squat down; my back screams at me so I fold into a cross-legged position instead. It's more awkward but my knees don't like the idea of taking my weight either. The grazes have scabbed thick and bloody and dry. Hopefully, there's something for me to clean them up with once I've done what I can for Kion.

The kit is packed. Good. I dry swallow a handful of painkillers and a stimulant, and then I clean and staple Kion's wound, using the handheld gun instead of a thread out of my dirty clothes. The inside of him isn't something I can help with now. I used Toby's power to hold the edges of a sliced vein together while I stitched it, but there's no way I'm gonna try that again without the benefit of telekinesis.

Dollops of antiseptic, thick pads of gauze, bandages, clean out the rest of his cuts including the ugly, jagged line splitting his hair into a new parting, and then I deal with myself as best I can.

There's sterile water in the kit, a small bottle, but I stick to using the grime clearing spray. The water has better use inside us.

When I'm as good as I'm gonna get, I dampen the corner of a bandage, part Kion's split lips with my antiseptic-wiped fingers and squeeze it into his mouth.

Leaf emerges while I'm baby-bird feeding Kion and passes me an opened energy bar. I scoff it with one hand while letting the wet cloth drop into Kion's mouth with the other.

When Kion has taken a quarter of the bottle, I pass it to Leaf. He takes a single swig, gargles with it, and swallows deliberately. I take two and then recap the bottle carefully and shove it in my pocket.

The whole scene has taken about an hour, and I can see the City on the horizon, sprawling wall glinting in the now reddish light. There's smoke unfurling sluggishly from several places, thickest above the gaping maw of the tube entrance.

"Almost there." I jerk my chin, and Leaf looks, and nods.

"You gotta plan?"

I shrug, not even bothering to inject false confidence or bravado into my statement: "Try not to die."

He snorts, pushing his hair back out of his face. "Hey, your guys hold the City; at least we'll get a hero's welcome."

And *shit,* the realization that the last thing that came through the tube line was a *bomb* hits me like a ton of bricks.

They're not expecting us, but they might be expecting a weapon.

I scramble; my wrist unit's nuked from the world falling on us, or the fight beforehand; Kion's bag with his tech in it is left behind on the tracks. They'll find it, but I'm sure there's nothing on there that could screw us.

"We have to get off. We have to message them." I look frantically for tech on the train controls, and Leaf ducks into the little cabin after me.

"Can't. I had ta take the wireless ou', or they'd've scuppered us back at Second." I see what he's done, pulled the patch panel right away from its wiring, the clips not accessible so sliced through leaving a tangle of shredded cables instead.

"Nuke. We have to stop the train, then." I have no idea how to do that, but a big lever looks promising. My heartbeat is fluttering in my temples, my wrists, my breathing shallow and rapid.

Leaf snags my wrist in midair. "And wha'? Carry the guy? You're fried; we've got no food, no water, no cover. He die fer sure and probly ya too."

"Not you?" I sneer, angry at the situation, at Leaf, at everything. Angry is better than scared. Angry is always better than terrified, frozen. A coward.

"Course no'. They ain't invented the thing tha' can kill me," Leaf smirks, but his eyes are serious.

"Well then you'll have to go overland and get help. We'll stay in the car." It's the obvious solution, only solution.

Leaf wrinkles his nose, looks at the still setting sun, the Wall growing in size on the horizon. "Yeah, all right. How close d'yah think we can get?"

I tug my hand free of his gentle grip; he doesn't try to stop me, but he nods when he sees the look on my face and settles his fingers around the huge lever. He puts his whole body into pulling it back, grunting with effort.

The engine brakes hiss, the car judders, slows, travels about another ten kilometers and finally squeaks to a halt.

Hopefully we're far away enough they won't think we're a threat; hopefully they're too busy dealing with their casualties to send a missile our way; hopefully the barrier would stop it if they did. Hopefully, hopefully, hopefully.

They might send a squad out to see what we are, but they might not. Kion doesn't have that long; his pulse is weak, and I don't have any more blood to give him. I'm lucky I'm the universal donor, as it is. A fact that always annoyed in the Institute, made me vulnerable, less easy to save, now saves my friend—or at least buys him some time.

"You'll have to stay on the tracks until the barrier's broken." I can't see the end of the sparkling effervescent death-bringing screen, but it must be down: a bomb went off *in* the tube station, so it must have taken out at least some of the towers. The towers are inside the barrier, making them more secure and impossible to take out externally, but they'll have been hit. They have to have been hit or Leaf will have to walk through the bomb site to get help, and that must be impossible.

He rolls his eyes at me, grabs the water bottle out of my pocket, and takes a swig before handing it to me. "Ah know, I'm not an idiot. If the big guy wakes up, tell 'im it's sixteen five."

"What?" I take the water bottle, squeeze it gently, and grab a clean bandage so I can feed Kion a little more, if he'll take it.

"He's saved my ass sixteen times, but this brings me up ta five." Leaf salutes me, slides past, and opens the door at the back; he's gone in less than a second, and I hear him softly-clattering up the back of the car, onto the roof. Smart, rather than risk tumbling sideways, he's gonna run on the top of the train and down at the front. Sure enough, I hear his footsteps, light but still audible as he makes his way to the other end.

I want to get up to watch him lope down the tracks ahead, but Kion stirs and I return my attention to him.

He takes some more water, and I have another mouthful myself. Putting the bottle down a quarter full is one of the hardest things I've ever done. My mouth feels like sandpaper; my body is crying out for liquid, but Kion needs it to stay alive.

There's nothing to do now, but wait, and I find myself drifting off.

A SCRAPE OF metal rouses me, and I jerk awake. It's full dark now, stars sparkling in the thick black velvet above the bowl of the desert.

"Leaf?" I hiss, unnerved and unsure. I reach out with my power, which doesn't work because it's completely scraped out, empty. I can feel the place where it should be, like nerves twitching a missing finger—I know what that feels like, thanks to my brother—that can't obey the commands sent to it.

It's not Leaf; he would have said something by now. It's not the ARC soldiers, because they'd have given me a warning. The night is too still, eerie. I have the hammer clutched tight in my sweating palm, and I ease myself upright, setting myself between Kion and the door and into a fighting stance. My bones hurt. My heart hurts.

It's the blindest I've ever been, night and lack of power combined to make me feel completely vulnerable. I can hear my heart beating in my own ears, the whoosh, whoosh of blood spiked with fight-or-flight and waiting to see which one I choose. I can't run, though—I won't leave Kion. And maybe it would be better if I died, taking Cassandra with me. In my head, she stirs, a smug amusement staining her presence, like she's not afraid that I'll die, not at all.

I force myself calm. I breathe. I tap a soft rhythm for my lungs on the side of my leg and ignore the protest of panic gripping my chest. I listen. I hear only the steady pump of my heart and the soft susurration of Kion's breathing.

My imagination, then. There's nothing there.

A light flares so brightly outside the window my vision is washed white, and then I hear a yell of fear.

Chapter Fourteen

TOBY

There are purpling bruises on my chest where a nurse gave me CPR when my heart stopped. Hundreds of people died during the attack on ARC, and I followed them days later, when Thea hauled my Talent, and *me,* out of my own body and across hundreds of kilometers.

Everyone's furious with her: Johan, David Jacobs, Serena. All of them spitting mad—it feels like everyone at ARC—except for me. I was *in* her. She would have died, and so would Kion, and probably even Leaf—the boy who showed up to help them—if she hadn't used my power. And I'm still here, only slightly worse for wear.

Johan's been screaming at me for like twenty minutes; he's not even paying attention to me, just yelling in the same place as I am. Apparently I let this happen and there could have been a psychic shockwave to shame the one I sent out when I lost my finger, and that's my fault too. Blah, blah, blah.

It's impossible to explain to him that there wasn't much to be done. Thea needed me; Thea took me, and she didn't do it on purpose either. Our power isn't mine and hers, separately, it's mine-and-hers, connected irreversibly. She thought about it, with the part of her brain that wasn't busy sewing Kion back together with knowledge she ripped out of the closest doctor, miles away though they were. She thought about how she'd be dead without the connection between us, dead like the kids were dead until ARC took them back. Dead like an empty meat puppet walking around and doing what it was told. Instead, she dreamed of me and stayed alive.

"Are you even listening, you smug little asshole?" Johan screams right in my face, dragging me out of my thoughts and back to reality. I feel like I should be more upset, about something—either that I almost died or that he's mad at me—but I don't have it in me to care.

"No," I reply, and flinch as I see the anger in his eyes ratchet up a notch; see the violence in him curl his hand into a fist—which is grabbed before he has a chance to do anything with it. I don't think he'd hit me, not really, but my body apparently does.

"That's enough, Johan," Serena says from behind him. I didn't even see her come in, my spacey thoughts leaving no attention for the real world.

"I..." Johan deflates, snatches his hand free of Serena, and storms out without finishing his sentence.

"You sure know how to scare the shit out of everyone," Serena observes, turning her head and looking behind her with a confused expression. "Yo, you coming?"

A raggedy teen slopes into the room, his hands shoved in his pockets. "Sorreh, I was lookin' at the damage."

I recognize him immediately. "Leaf!"

He slides a step backward so he's halfway out the door. "How d'a know mah name?" he asks suspiciously. He looks exhausted, his clothes are covered in dust and there's black circles under his narrowed eyes.

I fumble, not having an easy way to explain what happened, but Serena does me a favor and fills in the blank efficiently.

"Toby's Thea's brother, but they're twins, and their power is weird as nuke. If Thea knows, then Toby knows. It's just as annoying as it sounds. Leaf's come with Thea and Kion, but Kion's badly hurt; he can't travel. They're in a tube car a couple of hours out of the City. I thought you'd want to know, because someone has to go get them, and I'm needed here. You, on the other hand, have been marked down as useless." She gets to her feet. "I have a meeting. Leaf, can you fill Toby in on what you told me?" She raises her hand like she's gonna pat him on the shoulder and then drops it without making contact. Leaf grins at her.

"Yup," he replies succinctly and then sits on the end of my bed like we're friends, pulls a thread out of the blanket, and starts tying it around his middle finger.

My head hurts, and I locate the water I was drinking before Johan started screaming. I didn't even get a chance to tell him what happened. "Is Thea okay?"

"She's tougher'n my calluses, that one." He looks up at me with a calculating expression. "But Kion might not make it through the night, and it seems like people have enough on their plates around 'ere already. If ya tell me where I might find some transportation and get me someone ta drive, I'll be off ta get them myself."

Meeting. Serena's in a meeting. She's presumably scheduled on cleanup; there's still got to be people not accounted for, rubble to move. People buried alive. If they sent a team for Kion, it could cost dozens of lives here. ARC. Always trying to do the right thing by everyone. Nuke.

Why does getting out of bed always hurt so much?

Leaf figures it out pretty fast, all things considered. "Ah, you and me then, is it?"

"From Serena's subtle hints, I'd say that's about the size of it."

"Uh, no." The new voice surprises me, but Leaf's off the bed and looking for an exit in the time it takes me to jump slightly.

Aly does not look impressed. Regardless, I find my beat-up shoes under the bed and slide my feet into them. Even my toes hurt.

"Toby, you can't." She has that tone of complete conviction people get sometimes, like all they have to do is reasonably point out how stupid you're being, and you'll stop. Funny how people never seem to realize I know exactly how stupid I'm being.

"Thea and Kion are in the desert. At night. Alone. It's gonna get cold. Kion is bleeding to death." I state the facts very calmly, I think, but Alyssa's face doesn't soften like I hope it will.

She exhales, cocks her head at Leaf. "Who're you?"

"Leaf," he offers her a dramatic bow, and to my surprise, her demeanor relaxes a little. If I'd have done that, she'd have hit me for jerking around.

"Aly," she nods at him, like "Okay, got that out of the way then" and takes a step toward the bed. She pokes me in the ribs, hard, and I'm too slow to stop her, but I manage to stay on my feet. Although I do sway a bit, it's close. She grunts something under her breath that might have been "stubborn jackass" but then she kneels and does my laces for me. "Where are we going, then?" And just like that, there'll be three of us sneaking out of the City.

Leaf is a nuking magician, as it turns out. He hears people coming from down the corridors, makes us stop and wait and go and stop and wait again, but somehow we get out of the building without running into anyone who would order me back to bed and cuff me there.

I need to change my clothes. I'm still in the gray sweats and T-shirt I was wearing when I was helping in the hospital, which is gross from the sweat and other unnamable things smearing me, but more to the point, totally impractical for a midnight rescue mission into the desert. Fortunately, I'm not the brains of this...or any outfit.

"I'll meet you in the west garage; we should be able to get a couple of ATVs; no one's using them right now, I'd guess. You go, sign out two vehicles—and honestly, I don't know what you thought you were gonna do with just the two of you. If one of you can't drive, how would you possibly fit four on one bike to come back? Anyway, I'll grab some clothes and stuff and meet you there, idiots."

"Hey," Leaf seems to be a bit put out by being coupled in with me under the idiot banner, and I snort softly, concentrating on trying to work the stiffness out of my joints. I need to sleep and have a bath, and then sleep some more. For like a week maybe, how come no one ever talks about how exhausting war is?

Leaf and I walk across the grounds in silence. Either he's as tired as I am, or he's respecting the fact it's taking everything I have to function. Or possibly he's a quiet dude, I guess. We stick close to the building where we can, where there aren't piles of broken concrete waiting to trip us or shattered transal trying to slice our shoes to shreds. It crunches under our feet as we walk, sounds like sand at the volleyball courts.

"You helped them." I surprise myself by speaking as we turn off the main grounds path and head for the garages, for the squat building that butts right up against

212 - | Tash McAdam

the grounds of City Hall—now ARC—with a defendable entrance that I'm hoping no one is gonna try to stop us from using. It'll take a lot longer if we have to go out of the main gates and explain ourselves as we go.

"Kion's mah boy," Leaf replies, like that is an entire explanation of how he ended up coming on a locked-down tube and getting stuck here. Oh, and my slow brain puts together his name, Leaf, with the Leaf Serena's told me about from Second City.

"Oh shit, you're Leaf—like, Leaf and Abial and Serena pulling Sam out of the Institute."

He laughs at me, but there's an edge of pain in it. "Yep, that's me. An' we're down two from that story now, I hear."

I don't know what to say, so I don't reply, and we make it to the garage without having to explain ourselves to anyone. There's a soldier on duty at the booth, and I head over, trying to look confident.

"Hey, we need to check out two ATVs." I lean one arm on the sill of his booth. Beside me, Leaf has somehow become about an inch taller, wider, standing strong and authoritative-looking.

"Toby, right?" I don't recognize the soldier, but she clearly knows me.

"Yep, Toby Reynolds."

"Who's authorizing?" She sounds like she isn't suspicious, just doing the routine stuff, and I exhale, hoping for the best.

"Kion Arbalast, code seven-one-five-seven-zero." I'm good with numbers, my brain grabs them, and that was one floating around in my twin a few times. I might have mixed the digits up though. I cross my fingers at my side, subtly I think, but a sharp pain in my wrist makes me flex my hand. I shoot Leaf a dirty look. He's flicked me in a nerve and made my hand all tingly.

She turns around in her booth, rummages through a cupboard and hands me two sets of keys. "Seventy-four and seventy-five. Drive safe. They're both charged."

"'Preciate it," Leaf says, snagging the keys out of her hand and turning like he knows where he's going. Although as I start after him, thanking the guard, I realize there's a sign sprayed onto the gray concrete wall.

Alyssa catches up with us a few minutes after we get to the vehicles. I'm checking the charge and the engine, like we're trained to, and don't notice she's arrived until she touches my back as I'm leaning down over the front of the ATV.

I jump and hit my head on the handlebar; Leaf cackles at me as I straighten up. Fortunately, the handlebar is rubber-coated, and it's more of a shock than an actual injury. I don't think anyone needs a head injury to be added to our list of what's wrong with us.

Aly seems to have escaped the bombing mostly unscathed, but she's moving a little stiffly and looks just as exhausted as the rest of us.

I change into the clean stuff Aly's grabbed—black combat pants that are too short, a gray camo shirt that's too big, and a thick jacket with padded sleeves that fits me like it was made for me. I have to keep my beat-up sneakers on, but all in all, I'm much better prepared now.

"Leaf, you ride with me; it's a more even weight split," Aly points out, confidently swinging her leg over the seat of the olive-green ATV, leaving me with the navy blue. I shove my old clothes into the bag she lobbed me, grab an energy drink, pound it back, and shake my head to clear it before following suit.

"I am super hench; it's true," I joke, settling my feet onto the rests and slotting the key into the ignition, clipping the safety cord onto my belt—if I get thrown off, the cord will pull out of the key, and the power will cut, instead of leaving my ride to veer across the desert for a bit longer.

Leaf snorts, settling onto the seat space behind Alyssa and grabbing the handles near his hips. "Well, Thea don' weigh much, bu' you'll probly have ta carry Kion on the way back, so enjoy it while ya can, I'd say."

He's right, I realize, gunning the engine. Kion's big enough that it's gonna take some brute strength to keep him on the bike, even if we strap him to the driver. And Aly, Leaf and Thea are small enough that putting the three of them together makes sense. We need another driver and vehicle, but it's too late now.

Alyssa leads the way out of the garage, engines rumbling quietly. A couple of people nod to us, jogging from place to place, but we get out the back gate unmolested. The city streets are shockingly quiet, everyone hiding indoors, I guess. It doesn't feel safe anymore. There's a weird edge to the silence, like everyone's holding their breath. The purring whine of our engines splits the night air, our headlights stream over the shining road. The streetlights are out here, part of the grid that got hit, I guess. We're the only vehicles moving, but we still drive sedately, out of deference for the usually busy streets, maybe. Or maybe because Alyssa thinks I'll fall off if we go too fast.

A flash of light catches the corner of my eye, but I can't look because driving is hard, the rumbling of the engine is making my bones ache already and concentrating on following Alyssa's taillights is the best I can do. Leaf periodically twists around to check on me, giving me a flashing grin and sometimes a thumbs-up.

The city rolls past us, damaged buildings and broken slabs of solar panels giving way to the untouched, with a few people around, cleaning up or walking determinedly somewhere. The gate in the Wall is locked down, obviously, but a flash of my ARC credentials gets us through without further checking. They're busy and don't care what we're doing right now. I wonder if we could have gotten permission if we'd asked, but it would have taken time, time Kion might now have, and we can always apologize later. They're probably not gonna bump me down. I should just get some shitty duties to do, and I can handle that.

The slums are much, much busier than the center of the city, and a few people look far too interested in our vehicles. We speed up, cutting through ways I didn't know, but Aly grew up out here so it's not really a surprise she's more confident than me. At least no one tries to knock us off our bikes. I didn't even think of that until we started driving through the slums, with shadowy groups of people in dark corners. There's a lot out here who'd jump at a chance for two vehicles if we gave them a shot.

I speed up a little more, right on Aly's tail, and she confidently takes us around a few more corners and then our wheels are sinking into sand instead of churning over packed dirt.

"Toby!" the yell has panic in it, it's behind us, why is someone calling my name from behind us? They sound young, scared. "*Toby! Help!*"

I skid the ATV to a halt, looking around frantically. It could be a trap. I know it could be; the Institute could be here with a kid told they have to bring me in...but they'd wait till we were in the desert, surely, exposed and alone.

I can't see anything behind me, so I wheel the vehicle around, the headlights streaming down the slight incline and splashing against the few, crumbling walls. There's a small shape, a kid, running toward me. He's lit up by the lights, but I know who it is as soon as I see his feet, not touching the ground. Jake.

Gunning the vehicle down the hill the space closes rapidly, and Jake grinds to a standstill, his face frantic, "Damon, they grabbed Damon!"

"Who?" Aly's ATV throws up arcs of sand as she slides it down the slope next to me. Leaf's already sliding off, and he sprints down and melts into the darkness before Jake has a chance to answer or I have a chance to get off my ride.

"What do we do?" Aly yells, frenzied. I don't know. I don't *know*. We can't leave Damon, though, so I clamber down awkwardly. Aly's a good shot.

I grab Jake's shoulder. "Stay here. Stay with Aly. Aly, Zap out and ready, okay?" I'm already moving. My legs feel a little shaky, but they steady under me, and I pound down toward the buildings, reaching for my Talent, without thinking about it. Nuke, still nothing, the faintest shadow of sparkling power so faded I can't grab it; it slides through my fingers, sloshing sullenly in the base of my belly.

No power it is, then. I hoist my Zap out of my holster on the run, keeping it at my side. Yelling draws me around a corner, and I see Damon, sprawled on the ground, two men standing over him and...two more on the ground, in quiet heaps. Where's Leaf? One of the vertical thugs clutches his neck and drops to his knees, making his friend swear and run for it before I catch up.

"Toby." Damon's crying, big wet tears running down his cheeks. "'M sorry, we just wanted to see where you were going. I said we should go back." He's shaking, but he seems to be okay. I pat him down to make sure I'm not missing some life-threatening injury.

"Well, that was pretty stupid, as ideas go, but you're okay. I've got you."

Leaf melts out of the darkness. "Put him down before he could call any friend's he might 'ave."

"How?" It's not the most important question, but it's good to know what kind of fighters people are, in case we get jumped again. Not that we got jumped this time, exactly, just the ten-year-old boys trying to keep up with the ATVs. Shit, they're lucky we weren't farther out. I don't know that I would have picked up a Psionic yell. In fact, I'm sure they were sending their best signals out, and Leaf's a Blank and Aly's got nothing. They'd have been all alone.

I haul Damon to his feet. He's a little unsteady but he manages, keeping a tight grip on my hand as I start walking in the direction we came from, fast-paced.

Leaf flits forward, takes Damon's other hand in a surprisingly supportive gesture, considering he doesn't know the kid, and replies, "Blow gun. I have eleven darts left, if that was your next question."

It would have been. I nod in thanks, cracking my neck and waving with my free hand as we turn out of the dark street end into the open space at the edge of the slums, in sight of the vehicles.

"Damon!" Jake hollers and runs down the hill. I'd be annoyed about him drawing more attention to us, but the blazing lights of the vehicles have drawn a crowd, hovering in the shelter of the buildings, but I can feel them shifting. It won't take much to upset the balance and bring them down on us. Two ATV's, a couple of Zaps, and whatever else they assume we have on us. Aly probably grabbed more supplies and medicine, at the very least. We gotta get out of here.

Jake thumps into Damon, and I wrangle them both up the hill, pushing them ahead of me. Leaf glides forward and hops on the back of Alyssa's bike; she guns the engine, clearly feeling the same as I do. We can't stick around, and I don't think we can get back through, not the same way we came out. Which I guess means we're taking the kids with us. Serena's gonna kill me. Thea's gonna kill me, if I don't die of exhaustion first. Shit.

I basically throw the boys in front of me on the bike, barely able to reach past them and grab the handlebars. I can't see properly, but at least they're trapped in the cage of my arms and can't fall off. I slam the ATV into gear and spin it around, catching a glimpse of a few braver souls making a run for it toward us. I spit grit at them behind my wheels, as I zoom up the hill, easily outpacing their grabbing hands and gaining easy ground into the desert.

Wind streams past us, and I have to stand up on my toes to see. Jake is using my arm like a handle, and Damon is squirming like an otter, which lasts precisely till he elbows me in the balls. The air *oofs* out of me and I lose my grip on the handlebars, meaning we lose our steering and skid, but the engine also cuts and we're slowing down before I slide off sideways, landing with a bone-shaking thud and a loud grunt.

I lift my head far enough to ensure no dwells are about to slit my throat, but we've made a good 5k out of the City already, and then I just stare at the stars for a minute, counting all the ways things have gone wrong in the last few days.

"Uh, Toby?" Damon's head peeks into my vision; he looks terrified, and I make an effort to smile at him, lifting a hand and clambering to my feet when he takes it.

"Yep. Yeah. Just another bruise to add to the collection. Let's figure out the seating arrangements now we've got some breathing room, eh?" I force my voice to hide the irritation I'm feeling, and Damon gives me a weak grin, snagging my hand again as we trudge toward the vehicle, Jake perched on it, looking worriedly for us, Aly's ATV closing in.

We figure out a better system, Damon in front, Jake behind, standing with his feet on the seat pegs and his hands on my shoulder. I have not even a semblance of an idea how we're gonna fit Kion on board, but maybe Thea can drive, and Leaf and I can come back on foot. That's a problem for later Toby if ever I've heard one, though, and I concentrate on keeping the boys balanced and the wheels angled right on the dunes as they get deeper and deeper.

The tube car is in sight, finally; we're closing fast, headlights dipping and bouncing over the wavy sands, when Jake squeezes my shoulder hard and leans forward, yelling over the wind.

"Toby, there's someone there!"

Even with the warning, the flaring explosion of a flash grenade takes me completely by surprise. The ATV tips, and I can't keep it upright. Flashes of movement, Damon's wide-eyed terrified face as he's dashed off the vehicle, shadows racing down the hill toward us. My shoulder smashes into the ground. I black out softly, like a feather blanket's been dropped over my head.

Chapter Fifteen

E17

I feel a burst of panic from Toby, then nothing again, my power still drained and worn from yanking him through me. He's close, though. I feel that—close and with people to protect.

The light has faded, leaving a white wash over my vision, graying out my view of the world and doubling every time I blink, trying to clear it. Something—someone—grabs me, violent fingers digging into my shoulder, pulling me around. I react faster than I would have thought possible without Reading the move on them; there's a hand on my throat, pulling my chin back but I'm already moving.

I lean backward, into their body; they've come through the door and now my back is to them. They're yanking my chin up like they're expecting to cut my throat, but I get hands around their wrist and twist, pulling them over my hip and slamming them into the floor of the tube car.

An alien-looking face blinks up at me, something strange about the skin—it doesn't look *right,* but they're already trying to buck me off; a knuckle punch slams into the thick muscle of my forearm, and I don't have time to analyze because there's screaming outside, and I know Toby is out there.

Without knowing who this is, why they're attacking me, I won't kill them. I pull them off the floor and use my free hand to land a solid roundhouse punch to the point of the jaw. Their body goes slack. The whole thing has taken less than a minute, according to my internal clock, but I spend another thirty seconds immobilizing them with bandages from the first aid kit.

Satisfied they're not able to move, I flail for my next action: what should I do? I need to find out what's going on outside; if only my power were available to me. Nuke, is this how other people *live?* How can they bear it?

Kion's still unmoving, but breathing. I wish I could hide him somehow, wedge him under the seat or something, but I'm not strong enough. I have to leave the tube car, have to leave him. But there's some kind of force attacking us, and he's helpless.

I sit back on my heels, breathing too fast, and the window-smashing hammer jabs into my hip.

A faint semblance of an idea dances at the edge of my mind, but I need to hurry. I don't have time to sit and plan. Scrambling to the door, I run my hands over it, desperate for a way to lock it so I can leave Kion with something between him and whoever this new enemy is.

The handle twists in my grip, clicking around to push out the latch bolt, jumping out of the faceplate and pressing in to my palm. If I can break off the handle, then the door will stay locked. It's better than nothing, a lot better.

I clumsily jump out of the car, slam the door behind me, grab the hammer with nerveless fingers and hit it once, twice, three times and something breaks under the strain, the handle clattering onto the tracks.

I'm balanced on the crossbeams, metal under my boots, the barrier is down around the tube car, somehow cut off. I can see the sparkle of it twenty meters down the track. On the sand below me, an ATV swerves, a Zap gun blasts, lighting the night up in a shock of white.

I see everything. Toby sprawled on the ground, a small figure standing over him—Jake—a Zap gun in his hand. He takes aim at *nothing,* fires, another burst of light and then a shadow tumbling down the slope of a dune, resolving itself into a humanoid figure as it stutters to a halt, disturbed sand haloing it. Leaf has a gun. I don't see him until he fires, he's halfway up a dune scanning the area. His shot hits something I can't see, just like Jake's did, and then there's a body rolling down the hill in front of him.

Damon is crouched next to Toby, slapping his face, Alyssa is on the moving ATV, and she rams into something I can't see, leaving blood spewing behind her wheels. It's eerily black against the gray sand, lit by the receding glow of a flare and the spinning headlights.

A hand grabs my ankle before I can figure out how to get down, how to help them. I don't know what's attacking them, but I stomp on the fingers, the fingers *I can't see,* and my brain makes the connection; they're cloaking— whoever's jumped us is cloaking like Toby can do, except they can *all* do it. I don't stop kicking the invisible climber until the grip relaxes, and I hear a thud below, someone flickering into view as they hit the ground, lose focus.

And then I make sense of it, there's sand skidding under invisible feet, you can see the puffs of movement, six, maybe seven, plus the one I just dropped and the one Jake hit. Jake is spinning madly, pointing his Zap in every direction, and then he pops another shot off and another figure hits the ground. Good, he's conserving ammo, reading the area, taking good risks.

Toby stirs, and I feel my power ripple inside me in response, but it's still not there, not really. I can't use it and so I have to stop thinking about it, have to use what *is* available to me. I don't have a gun, but Aly probably does. She's using her ATV as a weapon, keeping them back, circling Toby's collapsed form and smashing into another running but imperceptible form.

Scrambling for a way down, I squat and try to see how the climber got up, a rope or something would be a blessing. There's nothing; it's a twelve-foot drop, at least. They must have climbed the bracing pole, hand over hand. I don't have that option; I have to jump.

My hands are shaking as I wrap them around the metal supporting the tube, push my feet over the side, and wiggle backward until I'm dangling down into the night. My full height, plus my arm length shortens the drop, but it's still a long way down. I inhale deeply, try to remember everything I've ever learned about parachute rolls, and let go.

Letting my legs fold up, rolling sideways, slapping the ground to take the force of impact on my hand instead of my shoulder, I end up flat on my back with the wind knocked out of me, but nothing broken as far as I can tell.

A shadowy figure detaches itself from the concrete pole holding the metal support beam, apparently this one doesn't know how to cloak or is choosing not to. A blade catches the light, glinting, giving me the split-second warning I need to twist away from that arm.

I hook their ankle with my foot, kick upward with the other, catch softness of a belly leaning over me, and take their legs out from under them. Before they can recover, I've crawled on top of them. I wrap my fingers around their knife arm; it's scaly under my hand. I twist and something snaps, the knife dropping to the ground. Then I punch them in the face until they go limp, and then I crawl off, breathing heavily. I take their knife, swap it out for mine. I know the heft of mine and how it will fly. I don't want to kill anyone, but I don't think we have a choice.

Down the slope, Jake yells, and I see him being pulled away by invisible arms. My heart clenches in my chest, sure I'm about to see his bare throat obscured by a spray of blood, but he goes soft and malleable in the hands that have him, unconscious rather than a trick, I think; and then...then he winks out of sight like he was never there. Leaf's racing toward where he vanished. He moves so fast over the sand it's like he's running on concrete. He's so quick, I see him dive, grab, but he's knocked down and hits the sand face-first and doesn't get up.

"Jake..." I scream, giving away my position, but if these people are all Psionics—and they're cloaking, so they *must* be—they knew where I was anyway.

The sand is soft and shifts under my feet as I half run, half slip down the gentle slope toward the place I saw him disappear. There's nothing there, *nothing*. I cast my powers out without thought, but there's nothing in me either. For a moment I feel like they're gone forever, that I'll never be complete again, but a twitch in the connection between Toby and I reassures me. Jake is gone...gone, and I don't know where he could be, but Toby is still on the sand, and Damon is still crouched over him, now without a gun protecting him, and I'm four steps too slow to be close enough to grab him when he's lifted into the air.

"No!" My throat rips the word out, and Damon's looking at me with such faith in his eyes; he sees me coming for him, coming to save him, and then he blinks out of existence just like Jake did in the arms of his captor, and my hands grab nothing but air as I catch up with the space he was in just a second ago.

I whirl around, my heart pounding, my knife in my hand. I see footsteps, maybe, dents in the sand that could have been from the wind, I dash for the same spot, but the footprints clear the dune, and I'm not quick enough, never quick enough and the far side of the dune is so dark I can't pick out a single undulation.

Zap fire makes me jump, my heart stuttering. Is Leaf up? Did he pick off another one coming for us; did he miss? I hope Aly's taking care of my brother. I hope Kion is okay. The fading light of the Zap burst casts scattered light down the hill, and Leaf's on his feet, running toward me, but it's no good, there's nothing to see, nothing to catch. He fires another burst into the air, light streaming, but the stillness of the desert in front of me is undisturbed. They could be standing two feet from us, and we'd never, ever find them. Not without a Reader.

I stand, uselessly, the wind whistling past my ears as I frame myself on the skyline for any enemy. If they come for me, I can hurt them. But the only hand that touches me is Leaf's, his face tight and worried.

"They're gone, jus' gone," he says, sounding like he disbelieves himself. "I could see 'em, but...they're gone now. Can ya feel 'em?"

"No." My answer is hollow. I turn, woodenly walk down the hill toward my brother, who's finally, finally sitting up, looking around with a confused expression and blood smeared on his cheekbone.

"What happened?" He's bleary eyed.

Alyssa, crouched by his side, is crying. "The Eaters...they took them. They took Jake and Damon."

"They're jus' a storeh," Leaf snaps. "They're no' true."

"Then how do you explain this?" Aly waves her hand at the empty dune bowl. "They took them, and we couldn't even *see* them."

"I don't... I don't understand." Toby mutters, rubbing his head and wincing.

"The Eaters. The people from beyond the deadlands. They have the kids."

"Kion." I remember he exists and turn, running for the tube. If they got in, he could be dead, lying bled out on the floor. I can't... I can't even think about it... It's impossible.

The door is still shut, I can see it, but that doesn't mean he's safe. Aly stumbles up the hill after me, leaving my brother and Leaf limping around the area, Toby's arm slung over Leaf's narrow shoulder. They stop by one of the attackers.

"I'm sorry," Aly gasps, tears still racking her words. "The kids followed us out and we couldn't take them back. We didn't *know*."

Of course, they didn't, because it's impossible—what just happened was impossible—but it happened anyway, and Jake and Damon are gone.

"We'll find them." My answer is short, brutal. As soon as my powers come back, I'll be able to follow them— follow them from this spot to anywhere, and they didn't kill them, did they? So they must want them alive for something, which means we have a chance.

Aly drops her pack and rummages, finds a rope and a hook and handily throws it up and over the beam, where it wraps around and around, clanging in the still night, and she tugs on it violently before starting up.

I follow suit, hand over hand, pulling myself over the beam and hoisting the hammer out of my belt, once again. Aly watches in silence as I smash the small window over the door, reach through and find the handle, unlatch the door and balance myself around it to climb back into the tube car.

Kion's where I left him, still breathing, no pool of blood spreading out under him, no dead eyes and unmoving chest. It's more of a relief than I realize, and my heart steadies.

"Okay, call the boys, we have to get him down."

Aly nods, still outside the car, and calls Leaf and Toby away from their rounds of the dead or unconscious attackers.

Toby's nerdy interests in physics end up being the answer to the huge question of how to get Kion down from the tube car. We pull together a sort of rope sling, muscle him into it, and lower him, ropes over the beams and into Toby and Leaf's hands, and brake ropes up top, with Aly and I providing a failsafe. He hits the ground gently, and we scramble down after him.

He's not bleeding through his bandages; my battlefield first aid has held up.

"Leaf, I'm sorry to force this on you, but you and I are going after the boys." My tone holds no space for argument, but I see Toby open his mouth to argue, and I cut him off. "You need to get Kion, and one of these—" I point at the body of the man I punched out after dropping off the tube lines. "—back to ARC.

"You go—you and Aly. I'll go with Leaf. It's my fault."

I hear it in his voice: the absolute refusal to think about what's best, what makes the most sense. I'm a Reader, I'll track them...but right now I'm powered out, and he's just as much of a Reader as I am, I realize, deflating.

"We'll send help; we'll find people," Aly chimes in quietly, her face set, the tear tracks visible on her sand-dirty face, but no longer flowing.

"Yer all dea' on yer fee'." Leaf frowns, scruffing his dirty hair back from his face, clearly not including himself in that assessment.

"We brought shots; hang on." Aly rummages in her bag, comes up with energy shots and glucose tablets, handing them around to all of us.

"This'll keep me upright, maybe let my powers juice up again," Toby chugs his back with the expression of disgust I associate with the bitterness of the refueling gel. I try to swallow mine without tasting it, but as always, am left scrubbing my teeth over my tongue in the hopes of scraping the remnants off.

"See ya." Toby breaks the silence, pats the Zap on his belt, and starts walking to the top of the dune the attackers—Eaters—disappeared over.

"Ah'm a deser' boy. If'n anyone can fin' 'em, I will." Leaf gives me a long, slow look and grabs both the packs off the floor. "Think we migh' need these more'n you." He turns, flicking a silly salute at Aly and me both and then loping after Toby's receding figure, leaving Aly and I to figure out how to get all two hundred and something pounds of Kion onto the back of one of our ATVs.

It takes a while, too long, my heart and body are so tired. I can't stop thinking about my brother and Leaf, traipsing across unmarked desert, looking for men who don't exist.

We strap Kion on with the belted webbing that's supposed to be for ammo packs, lash his legs to the handles and his torso to me—I'm stronger than Aly—to try to keep him on the bike. We picked the smallest, slightest of the unconscious attackers to lash less thoughtfully over the back of Aly's vehicle, leaving the rest bound in the hopes that they won't wake soon and follow after Toby and Leaf. We should be back in a few hours, or someone should be. I make sure the ATV has a GPS pin dropped at our location before we head back toward the city.

It's the middle of the night now, pushing 4:00 a.m., and even the slums are deserted. We get no trouble pushing back down the narrow streets and the soldiers on the Wall wave us forward, see Kion, and take over. There's a medivan on-site in minutes, and he's whisked away from me by efficient personnel, leaving Aly and I to be shuttled back to the base with one of the Wall relief convoys.

Word must have gotten out that I'm back, and Kion's back, because Ria hops onto our ride at the front gate of base and redirects our driver to drop us at the east end of the building for our debrief.

Thankfully, Aly starts talking before I have to, tells Ria what happened out on the dunes, and how Toby and Leaf are still out there, trailing the boys.

Ria radios Serena and David Jacobs to meet us, and I touch her hand while she's still on the line. "I need Oman and India," I mutter, the words thick and hot and full of shame. But I told Kion I'd let them help, and I won't be made a liar this way while he's fighting for his life. She doesn't reply, just relays the message.

The meeting is a blur. I stumble over the answers to simple questions, losing all my ability to report concisely and efficiently. It was Serena's face, you see. She marched in and grabbed me. "Where's Damon?" And my power had come back enough for me to feel the helplessness and rage washing through her, washing over me and scraping every nerve I have raw. It was too much, too deep. I retreated, pulling back from her, pushed myself down the connection restrung between my brother and I. He's with Leaf, of course, Leaf's walking half hunched down, a shielded light in his hand, following marks Toby can't even see. He seems confident, though, and it's given Toby just a little hope, combined with the resurgence of his powers flickering back to present and his sense of me returned.

Serena shakes me, fury smearing her features hollow and sharp. Ria yanks her off me, pushes me out of the room. Marty and a kind-eyed soldier take me to a smaller office. After I'm done reporting, they give me something to help me sleep, and then escort me back to my bunk. The medicine drags me into gray dreamlessness.

When I wake, Oman is by my side. He's very calm, very kind, as he leans forward and looks at me with his unnervingly intense eyes. "Tell me."

So, with my heart in my throat, I do.

Chapter Sixteen

TOBY

My back is killing me, my leg muscles screaming from the drag step needed to ascend and descend the rolling hills of sand. The people we're tracking seem to be taking a direct route, judging on what my GPS says, and the longer they keep heading due northeast the more confident I feel. They have to stop at some point; they don't seem to have vehicles. All we have to do is outlast them, catch up, and take them out.

My power is coming back, thank Google, because the state of my body isn't going to help much in a hand-to-hand fight. I can feel it tingling in my bones, but I'm not quite exhausted enough that I need to use it to strengthen my legs, brace my spine. I need to hoard it for the inevitable conflict.

A few paces ahead of me, Leaf holds up his hand, straightens from his awkward crab walk—I have no idea how he's kept that up for over an hour, staring the ground illuminated by some sort of glowing ball he has clasped in one hand—and sniffs the air.

I catch up with him, moving fast, and stop when he slaps his hand into my chest to let me know I've gone far enough.

He crouches, very, very slowly, and I start to ask, "What's going on?" in a low hiss, but he waves his hand in a clear sign for silence. We're high on a dune, but not over it yet, and even though my eyes are tired like the rest of me, I've adjusted enough that I can see the steps we've been following, kind of. The sand surface is pocked and uneven, but the fact our prey is traveling in a line makes it easier to see.

"There was five of 'em," Leaf murmurs. "An' now there's only four."

I guardedly shift around, scanning the surrounding area with as much focus as I can manage, looking for a puff of sand, a shift of air, a flash of movement. Anything.

Meanwhile, Leaf starts blowing on the sand in front of him, very carefully. I have absolutely no idea what he's doing, but he seems to be pretty familiar with the desert so I concentrate on what I can do, looking for anyone trying to sneak up on us.

After a few moments, Leaf touches my leg lightly, making me jump. "Toby, can ya lift this up without rattlin' it?"

Looking down, I see he's uncovered a metal circle about the size of my palm. After a split second, it resolves itself into the tin lid of a food storage can. Leaf's carefully moved the sand from either side of it, so it's sticking out a little.

I squat, taking a deep breath, trying to get a grip on my powers. Before I can start, Leaf looks at me very seriously. "Do not push it down. That there's a bomb."

My heart rate spikes and my hand trembles just a little as I extend it, wanting to use my physical muscles, my actual presence to bolster my traumatized powers. I curl my fingers a little, hovering slightly above it and send a tendril of talent out of each digit.

I snake them down the sides of the tin, feeling my way, curving them underneath and gently, gently pushing the sand back. I'm not breathing as I hesitantly lift it out of the sand bed.

Then Leaf grabs it off me like I didn't just about give myself a heart attack trying not to move it.

"What?" I yelp, indignantly, but he's already rummaging in the hole.

"Aha!" he grunts, and I didn't know people actually said that in real life, but I'm too overwrought to be amused. He's got something shiny and metallic in his hand; he spins it around his fingers. "Nail. We step on the can, the can goes down, the nail hits the metal and the bomb goes boom," he explains.

"Why didn't we just...go around it?" I hiss angrily, shaken up by the whole scene.

Leaf snickers and gets to his feet, poking the can into the bag he swiped from Aly and the nail into his pocket, "'Cause ya cin barely walk; we got two Zaps, both down ta half charge, and if they run after us, I'd like to leave 'em a surprise." He states, matter-of-factly, and the reasonable tone cools my indignation a bit.

"Oh. Okay. What about the missing man?"

Leaf shrugs a shoulder, starts walking up the hill again, his long legs striding over the loose scree with ease. "Who knows? Coulda gone on ahead; could be behind us right now. No real way ta know, so why worry about it? They don't seem ta have Zaps; this bomb is a slum kinda thing, smells like homemade saltpeter done with piss, so I think we 'ave a decent shot, *if* we catch 'em. Move it."

I scramble after him, impressed by his reasoning and smarts. Distantly, my connection to my twin thrums, and I feel her agitation, stress, but not fear or anything dangerous. Frustration, maybe. Nothing I can do from here. I try to send her a beat of calm, of faith, without the exhaustion that's been living in me for days behind it. I wonder when I'll be allowed to sleep. I wonder when this will be done.

We walk for another hour and twelve minutes according to my datapad, before Leaf throws his head back, sniffs the air, and then drops down flat to his belly without a sound. I try to mimic him, but not nearly as fast, because sound carries like a beast in the desert, and I don't think a rolling belly thud is gonna be helpful if Leaf thinks we need to be flat on our stomachs.

He squirms until his face is right by my ear, whispers so quietly it's like the sound doesn't even disturb the air. I can feel his hair tickling my cheek. "I can smell fire; they're close. Stay 'ere. Watch out."

I nod, and he gives me a wicked grin, from very close to my face, and then starts to wriggle away, silent and flowing over the ground like an animal. I sniff the air quietly but can't smell anything. Either he has an amazing sense of smell, or I have a terrible one. Or a bit of both, I guess.

Trying to be helpful, I wiggle onto my side and scan the area. I see nothing, and nothing, and nothing, empty expanses of dunes that are clearer than they were just moments ago. Dawn is starting to lighten the air; soon we'll be under the baking heat of day. I occupy myself by trying to remember at what time the desert gets to what temperature, and how much water we have. When we'll collapse from heat exhaustion. None of the numbers I come up with are very comforting.

Leaf slips down the slope above me, sending sand into my face and hair. I try really, really hard not to cough, shaking the coarse grains off me, and he gives me an apologetic grin. "Misjudged me angle." He settles in on his side, propped on one arm. "They're cozyin' up by a fire, our boys're there, trussed up good but awake, which is helpful. And I have a question for ya. So, these guys, they're powered up, right, 'cause that's how they went invisible on you all before. Right now, they're all visible, but they are also *covered* in sand. Like...second skin on 'em. Make's them hard ta see when they're lying real still. S'gotta be telekinesis 'cause ya couldn't glue sand ta your outfit, your skin; it's not possible. So, these guys're power' up and yet...when they took us down, they didn't attack wi' telekinesis at all. Not a single strike. So, why not?"

"I...don't know," I say dully, after a moment has gone by with Leaf looking at me expectantly. "Maybe someone at ARC would, but I have no idea. Still, gives us an extra advantage, right? Do you have a plan?" How the hell someone would have enough fine control to hold sand against their skin, the fabric of their clothes, I don't know. It sounds impossible to me. Maybe it takes so much energy that they can't spare any for fighting?

Leaf chews on his lip, eyes flicking around like he can see things in the air, like he's looking at data on a screen, and then he shrugs, "I'll circle 'em; come in from the northwest; you stay at this angle so we don't shoot each other. There's four of 'em; that's two each. Zap 'em from the top of the dunes and clean up on foot?"

I smooth my hand over the sand between us, making a flat patch and dragging my finger in a curve for the dune we are on. "Show me where they are?"

Leaf takes a second to think and then adds some crosses to the map for the kidnappers, and a circle for the boys. We divide them into two for each of us to take out, and then figure out the best lines of attack. When we have the plan solidified, I check the time on my datapad, 4:45 a.m. "We need a signal." I tap the screen. "You don't have anything to tell time with, right?"

Leaf looks at me, with a sort of patronizing grin. "Ah'm good at countin'. Gimme ten mins ta get into position." He squirms back onto his front and sets off at an angle up the dune. I check the time, set a counter, and then start painstakingly creeping my way up the hill. Embarrassingly, it takes me eight minutes to get to a position where I can see the tiny, shielded fire, and another solid minute to pick out the lumps of the people around it. If Leaf hadn't drawn them for me, I don't know that I would have realized they were anything but irregular masses of sand.

Thirty seconds.

We're gonna have to take our shots at max range, but the Zaps have a little popup viewfinder, and I spend my last twenty seconds practicing shifting from my first target, the one nearest the boys when I have the most time to aim, to my second. I squeeze the stock in anticipation.

Three, two, one, my finger tightens on the trigger and the night explodes. My shot is good, slamming into the first guy, sending him head over heels to sprawl on the sand. At this range, he'll have broken ribs at the worst, but he should be down for a few at least. I hear Leaf's shot explode at the exact same second, but there's no time to look for his targets.

I swing onto my second target; it's only been a second, but he's already moving, on his feet; two steps, I aim; he vanishes, and I keep my hand swinging on his line of motion, firing off three rapid shots. My second catches him; he snaps back into existence, and my third shot hits him in the face, the ball of light-energy throwing him into the air. He won't be getting up any time soon.

The sand slips and slides under me as I scramble upright, bolting down the hill as fast as my tight, worn muscles will allow, scree skidding out from the sides of my boots until momentum has me, and it's all I can do to stay upright.

Something slams into me, knocking me sideways, a streak of heat scores my ribcage—a knife, invisible in the hands of an invisible wielder. The missing member of the group, maybe, or maybe Leaf missed. He's half underneath me, trying to twist free.

The fall saved my life, I think, the blade is still digging into me agonizingly, but I'm on top, and I'm heavier but not impaled. I lift myself up with one arm, punch down with everything I have, the Zap still in my hand. Metal and plastic shatters into bone and he flicks into vision under me, sand-covered, sand-colored, sand grains coating him like he's been glued and dipped, but just after he loses his invisibility, he loses his grip on the sand as well, and it melts away. It's a woman I realize, before I knock her out for good.

Crawling off her, I lie on my back, padding my fingers over the wound in my side. It's not horribly deep, but it's bleeding freely. Great. I definitely wasn't injured enough, a stab wound was just the thing to complete my collection.

Hoping desperately that Leaf has dealt with the other two guys, I stagger to my feet, and down the hill. I walk past the guy I shot in the head; he's moaning faintly, most of his face pulverized. Nuke, it looks bad. I have a sudden surge of guilt, but then Jake screams at me through the sticky-looking gag over his lower face, and I trudge past the injured man.

Untying them, I look around for Leaf, while the two young boys practically drop me in the sand again, both of them have been crying—they're terrified and dirty and bruised, and they won't let go of me.

Aching and exhausted, I manage to get my non-stabbed-side arm around both of them, let them tremble against my ribs for a minute.

Leaf slopes down the hill. He has a knife in his hand, the blade glints red in the firelight. Blood, like the blade's been plated in it. He sees my eyeline and looks away, leaning down to wipe the blade clean on the sand.

"Even people who take little boys don' deserve to fry." He jerks his chin up, and I realize what he means. The sky is awash with orange in the east; soon it will be full day, and we can't take them with us as prisoners. We'll be lucky to make it onward ourselves. And with Zap wounds, they'd have died horribly of creeping dehydration and shock.

I grit my teeth as Damon's arm wraps against my fresh injury, and squeeze both boys for a moment, before detangling.

"You hurt?" I lean down a little. I'd squat, but I'm not sure I'd get up again. I need another shot, water, food...medicine. The list goes on. I'm not sure what we have with us.

"No, but you are!" Damon looks at his hand, covered in blood now, and I try to sound confident.

"Just a scratch. Leaf, do you have some bandages?"

He drops the bag, crouches, rummages, whoops quietly. The sound dredges a quiet grin out of me. The kids are still hovering close at my side, looking fearfully around the area with jumpy body language, not that I blame them.

Leaf finds bandages, clotting foam and gauze, makes a decent job of wrapping the long slash curling around my ribcage and pulls my shirt back down for me. Once I'm wrapped, I catch an energy shot thrown by Leaf and start checking the bodies for things we can use.

Hopefully there'll be people coming out soon, on ATVs, but we'll need at least three to get us all back, and that might take time to figure out. They have my GPS signal from my datapad, so we'll be easy to find, but I think we should start covering ground back from where we came. I don't want to stay here, at this campsite, even if it does look like a good spot, sheltered by a huge towering dune that will keep the killer sun off an area big enough to sleep in.

For all we know, this is a meeting place and more people could be on us any minute. If I had the energy, I'd bury them. Not for respect, or anything, but to cover our tracks. Hide the sight of what we've done here.

After I've checked the first body, Jake and Damon summon the courage to follow me, and take what I hand them. A flask of water, half empty, paste that looks like it could be sun protection, wide-brimmed hats that will keep the heat off our heads and necks.

It's a paltry selection, but Leaf has water in his pack still, and we let Jake and Damon glug some down eagerly.

"D'ya reckon we should give 'em the last shot to split?" Leaf inquires, twirling it in his fingers, the little tube calling out to me. I can feel the one I took buzzing in my veins, and I know they're easy to OD on, but that doesn't mean I don't want to suck the powerful refueller into myself, before trudging up yet more sand mountains, this time in the blazing heat of the day. I can already feel it drying the cold sweat of the night and the fight.

I think about it, looking at the kids. They're both exhausted-looking, matching dark circles under their big brown eyes. I wrinkle my nose. They're too young for the shots, really, but I'm too wiped to carry either one of them. Leaf is probably the same, although he's still moving lithely, and they don't look like they're good for much walking.

"Yeah, do it." We have to put some space between us and the bodies we're leaving behind. Nuke, we've all been running on chemical energy for a while, and now we're gonna pour some into the kids. Needs must, though.

I have a sudden flash of *bed* and just about drop to my knees at the mere idea of it. Thea's made it back; she's safe, and she's nuking exhausted, but that means help is on its way.

The kids make matching yuck faces as Leaf squirts half the gel into the back of each of their open, waiting mouths. Then he swings the bag up onto his narrow shoulders, gently pushes Damon so he starts walking, and gives me a grin before heading up the slope, nimble as ever.

The energy gel hits Jake pretty solidly, and the exhaustion piled up with the chemical boost gives him a serious case of the yammers, as my dad would have said.

It helps though, hearing him blather on, seemingly without the need for breath or to stop and think about what he's saying. It's distracting, keeps my mind off the pulling sting in my side, the bone-deep tiredness in my muscles, the headache that makes me squint against the brightening sky from under my floppy new hat.

The sun is hammering down; my mouth is dry and cracking, sticky saliva making me work my fat tongue against the roof of my mouth as I step, drag, step, slip, step, stagger onward. It's been two hours according to my datapad, and Jake has run out of energy also, staggering along at my side in stubborn silence.

Ahead of us, two figures coalesce out of the hazy heat hovering above the dunes, and my heart leaps in my chest—rescue, surely. I can sit on the back... No, those aren't vehicles, those are people on foot.

To my left, Leaf sees them, too, halts. We make eye contact above the heads of the kids, and my hand wraps around my Zap, of its own accord.

"No' nomads," Leaf hums, tilting his head and shading his eyes with his hand. I wonder if we should run and then realize I couldn't even if I wanted to.

The figures get closer, and closer. "What should we do?" Damon tugs my hand, frantic, but I don't have an answer for him. It's too far away to tell if they're friend or foe. If they're bracketed by invisible backup, I can't tell.

They're tall, both of them, a woman and a man, I realize, as they get closer. It's a horrible, dislocating moment when I make out the man's face, his high cheekbones and chiseled jaw. His blond hair, greasy now, but recognizable slicked back into a horsetail. I've only ever seen him in pictures, in my twin's mind.

Icarus.

And next to him.... Raising her hands in the sign of no threat, is Leah, the precognitive who left ARC in the middle of the night just after we pulled Thea out of the Institute.

Chapter Seventeen

E17

While I was recounting to Oman what I knew, what happened to me, Johan and India join us. They sit silently, though, let me get it all out of me. Inside, Cassandra rails, furious that I would dare to reveal her presence. It's with a swirling sense of dread I realize she's been steering me away from trusting anyone, driving the gulf between me and these people deeper.

It makes me feel sick, worn, useless. I tell them what happened as best as I can recall, how I tried to kill Cassandra, and instead, she flung herself into me. How she speaks to me, how I can feel her *always*. I tell them about the dreams, about Icarus in the desert with Pollux. About sleepwalking into the ARC servers and again in Fourth City, with Kion there to stop me.

Johan looks furious, gray in the face with it. I don't blame him. He must be sick of me, of Toby, of us putting ourselves first and trying to stay alive. I can try to excuse myself, ask how someone like me, raised the way I was, is expected to trust anyone, ever, but it's a weak and flimsy excuse. Really, I'm just afraid. I'm always afraid.

Toby's rebuilding power calls at me, begs me to take a little, just a little, so I can be strong, so I can bear this, but I curl my hands into fists at my sides, resolute. I took it because I needed it, because I would have died without it, but I don't need it now. Cassandra hisses disgust in my head. *Pathetic, useless, victim. You'll always be a victim, Epsilon 17.*

"That's not my *name*," I yell it, slamming my hands into the metal of the bunk, pain bursting in my knuckles. It helps me focus. I'm breathing in thick little pants, my stomach swirling. I concentrate on the smear of blood on my middle knuckle, the pinkness of the skin as it puffs and swells under the split. I zone out so thoroughly I jerk in surprise when a gentle hand takes mine, pulls it forward and dabs gauze on the oozing wound.

Johan is soft in his movements, but his hands are strong and broad, callused like a warrior. He could snap my arm in a moment. I knew it even without Cassandra providing a flashing sensory image of what that would look like, feel like. She's trying to make me run, I think. Make me leave ARC. Which means the best thing I can do is stay—she's played her cards wrong this time, given herself away.

"It's okay, Thea." Johan tips my chin with his free hand, still holding mine, so I have to meet his eyes. "It's okay. We're going to help you. I'm sorry."

Against my will, my eyes fill with tears, stinging and hot. Johan gives me a small, lopsided smile.

"Do you think you can sleep? India will walk with you. We'll all be here with you." His tone is the sort you'd use on a child, or a frightened animal, but it comforts me, and I swallow thickly, forcing the lump in my throat down.

"I can try."

THE STARS ARE bright in the desert, the sand clawing at my feet. My boots have long given up, cracked and broken.

I've bound them with fabric strips we stole from a small band of nomads, but the sand still gets in, it gets everywhere. I'm scoured and dry down to the bone.

At my side, a calming presence touches my hand, takes it gently and pulls to angle me down the dune we're traversing. A snake in front of me, where I would have stepped without the guidance, slithers away at the vibrations of her footsteps. I-Thea assume the other is Pollux, but the hand in mine is smaller, softer. Strong, but delicate. Icarus doesn't look though, so I can't discover who is with him.

"It's okay, Cassius," a woman's voice whispers, familiar. "We're almost there."

"Almost where?" Icarus's voice is husky with disuse; he's calmer than I've ever felt him. Inside me, Cassandra bucks and pushes, trying to reach him. *Icarus. Icarus.* She sounds desperate.

"Cassius," The voice is firm, reprimanding, and I finally place it. Leah! The precognitive who ran from ARC after they took me in, who left a message of destruction behind her. Why is she here? Why is she with Icarus? Why is she calling him Cassius?

Cassandra laughs in my head.

Be calm, Thea. This voice is not Cassandra, not Leah, not Icarus. It's strong and soft at the same time; it's comfort like being held in the hands of something much greater than myself. India touches my real forehead, and I feel the contact flow through me, gentling my muscles. I'd been shaking, I realize, afraid. Always afraid.

I see, India smooths his fingertips over the arches of my brows. I have two bodies; I'm in two places, but I am used to this sensation. It doesn't jar me; I feel safer than I ever have.

Cassandra hisses, twists, claws at the walls I push against constantly, trying to hold her back. It's exhausting, I realize through India's observation of the same. I spend my days trying to keep her locked away, trying to keep her imprisoned in my own head.

Abruptly, on the sand slope, Leah turns and grabs Icarus's face in her hands, looks deep into his eyes. "Enough," she says, and it's firm, echoes into me, loosens the connection between us. "Leave him. He is not yours."

She blows in his face. I feel it on mine, and I'm tumbling out of Icarus, out of the desert, back into my meat body with a shudder.

India holds me against his chest. I can feel the rise and fall of his ribcage, his old skin too thin over the bones. His body feels fragile, but his mental presence is strong, so strong. "You're safe. You're okay," he tells me, and a small part of me believes him.

They run tests, extensively. I want to be sent back to look for my brother, but they have the GPS, they tell me; they have Toby's datapad on the system; they know where he is. They're sending people for him. Serena is going; she pokes her head into the medical wing to let me know, and I feel like she's forgiven me for Damon, for letting Damon be taken again. She's taking a team. I don't have to worry. They'll find them and bring them home.

They test me, test Cassandra, try to find the limits of her within me. I'm taking all Johan's time, most of Oman's. But it's right they tell me; it's necessary. They'll help me.

After hours of testing, Oman nods, his face serious and exhausted-looking. "We can push her down. That will do for now. We'll help you hold her."

The idea of not being alone makes me cry, again. I'm not even embarrassed this time. Toby sends me a pulse of support, of love. He has the boys, I realize. They're safe and walking; they're coming back.

It's enough, and I wonder what the warm feeling in my chest is as I lie down on a white sheet, on a white bed, staring at a white ceiling before Oman lies next to me, cradles me against his chest like a child, and waits for me to settle. His presence is calming; I try to relax, try to let the walls that would keep him out down without dropping the ones that hold Cassandra.

Our breathing syncs. I close my eyes. Oman fuzzes into my head and calmly starts picking through everything that makes me me. He doesn't hold any memories. I can feel him scanning and setting them free without dropping into them, looking only for invasion, for Cassandra.

He finds her. He finds her *everywhere*. He finds smears and marks on my memories, on my knowledge, on my pathways. He finds hooks, and he calmly, patiently wiggles them free, pulls her parasitic presence out of my mind. Shoves her back and back and down, until I can't hear her at all, can't feel her at all.

I breathe.

I *breathe.*

Oman eases out of my mind, and I breathe out in a shuddery exhale. I'm *alone.* For the first time in so long, I'm alone in my head. There's no layer to my thoughts except the ones I put there. I'm not cut off, not stranded, but I'm alone!

I laugh with it, although I realize I'm crying as well, sobbing and laughing and safe from the voice that's lived in my head for as long as I've lived above ground.

Oman touches my back lightly, and I fling myself at him, burrow into his warm neck. "Thank you. Thank you!"

"She's still there. I don't know how to get her out, yet. But we can check you regularly, make sure you're coping." He strokes my back with reassuring hands, and I nod, his beard scratching at my face.

Someone clears their throat, and I wriggle clear of Oman's fatherly hug, sniffing and rubbing my face. I'm mortified when I see I've soaked his shirt with my tears, and he catches my eyeline, shrugs philosophically.

"A child threw up and then peed on me this morning; you're far from the worst I have to deal with."

"Thea," Johan's voice comes from the doorway, and I turn, clearing my eyes by blinking rapidly. "Feeling better?"

"Yeah, yes. Oman...pulled her out of me. I didn't know how deep she ran," I shiver just thinking about it.

"That's great. If you're feeling up to it, we need you." Normal Johan is back, brusque and dismissive, but I saw the pain in his eyes when I was telling him what was going on with me, I felt his distress. I know how much he cares, now, and it shocks me I never realized before.

"I'm okay." I slide off the bed, feeling lighter than I've done in ages, feeling energized and eager and ready to do whatever ARC asks of me. Ready to trust them now.

"The prisoner—" Johan moves out of the doorway, clearly expecting me to follow. "—He's strong. Very strong. We could use your help reading him." He looks me over when I pad out into the hallway, barefoot but still clad in my desert hiking gear. "After you shower and eat something." he sniffs, delicately.

I repress my giggle at his distaste and nod; I could do it now; I could, but if he says I have time to clean up then

I should take advantage of that. If there's one thing I've learned lately, it's that you never know how many tasks are going to stack on top of themselves and leave you running on fumes. I've slept, now, but I'm starving and dirty.

"I'll meet you in Q17." Johan claps me on the shoulder and heads down the corridor.

CLEAN, FED, AND wearing soft sweats, I knock nervously on the door to Q17. There are two soldiers standing guard outside. Johan is already there, with Oman, who gives me a gentle smile when I walk in, his brown eyes crinkling.

The room is dark, only a small light glowing in the corner, and the question must show on my face because Johan jerks his head at the prisoner. "He asked for it to be darker. Maybe it hurts his eyes."

The prisoner is bound with shackles on his wrists and ankles, strapped to the bed. I wonder if his kind of telekinesis doesn't allow him to escape, but I'm sure that the soldiers have thought of that. Maybe he's been dosed...but then I wouldn't be able to read him. His hair is dirty blond and matted, his face gaunt. His skin looks a little chafed, maybe from the sand he held against himself.

I shrug the thoughts off as unimportant; my role in this is small. Oman gestures to a stool that's been set up on the side of the bed, opposite him.

"Do we have any key words, any targets?" The Institute questions roll off my tongue easily, and Johan blinks languidly.

"We got some flashes; he's very strong. I'd prefer you to go in blank, so as to avoid possible influence if he was misleading us."

It makes sense, sort of, as much as any of this does. I inhale, sitting down, I close my eyes, once I find my seated balance, find a position my body can comfortably hold.

The man hisses, twisting on the bed, *You won't break me,* I don't understand the thought words, exactly, like a language I don't quite recognize, but with enough feeling under the unfamiliar linguistics, I get the gist.

I've interrogated people who speak different languages to the common tongue before; the nomad desert tribes have a different dialect, and this could be a distant cousin of that. I run over the questions I have for the man and place my hand on his forehead.

His skin is warm and dry. He's much younger than he looks, I realize, getting the shape of him. Maybe seventeen or so. He's faced a hard life, and it shows on his face, the lines around his dark brown eyes and the tumors riddling his body. I'm shocked at how many there are, how he can walk or speak at all, and then I realize there's tiny nets of telekinesis around each and every bundle of mutated cells, pushing them back, holding them in place.

No wonder they didn't attack us with telekinesis. They're all busy stitching their failing bodies together. I wonder how they have the strength to cloak, and he catches it on me, smirks a little.

He's pleased they have secrets from me, but he doesn't know I've barely begun to read him.

It takes a while to filter past his defenses, to crawl under the distracting memories he throws at me. He doesn't seem to realize that we know nothing of him and his people, even the emotion-fueled memories he thrusts at me—sex and violence and hatred and pleasure—are ones I can learn from.

His people come from beyond the cracked and broken black glass of the deadlands. They made their way here, drawn by flames of telepathic power that came in bursts, spun through the sky. Distant but full of promise.

I slap a picture of Jake and Damon up against his defenses, and I recoil at the craving that bursts through him. His body is dying, he's due for a new one...

I snatch my hand away as though his forehead burned me, reeling backward.

Johan grips my shoulder, saving me from a tumble off the stool and lets me lean against him as I try to shake the depravity of the new knowledge in my head.

They came for the boys because they don't shield the way adults can. We've learned to hide our emotions behind wall after wall, keeping ourselves separate from the world. Google, ever since the kids came up from the Institute, we've been sending up beacons without even realizing it.

This is not a seventeen-year-old boy. This is someone using the body of a young man, like Cassandra has tried to use mine. This is the way they live. Conquest, body theft, shove out the old and take their place.

I feel sick. But I'm not done.

Queasy, I place my hand back to his skin. It doesn't feel so normal now. It feels more like a corpse under my palm. I close my eyes and dive.

Images assail me, again. I sort and sort, looking for information we need, we can use.

Groups of people, out past the waste, living in broken, ruined cities. Not much language anymore, all telepaths, all of them. The weaker ones used for batteries for the strong, each new generation exterminated by the elders stepping into their bodies, except for a few special cases allowed to grow. This one is three bodies old. He calls himself Mando; he's shrugged off his own ruined self and taken flesh from the youth twice. He was going to get Jake, fascinated by his autokinetic power. Oh, you can only step inside someone weaker than yourself, or the transfer doesn't work properly, because they can fight back, hold the intruder at bay.

Inside me, Cassandra twitches, far away and faint.

I stumble back, half falling from the stool, my hands shaking. They're coming, all of them will come. Not organized or militarized, weapons pulled together from scraps and ruins, but all of them tuned to telepathy in a way that I never even dreamed possible. When I was reading him, I could feel pops of color, sparkles around me. Every single telepath here is like a firework, and the stronger and younger they are, the brighter they shine. No body jumper, no *Eater* could resist the buffet we've inadvertently spread out in front of them.

Instead of trying to vocalize what I've learned, I grab Johan's hand and let him read it out of me, flashing the information to him as fast as I can.

Just as he releases me, a shocked look of horror crawling over his deceptively affable face, his datapad buzzes. He catches my eyes for a second before checking it and swearing crudely enough to make my cheeks heat.

He exhales sharply, looks me over, "I always forget how young you are. Do you have another read in you? Your brother's back, and he's brought...company."

I nod, sniffing and trying to look tough, determined, tensing my jaw and dropping my eyebrows. "Who? More of them?"

"Worse." He fires off a quick message on his wrist unit and offers me a sympathetic look. "Leah and Icarus."

My heart drops out, down through my chest in a slow, icy slide that ends up with it dripping out of the soles of my feet onto the concrete floor.

Chapter Eighteen

TOBY

Icarus didn't say a word the entire trip back. We only walked for like an hour before ARC picked us up in dune buggies and took us home. He makes me angry, on edge, but Leah kept herself between us at all times and makes sure he's in a different vehicle to me. I ride with Leaf in the back of a four-wheeler, and the boys get stuffed in the front seat of another, not that worse for wear.

Our debrief is quick; clearly Thea and Aly told them everything already, and the only thing to add is that Leah and Icarus somehow tracked us down in the desert, but Icarus seems docile enough and didn't try to attack us. Thank Google. I couldn't fight a gerbil right now.

After medical clears me, I head straight for my bed. I'm dead on my feet, not even alert enough to shower before I flop down, face-first, on my bunk with all my gross clothes still on—I barely managed to get my shoes off. Leaf gets the bunk opposite me, Andrea must be out somewhere, and Jake and Damon climb up to the top bunks. For once, Jake's wriggling doesn't disturb me in the slightest.

I don't dream.

When I wake, the room is empty, and there's an alert flashing on my datapad, which has been hooked around the end of my bunkbed by someone while I slept. It says I should report to Ops when I'm rested, fed and cleaned.

Showering is nuking amazing and I cycle the same water through the filter system three times, basking for fifteen minutes in the warm spray. The cut on my head stings under the water pressure but washing the blood and sand out of my hair is worth it. I feel infinitely more human when I emerge, dripping, and put on some clean clothes.

The mess is pretty empty, it's late afternoon so most people have already eaten, and I scoff down a sandwich, alone and happy to be so. I'm exhausted, have too many thoughts rattling around in my head to want to talk. I feel numbed but violent, like my head has too much buzzing in it for it to get out of my mouth in one piece, or at all. And I'm due at Ops, anyway. I hope they have something for me to do.

My power's buzzing in me again; it feels like it's not up to full strength, but like me, is functioning, if worse for wear. I'm dressed for whatever. I'll be comfortable at a desk in my T-shirt and cargo pants, but I'll also be able to do labor if we're still clearing the lawns, and that's where I'm sent. On the drive back to the main building, it looked like it had been mostly taken care of, though.

When I get to Ops, a soldier I vaguely recognize is on duty. He checks my ID and gives me a judgmental once-over. "We're bringing people inside the Wall; you're on factory-clearing duty. District 17E, report to Spencer."

I thank him, accepting a pack that transpires to hold water and a food box, and head over to find my shift boss. She's a strapping lady who looks like she could bench-press me, hauling pallets with a mixture of telekinesis and brute force. She whacks a hard hat on my head with enough strength behind it to make my knees buckle.

I'm needed to shift machinery; the factory is out of use since we were cut off from the other cities, and it's full of rusting, dilapidated equipment that looks like it's been untouched for a year.

Another Projector and I join up, yank the holding pins out of the cement with a machine, and then use our power to heave the massive metal pieces out of the way, against the wall. We remove any blades or dangerous pieces that we can see, crate those bits up, and move on to the next.

We're hauling people inside for safety, apparently. I get the gossip as we sweat and shove. The word is out that an influx of dangerous telekinetics—the Eaters, I'm able to extrapolate—are on route, and we need to get people out of the slums while we can.

It's backbreaking, exhaustive work, and I'm shaking with tiredness by the time we get our relief. There's a half hour to stuff our food packs down our throats, and then we're reassigned to the intake.

There's unrest straining the streets, gawking citizens thronging the roads as slum dwellers are escorted through, carrying what few belongings they have, not understanding what's happening but thrilled to be Inside, where there are taps and shields and food packets being handed over to them.

I'm kind of on crowd control, but mostly I end up helping people carry their things, and in a few cases, their children, to the factories that have already been set up with mattresses and supplies. Tension is thrumming through the air, and I break up several fights brewing. Using my best calming voice and reasonable expression seems to work pretty well, and I do my best to soothe the violence threading people's expressions.

I wish I was paired up with Serena, or Aly—I don't actually know what Aly's doing right now, so I fire a message off to her when I get a second to breathe—because my coworker is happy to tell me what he knows but doesn't want to speculate further.

At one point I think I see Leaf, but he melts away through the crowd before I can get to him and resigned to being isolated and ignorant of what's going on with my friends, I carry on with the work I have to do.

Sporadically, I get bursts of emotion from Thea, and I do my best to send back reassurance, support. I don't know what she's going through, but she's safe, physically, if afraid. She's afraid a lot, though. It's something I've adjusted to. I wish she wasn't, but all I can do is try to help her feel safe.

Getting people settled starts to feel good, after a while. Actually, interacting with humans, but not hitting anyone, just helping people out in tangible, manageable ways. The factories that have been cleared are big, and a bunch of other massive buildings have been opened up, including the parks where tents have been assembled and a party-like atmosphere develops. I can smell barbeques and hear the sounds of guitars and hand drums from a few blocks away, as I walk with a family down the busy street. I'm carrying a duffel bag on my back, and a kid on each hip. They're twins, very, very cute, with golden skin and fuzzy brown hair bleached by the sun at the front where it's soft over their foreheads. I think they're about three; one of them has lost a hand at some point in her short life, and neither of them speak—at all, according to their mother who was reluctant to let me help her, but clearly couldn't keep herding them and balancing all her things— but the trust of their fragile little bodies tucked into my side makes me feel warm, good.

We trudge down the path, take the route marked out for this chunk of humanity, and end up at the main city park. It's...never looked like this before in my life, not even at fairs and festivals. There's a sort of excited energy in the air, and people from the City itself are wandering around, chomping on food that's somehow being made and watching dance circles. None of the strife of the walk here seems present, everyone seems to be pretty relaxed, and I recognize a few faces of ARC personnel, just wandering around making sure things stay smooth.

I drop my new friends off at the tent that's been assigned to them, getting gummy-handed hugs from the kiddos and a small smile from their mother. It feels like a victory. I hop a ride on the back of a truck back to the Wall and bring in the next batch of refugees: these ones headed to a gym that's been opened up.

Weirdly, I find a bounce in my step and a sense of balance doing the repetitive but varied work of giving directions and helping people travel to their temporary homesteads. Don't get me wrong—I'm terrified about the upcoming days. There's bound to be riots and fights and anger at the inundation of new faces in the City, and the dwells are going to feel entitled to take the things they've never had access to before, but if we can keep it together, repel the eaters at the gates and maybe, just *maybe* figure something out so everyone can stay inside the Wall, we might have a chance to heal centuries-old wounds.

It's with a sense of optimism I round the corner back to the main road, only to hear shouting and Zaps firing. I'm knocked off my feet as the crowd rushes me, panicked, trying to get deeper into the city, and I see the gates closing ahead.

My power stops me from falling, a tendril wrapped around that lamppost, pushing off that corner, rebalancing my feet as I push against the current of humans, desperately trying to flee.

The group of soldiers by the gate are firing outward. As I run toward them, I watch one of them get decapitated by an invisible blade in an invisible hand. It makes no sense at all for a split second and then my brain catches up, sees the blood spatter and hit the body that *is* there, just invisible, again. The Eaters are here; they're in the crowd, pushing and shoving and stabbing and causing absolute chaos in the heaving mess of humanity.

I'm bowled over, sent sprawling, someone stamps over my body, leaving bruises I can feel forming in the bones behind their hard, bare feet, before I remember how to shield, lock power into my skin and use it as armor, reinforce my fragile flesh.

There are spaces in the pushing, frantic chaos of people, spaces where heaps of bodies are on the floor and everyone is scrambling to get away from weapons they can't see. The gate soldiers are in the crowd now, hunting desperately for something to hit, something to hurt.

I can't *read,* I can't read, and people are dying all around me, and I'm useless, and then a hand grabs mine, an amazingly familiar hand, calluses shaped by years of handling weapons, connection to me honed by two years of working side by side.

Toby, left, Serena mind-yells, and I spin, throwing a ball of power out in the direction stamped into the words, watching the air distort ahead of it and then snap into a woman crashing to the ground, blasted out on invisibility.

The people sway, shift, and the woman is gone, lost under the violence of people finally able to see what was killing them. I hear her aborted scream, but there's no time.

There must be dozens of them, in among the dwells trying to get to the safety of the city, and the gate soldiers trying to keep control. It's a riot as I feared, but a riot with knives threaded through it.

Serena yanks me around, supernaturally fast, shoves me up with a mental command and a brace of telekinesis under my feet and gives me the height I need to throw another mental projectile at one of the invading Eaters. It slams into the hidden form, crashes him against a wall and into view. He's wielding a blade at least a foot long, plated in scarlet, and then a screaming teenage boy rips the knife from his limp hand and buries it in his throat.

Serena pings the attackers, she's the rifle scope, and I'm the weapon, firing blast after blast of power to knock them out of their cover. They're fast and have some weird ability to leap up walls, using the telekinesis they have that they don't use for attacking.

I find out why as soon as I try to keep my connection to the blast I throw at the next Eater. I planned on wrapping it around them, hauling them up in the air and chucking them on a nearby roof, where they'd hopefully be dazed by the blow and out of the fight but not dead, but he *takes* it. Somehow, where my connection to my power spooled out toward him, he *grabs* it and *pulls,* yanking me off my feet.

He'd have had me, if Serena wasn't anchoring, she's inhumanly fast—not even just by normal standards but ranked against telekinetics also. One of the reasons she's such an incredible fighter is that she's just so nuking quick. She has my feet back on the ground almost before they've left, and if it wasn't for the dislocating sensation of someone hauling my power out of me—a sensation Thea taught me just a few days ago—I'd be confused as to what had happened.

I let go of the power, and slam a loose missile after it, making sure I have zero connection between it and me. The recoil slams me back a step, as it always does—physics won't be thwarted even by telekinesis, but Serena braces me and fires her own blast off to someone closer, lifting him right off his feet and throwing him into the Wall about ten feet up; he plunges down and is lost from view in the raging crowds.

Something sharp burns across my hip, blade, attacker, on me, Serena and I spin as one; there's two of them, she reads for me, somehow able to pass me information, hold my hand and smash her reinforced fist into the throat of one of them all at once. I dance away from the blade headed for my sternum, bending backwards and inhaling raggedly as I reach up with my left hand, wishing I was ambidextrous more than ever, and grab my attacker's wrist, yanking him forward.

He falls with me. I twist his knife aside with a waft of telekinesis, and then someone grabs him off me and throws him into the crowd. Tudor hauls me to my feet by grabbing the entire front of my shirt and lifting me off the ground bodily, setting me down and giving me a crooked grin before plunging back into the crowd.

I turn, grab Serena's hand, and prepare to fight.

Chapter Nineteen

E17

The first thing I see are the manacles around Icarus's wrists. He's tied up, with reinforced restraints made with phenolated plastic on the outside, so the telekinetic can't snap the metal links with his power.

His face is paler than I remember, even though he was milk white always, traces of blue veins visible at his temples under the skin. He's gagged, thoroughly, but not aggressively. The gel strap over his mouth keeps his lips sealed without pain.

The fear that washes through me on making eye contact is familiar, and I shunt it away as best I can. He can't hurt me here. I'm safe. A burst of protective rage sings down the connection between Toby and me. It's laced with guilt; he's sorry he brought Icarus here, to me. That, of course, it's me that must read him.

The surgery gurney he's on, manacled at ankle, wrist, and neck, is positioned in the middle of the brightly lit room. He's shirtless, monitors stuck to his ribcage, wires linking him to the machines showing his heartbeat. It's incredibly normal, the spikes and troughs look just like every other heartbeat I've ever seen. There's nothing monstrous about him here, strapped to the bed, wide-eyed, and half-starved.

But I know better.

"Thea." It's Leah, and she's sprawled in a chair in the corner of the room, her hair wild and thick with desert dust, her face streaked with it. "If you don't help him, we all die."

Rage bursts in my chest, flowering outward, making my fingers tingle and my jaw clench. I'm two steps toward her before I realize I've moved, Oman touching my arm gently stopping me as thoroughly as if he'd grabbed me. I want to scream at her, to scream the things he's done, the things he is, but the words won't come, and I just stand there, uselessly. *He killed Sam*, I rage inside, *right in front of me. He looked at me and killed Sam for me, like a* gift. *He's broken in a way you couldn't understand. You haven't seen him.*

"I know," Leah says, like she's reading me, like she's read my mind, but she hasn't, I'd have felt her. "I know what he's done. I know everything, more than you. I know that he was a good boy, a good man, who had horrible things done to him. Look. Cassius, let me show her."

She called him Cassius *again*. "His name is *Icarus*."

Leah gives me a hard, dead-eyed look. "In as much as your name is Cassandra." It blanches through me, like ice water. What's she saying? That Icarus...isn't Icarus? That he, like me, has someone stuffed inside him? My knees give and I'd have fallen to the floor if Oman hadn't caught me, his strong arm looping under mine, holding me steady.

"Look." Leah says, holding her hand out for me, and I swallow the urge to vomit, before taking it.

She takes Icarus's...Cassius's hand and funnels him to me.

I lose my feet, again. Oman catches me and helps me to a chair without pulling me away, and I'm swept through

Leah's body into the boy on the gurney. I don't know what to call him now. I've never been inside him before, never had the opportunity or agency to try. I've looked in his eyes, of course, felt his madness pulsing out of him, but never understood.

There are *two* in there. Two powers, two people, two minds, one forced inside the other in the hideous kind of rape Cassandra has been attempting for a year. Icarus and Cassius. Icarus stuffed *inside* Cassius.

And then the memories hit me.

Like a trigger, like a wall has been washed away, like a block in my memories I couldn't even feel the edges of crumbles. His memories, finding mine. We did grow up together, Cassius and I; we were two Epsilon class students, him a little older but nevertheless bonded and paired and always together. Given opportunities denied to other students, a school, outside, the sun. No wonder I recognize him. I've seen his face more times in my life than any other. I know what he looks like in the rain. I know how his hair moves in the wind. What his hand felt like in mine as we ran, free and young and wild.

And then they took him.

One day, he was gone. And I screamed and railed and cried and *remembered,* until they washed him out of me, and I forgot he even existed until the tickle of memory in the back of my head the day I saw his face. But not Cassius, not any more. Not my friend. Icarus, Cassandra's son.

I burned. I burned, Icarus screams at me, inside Cassius's head, *You won't take me.*

Let me die, says Cassius, *please.*

Leah lets go of my hand and I snap back to my body, trembling, nausea rising. There's a bucket under my face before the bile comes up, and I empty my stomach into it, retching miserably.

Her hand is strong on my back, pressing against the tight muscles bracing my spine. She moves close enough to hold me, replacing Oman as a pillar of support. "They screwed up the transfer; he shouldn't be like this. They broke him. Cassius was too strong for Icarus to take completely. That's how it works; you can only crush weaker people out of their own meat, the biological tie is innate, strong. It's easier to take family, or similar power resonances." She's talking just to talk, to give me a voice to hear. I can feel it in her words, but I'll take it, sick and shaking and wretched. "But they didn't have time to find a better fit. Icarus was dying, burned alive beyond repair." She touches my side, the scar under my clothing throbs at the touch, the chemical fire I don't remember. "You were there; so was Cassius. They took too long deciding; he was already half mad with the pain before they gave him Cassius. Icarus should have died years ago. We're going to fix him and set Cassius free, but I need you to read him. You have to pull it together, and you and I, and Oman." I feel her look up, smile at Oman. "And the doctor. We can save him, and then he can save us all."

I nod, shaking, burning with rage and fear and years of helplessness. They leave me in the chair while they set up, and I wrap my knobby hands around each other, desperate for something to hold onto. The world feels distant, desperate.

The sound of the door slamming as Dr. Grey bustles in, rouses me. He's pushing a shiny tray of instruments, and Leah catches either my eyeline or my thought. "He's chipped; they have to come out too."

Understanding, I stretch my hands out, willing them to be steady and strong. They're shaking, but not as badly as they could be.

"We can't put him under because we need to do it all at once," the doctor states, pulling some kind of headgear off the trolley.

Icarus screams behind the gag, struggles against the chains, and Leah leans over him. "Cassius," she whispers the name like it's a spell and the tension falls out of him.

The doctor takes advantage of the stillness to plunge a needle expertly into the crook of Cassius's arm.

I look at the floor, the shiny tiles in white squares reminding me of the Institute, but somehow better than watching the boy being prepped for surgery. I hear the buzzing of clippers, run my hand over my own hair. It's longer now, almost as long as Toby's, a good two inches. The longest it's ever been.

There's rattling, movement, a cough, and then Leah steps back to me. "It's time," she murmurs, holding out her hand for me like she knows I need the contact to make it across the room.

She doesn't let go of my hand as we step across the room together, move to the far side of Cassius, and place our tangled fingers on his bare chest. His skin is warm under my crooked hand, alive. His eyes are shockingly wide, the pupils blown with fear and sedatives.

Leah doesn't let go of my hand as I reach out. She starts to move, but it's too late, and I already have the cold metal of a scalpel in my hand. She doesn't even have time to cry out before I bury the blade in her throat, red bursting out in its wake. Numb, I feel my body turn and fling itself at Oman, blade slashing red stripes against the sheer white of his shirt.

Epilogue

CASSANDRA

My son screams behind his gag, screams at me, but soon I'll have him out of there and we can leave together.

I finish the Reader with a precise slash across the carotid, opening his neck. I use telekinesis taken from the brother to hold the Doctor down as I fumble with my son's manacles, unlatching the complex clips and pulling him free.

"Icarus." It's strange to feel my mouth form the words, after so long inside someone's mind, and I see his eyes clear, the joy burst across his beautiful, stolen face. As soon as he's freed, I pull him against me, reveling in the moment of human connection. We're free. We're strong.

A sharp prick in my elbow makes me gasp, and I pull back, yanking myself away from my son. A needle, still in my arm, the plunger depressed. Weakness swamps me. *No, no, my son. How could you?*

I am not your son, he screams—the body screams—the boy who should have died screams, and his thoughts echo down through the blackness that washes over me, dragging me into the dark.

I'M NOT EVEN restrained when I wake. The idiots clearly shoved me in a cell while waiting for their superiors to tell them what to do. The glory of war, bureaucracy and idiocy abound.

I stand, stretch, feel the glorious, glorious sensations of *touch* and *smell* and *sound* not filtered through someone else's perceptions. The wretched, ignorant child squirms, tries to call to her brother. I snatch a thread of his power and use it to bind her, stuff her down where she belongs. I'll kick her out when I have more time.

I bounce on her toes, getting used to my new body. It's a good one, in much better shape than it was when we were holding her underground, but still, needs must. We'd have fattened her up if I'd decided to take her, which I probably would have been forced to do eventually if we couldn't pin down a young Epsilon on the outside. I was nearing the end of my last body's time, after all.

Sighing, I run through a quick kata, memorizing my muscle and reflexes. It's always disconcerting, being in new skin. Takes some adjusting to. I can't wait till I have her brother in front of me and can take his Projector strength to bolster her Reader power. When the doctor first told me they were to be twins, I was devastated. Out of time with my aging body, the first shakes starting to appear in my power, my control. We'd tried four times to breed me a new skin, and the perfect mix seemed to be at my fingertips. I was sure the child created would be the most powerful creature possible, and I had time then for a slow, seeping takeover. The subtle kind, instead of wresting control in one fell swoop.

And then, twins. Unimaginable. A disaster. The girl, with her lack of Projection, crippled in this world. The boy, a Blank...impossible to take even if I wanted to. And then the revelations that had followed—he was a Projector after all, and further, their power was connected. That's when I *knew I* had to have them. Once I'd absorbed their power, sucked it out of their bodies to bolster my own, I'd be even stronger than I'd ever imagined. A solid ninety on both scales. Unstoppable.

Still within reach.

I can feel the boy, his presence. He's fighting, presumably against the Eaters. I knew they'd come, eventually. They always do. The only thing you can do to keep them away is bury the children until they learn to govern themselves and kill the Eaters who pilgrimage to find a new body here anyway.

The girl is physically stronger than I'd realized, muscles built with hours of work, every day since she broke out of the Institute. It feels good to be inhabiting this flesh. I missed sensation more than I thought I would. She's not as tough as my fourth body, but much better than my last one, and she's young enough I can build her higher. I thought once that I should take a male body, for the strength, the physical force, the way women are always just slightly afraid of men. But when I tried it I was never comfortable with it. So, a strong female is the best I can aim for. This one is quite tall, as well. I like it.

I'll have to do something about her hair, and her posture is terrible. She has nervous tics ingrained in her musculature that will take a while to unlearn. Her shoulders are too tight; feels like I could use a bath, a massage and an orgasm, in that order. But there's no time for that now.

It takes me an hour, maybe, to acclimatize to my new flesh, to settle in and feel at home. For the neurons to fire properly. I won't be up to 90 words a minute typing any time soon but I think I can handle the basics, and all I really have to do is sneak out while ARC is busy with the savages from the deadlands.

The room is sadly underequipped, I know they've been keeping an eye on her, but I feel only one guard outside the door, and he's lazy, playing a game on his datapad and not paying attention. I should be able to take him out if I can figure out the lock. I send a thread of stolen telekinesis at the camera and knock it to face the bed before getting started.

She had been given a wireless disabled datapad for watching vids. There are no tools available to me, but a piece of wire extracted from a small light fitting, a safety pin from the mattress tag and the girl's only unchewed nail allow me to get the backing off the datapad and connect it to the electronic lock in less than an hour.

I think wistfully of the technopath boy we were hunting; that would have been a body I'd revel in, male or not. The addition of that kind of power... I shiver just thinking about it. Impossible now, though. Dead at the hands of my son.

The door lock clicks to green both more rapidly and with a sound louder than I anticipated. I'm not quite ready but I have to react. I've always been good at adjusting. I throw the door outward, reading the guard's movements perfectly and smashing him in the bridge of the nose as he turns toward the moving plastic.

He's down, but I snap his neck anyway. Can't be too careful. I drag the man into the cell, strip him, and arrange his body in the bed. Passable at a glance.

Pulling the uniform on takes a few minutes, but now I have a disguise, a Zap, and a datapad. It's the easiest jailbreak I've ever committed, and I have to repress the urge to whistle as I shut the door behind me and head into the bowels of ARC.

Inside me, Epsilon 17 twists and rails uselessly. I squash her without a hitch in my step.

Acknowledgements

Book three down! Approaching the end of the journey for this series, I want to thank everybody who has shared these books, who has reviewed them, and who has passed them on to their friends. To all the people who have connected to my stories and told me so... Thank you. You're what inspires me to keep writing.

Marie, my almost-wife, deserves all the thanks for everything ever. She's the one who puts up with my complaining, helps me untangle plot threads (when she has literally no idea what is going on), and makes sure I drink water, eat food and otherwise take care of my bodily requirements when I'm deep into it.

The biggest debt of thanks for this particular novel go to the big three, who are not just my friends, but my first fans. Lianna—who helps me figure out answers to all my weird questions, Lori—who inspires me to keep going when things are so so hard, and Dylan—whose passion for these characters and their stories made me believe it was worth writing.

My stalwart support team who always show up, here's a token of my love for you! Alix, Sinead, Leah, Ali and Peter, Anne and Dave, Eva and Kyle, Tosh and Richard, School Dad, Danny and Matthew, Erika and David, Zach and Reine, Mary Fan, Meryl, Angela, Team Morgan-Boalch, Team Tann and Team MacMillan, thank you from the bottom of my heart. And a special shout-out to grandma Glo for being my cutest fan!

To the folks of the awesome babes server, thank you all for listening to me vent, cheering me on and being the best.

My lovelies at the Trans Tipping Point Project, who recharge me with their amazing energy and passion.

My family, Mum, Dad, Alex, Dave, Arianwen, and my BRAND NEW nibling Seraphina!! Thank you for your love, care and support on this journey.

And last, but certainly not least, my wonderful team at NineStar Press, BJ, Rae, and my team of editors. Without you, none of this would be happening. Thanks so much for your belief, and all your hard work!

About the Author

Tash is a Welsh-Canadian author and teacher. They've been published in multiple anthologies, and their first personal release, a YA novella called SLAM was an international bestseller. Their debut series, The Psionics, is being released in full over 2019, from Nine Star Press.

When they're not writing, they're usually found teaching either Computer Science or English in Vancouver. Tash identifies as trans and queer and uses the neutral pronoun "they". As an English teacher, they are fully equipped to defend that grammar! They have a degree in computer science so their nerd chat makes sense, and a couple of black belts in karate which are very helpful when it comes to writing fight scenes.

Their novel writing endeavours began at the age of eight although they will admit that their first attempt was derivative, at best. Since then, Tash has spent time falling in streams, out of trees, juggling, dreaming about zombies, dancing, painting, learning and then teaching Karate, running away with the circus, and of course, writing.

They write fast-paced, plot-centric action adventure with diverse casts. They write the books that they wanted to read as a queer kid and young adult (and still do!)

Email: tash.mcadam@gmail.com

Facebook: www.facebook.com/tashmcadam

Twitter: @tashmcadam

Website: www.tashmcadam.com

Other books by this author

I Am the Storm

We Are the Catalyst

Also Available from NineStar Press

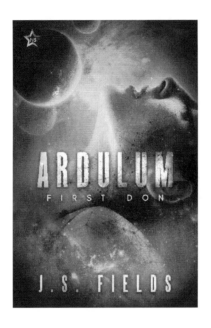

Connect with NineStar Press

www.ninestarpress.com

www.facebook.com/ninestarpress

www.facebook.com/groups/NineStarNiche

www.twitter.com/ninestarpress

www.tumblr.com/blog/ninestarpress

Made in United States
Troutdale, OR
11/25/2023

14950765R00174